CHILD SUPPORT

CHILD SUPPORT

Hisoka Takara

AuthorHouse™
1663 Liberty Drive
Bloomington, IN 47403
www.authorhouse.com
Phone: 1-800-839-8640

Published by AuthorHouse 04/04/2012

ISBN: 978-1-4685-6526-3 (sc)
ISBN: 978-1-4685-6525-6 (hc)
ISBN: 978-1-4685-6527-0 (e)

Library of Congress Control Number: 2012905190

This book is printed on acid-free paper.

Contents

Introduction

A talented young lady fighting for her identity, erasing the person she once use to be, developing her new self, possessing children as early as 15 and still continuing her education. Making a decision to let the children live with their father, so they can develop a relationship with them and learn ways of a man, only to fully develop her character and find her place in this life. Placed on child support by the co-parents and step mother, she then had to fight to justify her character as a mother. Getting to a point in her profession where she serviced elite and substantial women in areas of the fashion, social industry, and building a good relationship with them. While making a name in the makeup industry and building a business from the ground up, she runs into the love of her life. Getting to the peak of breaking full circle into the makeup industry she undergoes the most tragic situation. There are characters in this book that names are altered for their personal privacy, which is very much respected. The book is not to blame anyone for the mishap that she encountered, but to express how sometimes the good people a person think are in their corner to support them in their growth, aren't. It displays the strength the enemy and how a person should never underestimate how far people will go to destroy what a person creates for themselves. It exhibits God taking away the first to establish, the second and how if a person applies his word in their heart it does manifest into their life vividly.

People usually hear about men being placed on child support, but have we ever heard about a women being placed on child support. If it characterizes a man in a different ways what does it do for a woman? There are women on child support as well as men and their stories are never exposed to the public. They share the same experiences as men, but I believe even worst. The integrity of that mother or woman is questioned because of her title in that child's life. I do not believe a mother is bad for recognizing and acknowledging she didn't have a child alone. In regards of how she feels about the co-parents as a person, she trusted those men at one point, lying down with them, taking the chance having unprotected sex, and having their children. The mother in this book was active in the nurturing years of the child, but wanted a chance to establish herself in other areas of life. Thanking God that she had children with men who did not shy away from the responsibility of being the other caretaker for them as you here from most women. The two parents coming to a sensible agreement for the child to come in terms of new living arrangements to further push the child in a good direction.

Get involved in this persons experience that is not here to hide her flaws from anyone, a person who is here to connect with people in their change process. When we hear about vast leaders in the religion industry they say, they understand because they have been their too, but where was their there? They give you an example, but don't always tell their story completely. In this book you will be met where you may be spiritually and understand that change in a process, reading this story can make you free better about your own story. I do not want and will not step on anyone's toes in a position greater than mine, I can understand after you have arrive at a place in the road that God has chosen for you getting into details about how you got to that point becomes irrelevant. Most leaders could reach more souls if they became more accessible to being dissected. People associate themselves with people they can say are like them or have been like them.

I know many women would not share most of the information shared in this book about themselves it would be too personal. They would not want to be judged, every woman has done something that she is not proud of and would take the incident to her grave before exposing it to anyone. The young lady in this story just can't be embarrassed telling any and everyone about events she has surpassed, being too proud of the woman she has developed into because of those choices, mishaps, and mistakes. I laughed at some point in this writing because I may have left out some stories, honestly I know I have, but I would have to write another book. If a person was to speak to people in this persons past they would have more stories to share, the young lady rejoices that they are sharing old stories, nothing recent, speaking about how she use to be speaking about how they are now.

Childhood

It's hard to keep your head up with so much against you what do you do? Keep praying is what I can say now. What I would have said before I got focus more on God I don't know. It took many tribulations for me to become the woman that I am today and I can truly say I still have a ways to go for it is not to strive for perfection as much as it is to strive for correction. My life has never been easy so I know my day of greatness is near or on my itinerary before my eyes seal shut. I am named after my mother's mom Paris. Great lady strength like the bull of her astrology sign, but often hated on for overcoming challenges, which I feel was passed down to me, they say be careful who you name your children after. She was known for hair weaving, fashion and her talent in singing in our hometown of Tampa, Florida. She was a very opinionated woman and carried herself very ladylike in her approach toward any situation positive or negative. Like us all she started off ruff around the edges with all good intentions later turning to Christ after the grandchildren started adding up, she recognized the blessings stowed upon her life, the long way she had come with the grace, and mercy God had given her. Like so many of us she took life for peaks sake, she influenced so many by example in the way she carried herself. My granny was the concrete of our family, when she spoke we listened and took heed like most Madea's of their family. Her and my mom had a weird relationship out of all her children I think it was, because my mom was most like her. My mom admired her character and wanted to be like her, even better, all my grandmother's children had a skill like her, but my mom had most. Mom was a little rebel at heart and dated my father despite my grannies opinion of him not being good enough, he was a little older. I consider myself a love child, my dad and mom were just physically attracted to one another more than anything. They were both hot items all the odds were against them making it together, as what would look like the perfect pair. My dad had two daughters before I came along and manage to have one after I came all while having some form of relationship with my mom before finally marrying her when I was four. So, this made four girls for him in all, all by different women. Out of the four girls my dad had, I was the one he spent the most time with, showing somewhat his character of a man to, and what he was capable of as a father. I also endured, saw, and experienced the ups and downs of his wellbeing. He was a good person until weed turned into cocaine and cocaine turned into crack. The Cosby spin off that could have been, died. My family went from eating together every evening, going to the park, having beautiful holidays, to my dad being abusive toward my mom who he always adorned and still does, abusing, neglecting, and even molesting me. I since a child always have had a figure eight shape, butter brown skin, nice texture hair with length. Almond shaped eyes and a very warm spirit, when my dad went as far as putting his finger in me I was very confused. I remembered the day like it was yesterday, he was high out of his mind and referred to me as his Janet Jackson. Shortly before my mom and dad separated, dad started hitting on her, it became more than enough to deal with, and so we went to live with my granny. Once we had that distance I decided to tell my mom about what, I experienced with my dad. By them having a recreational bond (smoking weed) along with being legally married they communicated regardless of the separation. One Saturday my mom took me to see my dad, so he could watch me while she worked. At the time she was at Home Depot in Clearwater maybe like 25-30 minutes from Tampa. They had a small conversation as I stayed down stairs and watched WWF (that was one of me and my dad's favorite programs) when they came back down she was left out for work. Dad sat down rolled a joint and asked, "Why would you tell your mom something like that?" as if he had forgotten what had happened. I never answered the question, because I knew he was about to go off into abusive mode. I was taught never to repeat what I saw or heard let alone endure, but I felt nasty since the incident and was uncomfortable around him. Before I could blink there went the famous back hand to the lip, with the repeated words, "you talk too much." You better not cry he often kept the inside of my lip raw from the back hand slap; I was use to it at that point. I remembered taken a nap, waking up to peanut butter and jelly, going outside to train on the boxing bag with my dad. His missed his opportunity of becoming a boxer running the streets, the man was known for his quick hands and bad temper. We hung out for the remainder of the evening until my mom came and got me after work. I was thinking when she got me, "why would she leave me in a situation like that" trusting that I would to be all right. I never knew why my mom would trust him with me, after what I told her. I knew from then I couldn't tell her things and she trust what I said and protect me. Her and my dad's relationship was not going anywhere; she was hoping that he would straighten up and get his life together for the sake of me. He was just getting worst in his drug use, the man slept under my grannies house one night claiming that he could hear my mom in the room with another man. My granny almost shot him that morning ranging the doorbell repeatedly, cursing, and threatening to kill us. My granny had to start walking me to and from the bus stop, because they were afraid that he would kidnap me or something. My dad got to the point of stalking my mom and me, when she tried to live over to her girlfriend's house he came by one evening with a gun. The police had to come and restrain him from the property, it was a hot mess. My mom was waiting to save enough money to move and start over with it just being us two; she wanted her husband regardless of the drama just to clean up his act. I remember her begging him to come with us to Clearwater, Fla. when it was time for us to move. I was thinking to myself, "let that man be crazy" dad or no dad it was too much, I was tired of running and hiding all over the city, within a year's time we moved with three of her friends and he found us every time. When I would go to church or choir rehearsal with my granny, I would pray for his healing and that he wouldn't hurt my mom any more. I used to hate that she was so weak for his character; I would talk to my granny about it, and she would agree. Granny and I were extremely close; I felt comfortable talking to her about things, because I knew that she would do what she could to protect me. She never liked my dad from the time he came to my granny to tell her to mind her business, she ran him out of her house with a knife following behind him. Granny was one lady he would not cross the wrong way; my dad's mom was different. She past when I was in the fourth grade, she was a very good grandma as I can remember; she taught me how to say my prayers at night on my knees. My dad treated her bad in her last years; being on drugs really bad around those times. He was in prison during her funeral and was escorted by the guards in shackles under his suit. They pulled up in a patty wagon to the front of the church. I was thinking to myself, "that was not the way he should have come," but he did not have too much of an option. My dad start going to jail and prison a lot, it was hard keeping up with him for a moment that was my dad. Having the respect of him being the man the God choose for me to have with that title what more can I say, but I love him.

My mom and I moved to Tarpon Springs, a little town outside of Clearwater by her job. We started a life there with all confidence that my dad would not be able to find us on one of his intermissions from jail or prison. I had to be more independent than usual, because my mom had to work, so she would get me ready for school, I had to walk to and from. I had to sit home patiently until she came in from work; I use to do a good job with myself alone. It was no time before my mom met a man named William that was from the town we lived in; his entire family resided there as well. He was very popular in the town, because he played football and had a chance on making it pro until he hurt his knee in college. They started dating and the word spread, our neighbor that lived across the walkway from us started babysitting me just to get in my mom's business about William. William was cool, he was established, had a good job, and a nice car all the things that a woman would considered. William just had one small glitch he had nine children and was barely active with them. They saw him when they needed something financially, but quality time was out, he was busy trying to be too popular. William was acknowledged everywhere he went, my mom was the "who's that girl" of the town she worked most of the time and didn't hang out much but was noticed. They were the talk of the town, she had a sweet demeanor, and people wondered how she was going to handle his glitch. My mother accepted William and his glitch, expecting something different than what she heard. Would I have done the same, probably not, nine step children would have been a bit much for me, but William was a provider and I think my mother considered the resources between the two and was willing to make it work. She likes challenges, I think, the men that would be more difficult to settle down with. My mom and dad were not legally divorced at the time, she had tried, but he threatened to kill her and was not signing anything that stated separation. My mom and William started this relationship, and it was the talk of the town, they made a nice looking couple and the ladies that liked William were jealous, even the babysitter. They would get around my mom anyway they could to throw William under every bus they could find. She heard things from his past true or not, she was not satisfied not winning or achieving her goal with getting this man. She wanted to be the one that changed the talk of the town, no matter what it took. I really didn't know what my mom told William about the marital status between her and my dad, but William had been married and separated before, so I think he would understand whatever the situation was. I never remember my family from Tampa visiting us in Tarpon Springs, we always went to Tampa. My mom was too much of a disappointment to my granny, and it was known throughout the family. My mom took William to meet my granny; she was cool with him, because he was a stable man. Regardless of how many children William had, he was stable. Shortly after the meeting of the families started taking place the children started coming around. William's ex's was so jealous he called himself moved in with another woman and helping her with her child, they started dropping children off. I can't begin to explain how many weekend and holiday's I went through sharing my room with them. I look back on those times now and really commend my mom for being that type of woman, it's not many women that would do things that she did for another person's children, but she had a good step dad once in her life and took notes. William and I had a cool relationship; I never really respected him like my dad, because he never really stepped in like my dad. He stepped in like a man dating my mom and was good for money when she needed, he wined and dined her, but I was never there. She would get money from him for me, but I was never with them, spending time together as a family. I would imagine if he were not doing that with his own children why would I be so special, but to the outside it didn't look like that. People thought because he was staying under the same roof as I, I was getting the treatment, I can remember times, him being home, and we wouldn't even talk to each other unless I needed to ask for something. He never had anything to talk to me about and I wasn't at the age where I could just spark up a conversation, I was nine by then. My mom shortly after got pregnant with my little sister, I knew things were really going to be interesting; William was going to have 10 children, and a step daughter. I was ready for the little sister, it was going to grow me up a lot, but I was ready. When my sister got here I don't think William was mentally ready, he had gone so far into the relationship, had so many odds against him, and he had to face up to the responsibility. The night she was born William didn't get to the hospital that night, as I remember until my sister was almost born; he was drunk just coming from hanging out. My sister out of the 10 was the only one William had saw delivered, I guess that was a step toward change. My sister was like my baby, I had to be a big sister for sure; William would leave and go hanging out while my mom went to work. I was singing in the children's chore at William's aunt church, and I would take my sister with me. Get her dressed, make her bottles like my mom taught me, and walk with her on the other side of the town. William would have to call around looking for me, I had things to do, and I was not waiting for him to come home. If I had to take my sister with me then that's what I had to do with no complaints, she was so cute to me like a black Barbie. My mom was climbing the corporate ladder at Home Depot; they offered her a position in the corporate office in Atlanta. She had to relocate unexpectedly and William would have to figure out what he was going to do about his job. He had been with the company for at least 10 years; he had a little money invested that would support the transition until he could get employment in Atlanta. It was him leaving his comfort zone that was his biggest issue. My mom was going to wait until the following school year to move me with her; she had to start the job at a certain time. My mom took my little sister with her, her being an infant, but I had to go move with my granny to finish fourth grade with my God sister who was a teacher at a elementary school I would attend. It was a ruff school, but no one was worried about me keeping up with that I could handle myself. I was not the run-over type and I didn't mind trouble, my god mother knew that, she would warn me all the time. Telling me not to get into trouble or she was going to deal with me, I was coming under my god sister's image and I was not going to embarrass her name. I was thinking, "whatever" if it came to me I was going to deal with it and deal with my consequences after that, and that's very much what I did. I was cute and my granny dressed me in the things my mom left me with every day, she took time with me every morning. I had a jerry curl then with a nice length, I was known for having the best banana clips that matched my outfits. I kept a clean pair of Keds and had an option what I wanted to do for lunch, eat with my god sister, school lunch, or my granny packing me something the night before. The boys liked me and the girls hated me, it was only three cute girls in the class, as I think back and I was one of them. I use to get attention, because of who my god sister was. The teacher or students would go up the hall to tell my god sister, I remember I was fighting and arguing with the teacher one Friday. My god mother called for me to come see her that Saturday morning early, when I was at my grannies. She had me to lie under a coffee table, and she beat the bottom half of what was lying out from the table. It was crazy; my god sister could have looked out for me not telling, after she jacked me up in front of everybody that day and embarrassed me, I thought that would have been enough. I was thinking man where is my mom, it was a little longer before school was out before she was coming to get me. The odds were against her moving out of state away from her family, it was much being said from the family because my mom and William were not married. It was more security when you were married to the man than you just having a baby with him in my grannies eyes; that was the way she saw it. I was just ready to leave Tampa, I was missing my mom and getting beat for everything I was getting into; my mom never beat me like what I was experiencing. It was just punishments with her, I can remember a time I was hiding food under my bed, because I felt like William was eating all the food. I had cold items under the bed and a fan blowing under the bed so the food can stay cold, black ants started coming from everywhere. She punished me, if I would have been around my granny or god mother, they would have given me the business with a switch or belt. I don't think my god mother wanted me to go to Atlanta; I had to be responsible for too much at an early age helping my mom. My god mother wanted me to experience a kid's life, she was the one that took me to plays and spoke to me about how lady like situations the most out of everyone else. My mom had everything worked out for us in Atlanta by the time summer came. I was excited, I had been to Savannah, Ga. with my god mother; we rode horses there, but not Atlanta, Ga. We moved to Smynra, Ga. in a cute apartment like 10 minutes from my mother's new job, I was proud of my mother. She was doing so well; things were changing for the better, we were experiencing life. No drama from my dad, my mom I can say was different as far as drama, she really was not that spirit, and she was a peace seeker and maker. She always found good in things that another person would have saw nothing but bad, she was a very humble person. It was one of the attributes I liked that about her, it was like I was mixed with a poodle and a pit bull between my mom and dad. William didn't come up with us right away; he had to get some thing squared away with his job first. I think the change was too big for William; he was a little scared, him coming into this bigger city, coming from standing out to blending in. We had a routine, I would watch my sister while my mom was at work, and she would get everything prepared like the bottles and what I was going to eat the night before for the next day. I was like nine or 10 doing big girl things, me and mom were like a team, it flowed nice. My mom was always good for meeting people and not just anyone people that wanted to help. The lady that lived under us was home most of the day, so she listened out for me up stairs, during the day. I was going to the fifth grade that year; it was going to be more interesting than the last school I attended, since I was in a 60% white area. I had to adjust so to speak, I would be going to Teasley Elementary. William was coming up and I was curious to see how this was going to be, I didn't hear many good things about him making this move. It was in between him and my mom; she wasn't divorced from my dad so I wasn't really concerned about much out of their relationship. He had to be there for his daughter (my sister) and I could understand that, I was glad he was at least concerned to that aspect of their relationship. My body was starting to form were grown men was starting to complement me, when I would go play outside I used to have a hard time dealing with it from what I remembered from my dad. One evening when William and my mom were out I locked the top lock, and they couldn't get in the house. They had to knock on my room window to wake me up from out of my sleep to open the door, William was a muscular guy and his strength broke my window with the broom stick he was using. It was a winter night, so I had this nice size whole in my window until it was replaced. My room was on the second floor, so you can just imagine how cold my room was getting. William wasn't working at the time; we were on winter break at school, so William stayed home me and my sister while my mom was working. Early one morning I was in my room sleep, I felt someone touching me in my private area, I opened my eyes slightly, and William was looking in my vagina. I was so shocked I opened my eyes completely, he just looked at me jumped up, and started talking about he was putting more padding in my window to keep the room from getting colder. I saw William as a nasty man, what was I going to say to my mom, I had been through this before with my dad and she didn't believe me or didn't display her protective nature like a mom should. She told me that my dad said, "that never happened," what was she going to say about this incident. My granny was too far to get involved, I was just so disgusted. I balled up and stayed under my blanket, thinking to myself, "this body shape thing is over rated and it's getting me in bad situations with my mom's relationships." I stayed in my room all that day; he came in later asking me, "What's wrong, are you hungry?" I was thinking to my self this man has some nerves to even be still here, he had a nervous demeanor, I can imagine he was thinking I was going to say something. I asked him, "why did he do that to me this morning," and he said, "I don't know what you are talking about," explaining I must had been having a dream. I was thinking "that had to be some dream, a vivid one at that." He was out of his mind to think that I didn't know what happened, he must not have been aware of what happened with me and my dad. It was weird day that day William asked me not to mention what happened to my mom, because it was going to upset her. I thought that was bold, but what he didn't know is, even if I told her she wasn't going to believe me anyway. I stayed to myself that day and I just ask God to take care of me and what happened. I learned from my dad's mom to pray at night when no one is watching, God will hear you, and answer you openly. I would always remember her saying those words to me they stuck like glue, and before I moved to Atlanta I stop praying every night like I once was. I started back after that incident with William; something told me I was going to need God more than ever. We started going to church and that was a good move, we all needed it, William wouldn't come, but that was cool. William couldn't handle the pressure of the change; he was thinking insecure because he wasn't working. William went back to Florida for a while leaving my mom with the responsibilities, I believe the money he saved had run out. We shortly had to move from the apartment we were in, because my mom just couldn't afford it all by herself. It was in the middle of the school year and I was moving to another fifth grade class, I was going to Norton Park Elementary School not as nice as Teasley. The apartments we moved in was a down grade from the one we moved out of, it was some of everything going on in the complex. Our clothes would get stolen out of the laundry; you would see people walking around in them along with one section of the complex I couldn't walk in because it was some drug infested. My mom got a settlement with Norton Park for me getting hit in the eye with a baseball when I was not actively involved in recreation. I can remember that day like it just happened, I was outside being a bully to this girl named Kesha. We were arguing over the same boy that in the end dumped me when he saw how big my face had gotten from the ball hitting me. I was telling Kesha to come outside, when I turned around the ball came from the other side of the field, and socked me. I took it like everything was tolerable, and even tried to walk home, it didn't start swelling up until the bus ride home. It was funny when that boy saw my face he said, "Kesha I will walk you home." When my mom came home from work, she rushed me to the hospital. My mom was dating a new man by then named Ace, moving him in and everything, he stayed at home with me while she worked. He was cool until the day we were playing and he tried to tickle my butt, I was tired of my mom's men dealing with me in sexual ways. I went off and from that day he started having step child issues from me. We moved from that apartment to a nice townhouse, by the time I was going to the sixth grade. I guess my settlement money gave my mom a push and Ace helped her too, he was very possessive with her. I went to Nash Middle School, and it was the year the R&B group ABC had their album out. I would see Romel from the group all the time changing classes. I wasn't cool enough for him then, I remember Ace taking me shopping, and getting me some of the cool girl gear. My mom would ask him to do little stuff for me to get us to have some type of bond, we would fight and when he would try to tell me something, I would ignore him. He thought he could force me to respect him, which only made me rebel worst, he was not my dad, and I made that clear. He would get so mad, because I think Ace couldn't have children, he had been in prison and was trying to start a new life. He slap me so hard one day after I weld on him for pushing me in my room one day, I was so over Ace's presence. The only positive I can remember he liked for us to eat together and even then I would give both of them the hardest time. He later became a stalker, running for a crime he commented in another state; the police caught him hiding in the house one night coming to the house to arrest him.

After Ace left, William came back and my mom started hustling hair from out of the house on weekends, she would have the kitchen booked from Friday night thru Saturday afternoon. The word got around about her weaving hair and how good she was, one of the talents she picked up from my granny. William my mom in fact went to the courthouse and got married, being able to have my dad sign the papers in prison. I noticed when my mom was working her job and part time from home, she was so focus and happy. She was easily distracted is the only accuse I can come up with, because when Sophia and her started hanging my life hadn't began to become interesting. Sofia was a lady my mom met through the lady that lived under us in the first place we stayed in. She started coming around as a client initially; she had two boys same ages as me and my sister. William was really trying to do the right thing at this point; he was partially working and trying to help out as much as possible. The relationship was doing better than before, I was not really concerned about the relationship me and him had, because I was still bitter. What he and my mom had was in between them and if that were what was going to make her happy continuing to form into a better woman I was cool. She didn't live for my happiness, I had put that in my mind and left it there, but I was content. Her and Sophia's relationship was developing more, Sophia was seeing someone at the time, but it was not as stable as what my mom and William had. Sophia was the type of person to call out every flaw she could find, she looked everywhere else, but at herself. She was a very funny lady, had a personality, she was not that attractive, but her personality over seeded that. She was attractive through her demeanor, she came across as perfect, but she came from a good background. Her family bond was tight the only girl out of three children, her mom and dad had been together her entire life. Sophia would bring her children with her when she came over, and that's when I met Justin her son. Justin was a cool dude we had much in common; we were friends more than anything. We were attracted to each other it was like I wasn't the girl boys would liked for a long time, they thought I was cute; I was rough around the edges they would always find something more in another girl. I was a fighter then; I can remember when Justin came over once I was on punishment for busting a boy in his nose, suspended from school for a day. William was more upset than my mom, but I wasn't interested in his cares, I was talking about the boy pants in class (being a class clown) and he wanted to fight me afterwards. I think he was just embarrassed I about me making everybody laugh at him, he hit me first and we just went at it. So, when Justin came I had to stay in my room. Justin seemed more like a friend that would have always like me regardless of how I was. We made an agreement in the 6th grade that we were girlfriend and boyfriend, our moms started hanging to the point that William was getting jealous. My mom and Sophia had one major thing in common they both smoked weed, and they liked to have a good time. Sophia brought another side of life to my mom that distracted her from the life that she was creating for herself with her husband and children.

They hung out so much that by the time the end of sixth grade came; William was leaving going back to Florida, and Sophia and my mom were moving in together. I don't know who came up with that big idea, but that was the plan. My mom got terminated from her job a couple of months before schools ended and I guess they thought moving in together it would help one another out financially. Well, they got this big house on the other side of Smynra, I would be going to another middle school I was thinking, and this was my third year in Atlanta with attending my fourth school. I would be going to Griffin Middle School, Justin and I was still in our little secret relationship. I thought, we hadn't seen each other because he was in Michigan for the summer. We hadn't broken anything off so, I thought maybe since our parents were still cool, and moving in together we were still cool. The house they moved in was big enough that it separated everyone fairly, Justin and Erling, his brother, shared the downstairs and everyone else were upstairs. Justin and I got closer once he returned from Michigan, our moms would watch our interaction, and we had to act like we were not together and just friends. It was funny explaining to people our real living situation, so we pretended like we were cousins; I would even talk to other boys. I became a hot item when I got on that side of town; the older boys were digging me. It made Justin jealous and his mom talk about me so bad; my shape was becoming a big discussion in conversation. My mom was buying me those biker shorts with the shirts to match; honestly I use to think Sophia was jealous of my figure. See she wore tight dresses, daisy dukes and my mom later started wearing those things too. They always had their butts hanging out of some outfit; I don't think they really set a good example for me. I followed what I saw; I wanted that attention they were getting, I had a shape, and it wasn't so bad to expose it, if they were doing it. Sophia kicked it to Justin like I was a tramp, and to keep away from me. I was cute but off limits, she had no clue we were kicking it together the entire time and what she said never bothered us.

Getting my boys

They slowed down on leaving us alone so much when they caught us almost about to have sex, I would have lost my virginity then if it would not have been for them catching us. We both got our butts tore up Justin got beat with an cord, my beat down wasn't as bad, my mom was shocked most of all. My mom wanted to give me the talk then and Sophia wanted to be there to coach, but when it was time to respond and express myself. I stuttered and always had from a child getting it from my dad, he stuttered too. Sophia and some people thought I was slow because I wasn't able to express myself verbally as quick as they, so often they would use that to have the upper hand on me in conversation. It was said I was dumb, because of how I talked and when I use to get upset it got worse. One point in my life my mom had me in speech therapy class in Florida, I wasn't really teased about it until I moved to Atlanta. I would ignore it because of what Justin and I would talk about when we were alone; Justin would take the teasing to another level when he was in front of our moms. When I was teased nothing was said, sometimes my mom laughed too, I came to the point by then my mom was with whatever was going outside of me. My sister was still too little, but her self esteem was tampered with as well. They called her a dummy and talked about how dark skin she was, every flaw she had was exposed to her by the time she was four. She would cry and Sophia would pop her for it, Sophia even blamed her for her finger slammed in the car trunk one day, I personally thought Sophia did it on purpose. It wasn't easy getting adjusted to living with Sophia and the boys, it seem like her and my mom got closer the more things got difficult. We couldn't afford to continue to live in the home by Griffin Middle anymore, so the following year we moved to the City of Atlanta. The West End area, I would be going to Sylvan Middle School, it was a very ruff part of town different from where we were before. Justin was in Michigan of course for the summer and I was in Atlanta, so by the time he got back we were at another resident. My relatives from Florida came up before school started my cousin Farah, her mom Pearlie, my granny, and my youngest Aunt Jacey; they stayed over my granny's friend house. They heard so much about all the moving, and the calibration between Sophia and my mom, my granny thought it was fishy; she looked at my mom in two ways, gay and weak. She was confused how William was out of the picture and Sophia was in, she was so disappointed in my mom's decisions and my sister and I involved. Farah, Justin, Justin's friend and I all went to hang out downtown at the CNN; the theater was the spot on Saturdays. My cousin and Justin were looking at each other throughout the time we were out, my cousin knew Justin was the boyfriend that I had since the six grade but she really didn't care, she was here for four days and having fun in the meantime. We went to see Bebe's Kids that day and later were back at the house; the parents went out for the evening and left all of us alone that night. We had a screened in front porch that we hung out on, Justin had everybody laughing telling them about my fight stories from the spring break in sixth grade and fights in the seventh grade I was in that got me in or out-school suspension. We got our hands on Hennessey that was left behind and started taking shots, that's when it got interesting. Justin and my cousin started flirting with each other instantly, he said, "it's her sweet smile", that attracted him, I was a little disturbed, but what was I going to say. I didn't even know if we were still in a relationship at that point, I was going on hopes. I right away decided I wouldn't get angry or put fought on anyone, I had to live with Justin after her visit. I was more hurt that he would go there with a family member. Love wasn't involved it was four days, it was basically attraction, she wasn't interested in explaining anything to me knowing I had some sort of history with Justin, she was going home in a couple of days. I just thought it was funny how I was always blamed for being the fast one; my Aunt Pearlie would have never saw her daughter being capable. I knew the family heard about me and Justin getting caught almost about to have sex before. Until this day I don't know if Justin and my cousin had sex when they left the front porch, I left the scene and stayed where I was. When my cousin went back home, Justin and I talked, I got the awareness we were friends and just that, he liked me, but I wasn't his type as he put it. I was more of a buddy, what we went through last year was a fling, even though we still flirted like we were together up until he left. I could only accept what it was, I was a flirter too, and I never liked anyone more than they liked me except Justin. School was starting and I had to adjust to this new surrounding, Justin and I lied again telling people we were cousins, our moms started claiming to be sisters. It was going to be different from the last school we were in, and then Justin got a ride from his mom while I walked. We were going to be walking or riding the school bus together this time. School was starting and once again I didn't have new school clothes, I went to the point last year too stealing my mom's little skirt to where, so I can be cute, and get attention in the neighborhood. It was hard to see Justin getting things from his grandmother and dad and I not get anything. My granny use to buy me things, but her being angry at my mom for the decisions she was making was taking out on me. I would have to deal with it and keep it moving, I wanted to get more involved in extra curriculum activities, so I can stayed busy. I had not been in anything since I played the clarinet in the sixth grade, the reeds were starting to get expensive, the clarinet I had was from a secondhand store and it started giving out on me. It was too much for my mom to get the corks replaced, so she just gave up that was the first and last thing I had been involved in. I stood out in the new school, it was a hood school and these kids were use to the worst of a situation. I was thinking of a way out of poverty, they were comfortable in poverty; the life they saw was all they knew. This school was all about who could fight the best or who was the rudest. If you could fight you were popular, everybody respected you, and did what you asked. I was a fighter, but these girls were warriors you just are not punking them and getting away with it. I had to make some type of name for myself and I knew it, how and when I didn't know. I began trying to get recognition the right way, extracurricular activities; I tried out for the drill team and made it. I wasn't supported at home, but that was the least of my worries I was involved in something. Sophia was an unhealthy competitor, I felt like she persuaded my mom to the magnitude that if she supported me it was wrong, because if Sophia didn't approve of it my mom was not that interested. Justin supported me, he was really proud that I was doing something positive. If I didn't know anything else I knew I was going to be good at performing, my family in general was always known for dancing in Tampa. I did really well on the drill team when we had pep rallies and games; I just didn't want to do the schoolwork, it was too much distraction in class. When I got home I was so entertained spending time with Justin homework was a bother. I had a problem reading aloud in class, because I didn't want to be teased by my classmates about my stuttering. It wasn't like I didn't know the work or I wasn't listening, My speech caused me not to participate in class, which wasn't helping me pass the class to stay on the drill team. My grades didn't allow me to stay on the squad, if you tested me I could answer enough to pass, but everything else I was a mess with. My surroundings started getting the best of me I wasn't being accepted for the good deeds by my peers, so I had to prove I could hang with the crowd. The eight grade class queen was even hardcore, she was a twin and both were known for fighting and playing basketball they were my target. I was cool with them because we lived by each other, and we would walk home together sometimes. I had got kicked off the school bus for wrestling; we use to have matches between the boys and girls every afternoon. I joined the basketball team just to stay cool with the twins and played for a while before they cut me once again for my grades. I was very good though, I was second string point guard, and did my thing when I had the opportunity. Justin and I would play basketball together all the time that's what helped me get on the team. I was unnecessarily angry from what I was around; it was a ruff area I heard and saw things I had never since seen. My home life was getting worst as well we were struggling, it was times we had no heat and had to boil pots for hot water to bath with, get electric heaters to put in the room we were in to keep it warm. My mom was the only income, and she was hustling hair, her clients were from our old area, and it was a different atmosphere for them, so business became slow for her. She hustled as much as she could, but it wasn't enough most of the times. We ate Church's Chicken every night $4.99 eight piece special for months with no sides; it wasn't the best situation to be in. Justin and I became very close, we often talked about how we were living, while our mom's were always in and hanging out smoking and partying. They had the best times in the rough times which made our little minds turn, the type of habits they had were not cheap. My mom was the real go getter out of the two; Sophia didn't like the fact that my mom would meet men that always wanted to help her out of her situation, why she would decide to stay in it, I never knew. She would have to leave Sophia were she was and that's one thing she wasn't going to do, they were in it together. Weird now I think about it. Justin would tell me how my mom was a whore; both of our moms would wear the sleaziest outfits they could find. My mom was the bigger one out of the two and it pulled the most attention, they would look like they were working the corner. I was thinking that my mom was keeping up with Sophia, Sophia was always wearing something little and fitting. She wanted attention however possible, my mom was too big to wear those things, and she dressed differently before. It would embarrass me, but what could I say to make her change we rarely talked. Justin would disrespect his mom to all extents telling her he wanting to kill her and pulling knives on her. They would fight to the point where my mom would have to jump between them to stop them, it would not happen all the time, but I think Justin tolerate level reached its highest point dismayed in his moms behavior. Justin and I were alone often, and we would play around with each other sexually; he would do oral sex on me every time we had these moments for months. One day he finally talked me into letting him have sex with me, I would never forget the evening we were on the couch and our moms were in the room, smoking. They use to be in the room for hours at a time to the levels we had enough time to have moments with no interruptions; it was like they only came out to make sure we ate, and fuss at us for something we did or didn't do. It was an experience that was scary, fun at the same time, I think we got closer with each other because of that connection we experienced being each other's first sexual partner. Our relationship at that point became my only life; we spent every moment together after that. Justin having ways like his mom challenged me positive and negatively, it was mostly negative though, I was dogged all the time, so for a while I started believing I wasn't good at anything. I was a mischief at times developing the character they spoke about, I stole money out Sophia's purse to pay a debt I didn't really owe (the most dangerous girl wanted to fight me, I wasn't ready, and I paid her to leave me alone), fought after school, and stealing out of the corner store, and getting caught. I was in a gang by spring time. My mom had to come get me out of juvenile for a burglary scene that happened before I got to the gang's house, I still ended up getting locked up for being there when the police arrived. The reputation for me defending myself became the gossip to the point where it made the girls in the gang jealous; they actually rolled up to the house looking for me to jump me. That was something else to talk about within my household; I wasn't home at the time. Justin and I were hanging out downtown, I heard like six to eight girls showed that day. Two weeks before school was out, I brought a knife to school and challenged all the girls that showed at the house, the knife I had was the biggest I could find in the house, and it was dull. I just had to prove a point that whatever they initially thought was not going to be the outcome turned out to be. I was cute but was not going to be easily chump off; I was not the hardest and wasn't going to get jumped. I thought they were scary for wanting to jump me and not fight me one on one. Well, I got caught with the knife because one of the girls went and told the Assistant Principle. My mom came and I was not to return for the remainder of the year, so that was 8th grade for me. The only positive that happened in that time was, I was asked to go with a client of my mom's that took me to participate in a music video with TLC; it was the song "GET IT UP," off the soundtrack Poetic Justice. When the video came out I was disappointed, because it wasn't the same video we shot that night. I guess the producer wanted something different, it was a great experience over all. While all that was going on Justin and I were still having unprotected sex every chance, we got with no concern about getting pregnant, just having fun before he left. Justin was moving to Flint for a while with his grandmother and father, so Sophia could get on her feet. I was going to remain in Atlanta with my mom; she got hired with Bronner Bros in the West End. Well, plans change when our house got broken into one night after Justin left, Sophia got stabbed 17 times, my mom once right above her heart, the story made news. My mom thought it was a good time for me to go back to Florida with my granny while she recouped and get herself back together from the incident. I wasn't ready to leave my mom under her conditions, but she thought it was best. At the time I didn't know I was pregnant this was like the beginning of August. School was starting and I would go to high school with my cousin Farah, I hadn't seen or spoke to her since she visited that previous summer. I got into Hillsborough High with the promise to the assistant principal that I would stay on my best behavior and not get into any trouble. Hillsborough was known for education and sports, a good school to attend. My records from Atlanta were not good, my grades were just enough to pass, but the behavior record was bad. I got in on a good leg with school, personally I started going through the nightmares. Thoughts in my mind of things I saw that night Sophia and my mom were stabbed. The man jumped on my back and out of reaction I hit him with the lamp that was close, the police saw were the lamp had been thrown. I did the best I could internally to deal with it and focus on school. Moving back to Tampa I visited my god mother who of course heard about me and Justin's love affair at one point while I was away. She told me it would hurt her for me to get pregnant and all boys wanted was what was in my panties. I respected her and didn't want to disappoint her in no way, not knowing things where growing and forming in other areas of my life. I really had my mind made up that I was going to be the person that made the naysayers quiet. I came up with a "don't give them anything to talk about" motto, everything I did would be good something positive to get me noticed in another light. That was what I did, I was doing so good in school and at home with my aunt and cousin, I was very grateful for her welcoming me in her home helping my mom in her time of need. I was content in Hillsborough High School, meeting new people and getting my mind free from what happened to us in Atlanta. I got hit with the when was your last period question; I wasn't too concerned about the period coming every month at that time. I had only having them for a year or so and wasn't really comfortable with the every month proceedings so if it haven't shown, I was content. In Tampa the elders kept up with making sure no mistakes are made without them knowing. They watched me a little more than my mom would have and noticed my body changing more than I had. I figured it had been a while since I had sex; pregnancy was the least of my interest. I was scheduled an appointment, by the time I got to the checkup I was almost 5 mos. I can't even explain to you how I got that far, it looked like a 3 month bump. I was so small. That's when the change started in how they treated me, the comments "I knew you were fast", "you hot in the ***", "who baby is it." Well, when they got to that last comment that's when I had something to say, you can say whatever you want about me being in the position, but I knew who got me in that position it was only one person. Justin James. In regard to Justin, he denied ever being with me once the news got to him. I wasn't really worried, because I had real facts, and it was going to be proven when I had the baby, plus Justin was saying this because we had distance.

My granny suggested that I put my baby up for adoption, give him to the care of one of my Great Aunt's whom adopted children, a chain smoker in Plant City, Florida. My granny had good intentions, she did not want to slow my life down by no means; I was a baby myself. I just didn't have the heart to carry, deliver, and then pass him on to a person who I thought would not love the way I would have. I was young, but I knew that I would adjust and make due, they were going to talk about me regardless. They even took me over to discuss everything with my Great Aunt; I turned it down. When it got back to my school that I was pregnant, they suggested withdrawing me and sending me to an alternative school for expecting young mothers until I have the baby. The remainder of my 9th grade year that's where I attended high school, a school designed to support and educates pregnant teens. I even took a child development class that was required, it educated me on child birth/care, CPR, etc. I was learning on my grade level and adult as well, it was the best thing for me when I think about it now. I knew things about taking care of a baby naturally helping my mom so much with my sister growing up, but this was different. I needed to know everything I could to take care of my baby and that was something I didn't really have an option on doing. Micah R. D. was born in Tampa General Hospital the same hospital as I. When I had him all I could think about was how, I would love this kid that I had not asked for and what would I do with him being so young and raising him all alone. I had the support of my Aunt Pearlie in the delivery room and cousin Farah who fainted. The call was made to my mom and Sophia who was also denying that it was her son's baby. It made me feel bad being doubted and the fact that they were denying Micah, I never worried about going out of my way to prove anything or arguing over the fact that he was Justin's. His mom supposedly called and asked him was it his or could it be his, he told her I had been with other dudes and I had him mistaken. I knew once they saw the truth it would make their face break with shame. They had a habit of displaying the perfect family scene, so Justin having a baby young was beneath their family standards. I adjusted easily with the push and support from my aunt, granny, and cousin, we were making it work. I used their negative words along with their help to get through. I really had no other outlet in the situation; my god mother was not speaking to me not all after hearing I had a baby. I can remember getting off the city bus from the alternative school, her passing right pass me and my son like I was a stranger. I cried like crazy to my granny who really felt bad for me, but understood the level of pain and disappointment from my god mother as she shared the same feelings. I made sure I keep my grades up in school; I was on welfare, food stamps, and W.I.C. I contributed to my aunt's household as I did not have a choice, but it taught me another level of responsibility. I did very *well* for myself under the conditions and terms, since I had a baby I was the person to watch like a hawk. I was bold in action if I did it you knew it, I was never good at covering up things. I figure since I was always topic of discussion what was the point in being quite and sneaky. My cousin Farah she was off the chain on the down low, my aunt didn't want it to be her daughter solely, because that would have made me look like I might have had good sense. My cousin and I got in our dirt together and separately regardless of how it went, I was always the mastermind let the story be told. We had a dance group that helped us stay out of trouble for most of the time; we won our high school competition the following year when I was back at Hillsborough High and performed for different events in the area as well. We became popular around school from upper classmen because of how good we danced. I was known as the stronger vessel and I stood up for my cousin without a thought. Everyone knew I had the baby; at that time I think I was the only one in school with a baby by 10th grade year. My peers respected the fact that I had not giving up on school and made solid decisions. My cousin's decisions weren't as solid; she developed a reputation for having more than a couple of sexual partners. Peers liked her, thought she was cool, but they took her character lightly in comparison to mine. We had a good time with each other; it was like we were sisters despite everything else. As Micah got a little older it was things, I had to slow down doing, I was left home more and even replaced in the dance group at one point. It was like majority of the support was in the beginning, but the more I started standing out the more the reminder of my responsibility was thrown at me. I feel my Aunt Pearlie showed favoritism at times, which was understandable. I was living under her roof and had no choice, but to accept what was going on, I had a child. I wanted him to be treated a certain way and get use to a standard that I did know or a standard better than the one I knew. It was hard to do being that I was a child still being raised myself. I had a relationship with an upper class man named Leo; he was nice, introducing me to the treatment of a Lady at a young age. He got a job to support and help me out with my son, got his car fixed so we could get around and taught me how to drive. I even used his car for my Drivers Ed test and passed. My aunt really didn't care for our relationship; he was treating me better than the man she had been with for years. She respected our closeness, but didn't care too much for it. I went to his junior prom had a blast; my cousin went as well despite the trouble she was getting into. Leo would get upset with my Aunt Pearlie because it were things I believed done unfair to me. It was getting a bit over bearing and I was ready for a change, it was time for me to go back home to Atlanta. My mom agreed that it was time for me to come back with her and my sister by the end of my 10th grade year. I would have to leave Leo behind; I was going to miss him along with a chance of getting back into the dance group. Who knows where the continuance of dancing could have gone if I would have stayed involved, it was a very constructive activity for me. I moved back as soon as school let out, my mom had connected me with a job where she was hired before I left, Bronner Brothers. Justin was living in the Riverdale area with his mom, about 25 minutes from the City of

Atlanta; we really hadn't talked since I had the baby. My Aunt Jacey brought Micah up once in between the time we were in Tampa. Sophia and Justin wanted to see for themselves which were not a problem for me; I was ready to prove them wrong without words. My mom was finally in her own place, after another bad relationship breakup. My mom was dating this loser that was beating on her; she turned into this semi Muslim, just to establish more of a bond with him. It was not as negative as I initially thought; the religion changed her from where she was, so it was a good thing to an extent. She studied and followed some of their beliefs growing as a better person for herself. I had an opportunity in meeting him when I was visiting for spring break, he and I got into a bad argument during a short period. I just couldn't see myself being hit on and talked to like I was trash, when he didn't know me. My mom inherited some bad habits from Sophia, she described me to the man like this trouble child, who had a bad attitude and was hard to control. So, his approach was instantly aggressive toward me, like he was going or had to straighten me out. When I left we got the message that he beat her with a belt buckle, I would never forget how bad my aunts cried for her. My Aunt Pearlie was in a bad relationship like that with her ex husband, so she could relate. We was glad to hear she was in her own space, stable enough for me and my son to living with. I worked the job she got for me and the babysitter that watched my little sister at one point watched my son. She was a nice older Lady with an in-home daycare that was affordable and Justin started watching him on the weekend. Our moms were still cool, but they were still mad we made them early grandmothers, so, they didn't allow us to see each other. When school started I attended Terrell High School in Southwest Atlanta. My mom had grown attached to the West End, her job would have been a good excuse why, but she lived there even before the job. I personally would have moved far away from the area that stunned my growth, if I had better options. I made up my mind that I was not going to let my mom's decision slow my progress down at any point, when I had a good opportunity to improve myself I was going to take it. My goals at that time were to keep my baby looking good; his childcares paid, and finish school. Justin was not working and our baby had to have certain things, I really never pressed Justin about getting a job to help with the baby. I understood that he was going to develop into a man at his own time, I was glad he had accepted that fact Micah was his, after the first look at him. Justin watching him was creating a bond between the two that mattered to me the most. I was thinking Justin would want to see his child with certain things, and he would do what he had to do to make sure his child had them. I was still hurt that Justin denied Micah, but a man with fear would say the things he said, I can imagine. Before summer was over, I had to quit the full time job and find a part time job to keep Micah in daycare. I got a job a Dairy Queen close by our house, it paid like $125-175 a week. That was enough to cover daycare, my pager bill, and extra for Micah's wardrobe. I was always complimented on how he looked and I liked that. It made me feel like I was taking good care of him for my age. I was really not into what I was wearing until school started, I didn't have the resources to buy me any school clothes I wore what I had from Florida the previous school year. I wasn't looked at much because of what I wore, I was cute in the face, but I was known as the chick with the baby, people would see with Micah in the neighborhood and at the local mall. It was obvious I was taking care of my son, when you saw us together and noticed what I was wearing. I had to figure something out to take the attention of my wardrobe, so I started becoming the bad girl I left off being before I relocated to Florida. It wasn't hard, some people remembered me from Middle School. I became a little cool for driving; it wasn't many of us able to drive to school at that time, so those that did stuck out. I was going in another direction from when I originally came back to Atlanta. I displayed the, "I don't care how I get noticed attitude"; taken account how the boys in school responded to me, asking for rides everywhere. I got to the point of taking the car at night driving to Riverdale, sneaking in Justin room window to have sex periodically. I got caught when the insurance went up from getting numerous speeding tickets; my license got suspended for missing court appearances. Driving the car ceased after I was in the open, I had too much freedom and wasn't making wise decision. I didn't even want to see the school parking lot once that took place and my peers didn't want to see or speak to me. Mom couldn't maintain the house long after the man she was dating moved out. I think it was because mom had got pregnant; she ended up terminating the pregnancy. I drove her to the clinic and got the procedure done, thinking it was dysfunctional, but that's the support my mom needed from me at the time. I told mom the guy wasn't going to last long, glad for whatever reason they were splitting. I wasn't his biggest fan after his performance at Dairy Queen one afternoon asking my manager to let me go because I was working against labor laws. I wasn't interested in the labor laws; I asked for extra hours, they gave them to me. I end up losing that job when winter came half because of that episode. Mom and I moved with Sophia to Riverdale, it was a total eight of us in a three bedroom, one and a half bath house. I was allowed to drive again to finish the school year out until Therrell kicked me out. I got into a clash with the coach that checked book bags at the metal detector in the morning; Therrell gotten really bad with fights and kids bringing guns to school, so they put up metal detectors at the entrance. The coach reached in my purse taking my pager one morning and I reacted, slapping the man in his face. It was close to the end of the year, so it was easy for them to tell my mom I couldn't return when she came up there to get the pager for me. I was transferred to North Clayton High School and that's where I would be attending that upcoming year. Even though I was living in Riverdale getting transferred North Clayton High was a joy to Sophia, Justin was going to Riverdale High, the school that was in our address district. Sophia didn't want us to go to the same school, not wanting her son's image tarnished to his peers by them knowing he had a child that young. I had a standing reputation by then; I was nothing that you wanted to be bothered with. I had been to jail for stealing blunts out of Kroger which Justin mom came and got me completely throwing her hands up with discredit for me being the woman her child had a child with. My mom by then had quit Bonner Bros and started building her own business was not into leaving and missing any chances of making money, she had been on her own for about four months by then. Justin mom would tell me I wasn't a good mother and I would question what she was saying because I was the sole provider for our son. I went only a couple of months unemployed; I kept a job making sure he had childcare and his necessities. I would go to the Riches (now called Macy's) in Greenbriar and steal Micah's clothes until that stop when I got caught. One more arrest, mom came that time to get me I was taking to juvenile and my legal guardian had to sign me out. I wasted time in this stage of my life thinking back to it, discovering elements of life I had no business compelling. Justin was quieter that I was, but down for whatever I was doing knowing I had good intentions. He never had the heart I did, for what I called "spontaneous missions." When I got to North Clayton, it was funny, because everything I did at Therrell got there from a couple of boys that had cousins at Therrell and remembered hearing my name, so I had the bad girl image. The image I instantly had I didn't portray I like the attention my look was getting, everyone thought I was cute. I didn't pick up on it for a while, but when I did it made me act differently. My old peers at Therrell were so jealous hearing my name at North Clayton being more accepted. They labeled me "high class" I was puzzled about the comment, because my wardrobe had not improved from when I first moved back from Florida. North Clayton made me focus a little more in school; being accepted made it easier to walk through halls. The girls wanted to hang with me, because the boys thought I was cool. It was funny because it was like the girls were taking notes and I was just being me. I had upper classmen around all the time, everyone knew I had a baby, but I was still making the effort to get through school that alone gained me more respect. When I was at Therrell it wasn't that easy, so I welcomed the love. I was nominated for Miss 11th grade, which made me feel really pretty. Even to this day

I have no idea how, I got pushed into it, I just know I had to where the plum gown the school designed for us, my mom came, did my makeup to further advertising her work. I didn't even make running up, but the gesture gained me more recognition with my peers. I think the speech part messed my chances up during the campaigning process, I didn't know what to say and stuttering did help, I got on the lectern saying, "You know what it is." They thought it was hood some laughing; some booing as I quickly walked off. Justin supported what was going on, but Sophia was not interested at all, it was too positive for her. I had a graduate from the previous year picking up his sister notice me; that's when I took note I was the girl to have. The relationship with Justin was what I had once I got home, I never thought about him before then, I was a social bug in school and our relationship was nothing I discussed. We moved to another place, not far from where we were before Sophia, her children, my mom, and us. Sophia's brother's had finally made their way to another place, which was the best thing they could do for themselves. Justin and I talked about trying to be more of a couple for Micah, but honestly I was still flirting at school and out of school. I moved around a little more than Justin wanted me too, I had a mature habit by then, I had to hang where the smoking weed was taking place. He understood and accepted it; I paid for everything we did for Micah and with each other when we had a chance. Justin became my at home man, it was like I had another life, so I continued doing what I was doing. I continued to build my popularity; I stayed in school more than I did at Therrell, so that aspect was improving. I was just picky about which classes I did and didn't want to take, those I didn't I would leave, go smoke or eat, and come back to the class I did like. A guy started school named Mason was in my Science class. He was the most interesting person I had ever seen at this school. The way he dressed, talked was so unique it made me want to know about him. He didn't pay me any attention like everybody else, odd, but I liked that about him. It was a while before we made conversation in class and when we did have a conversation we never agreed on the same thing.

He became a challenge (I was developing one of my mom's bad habits looking back on this time), it was more than a month, and a half before we became cool in class, and exchanged numbers along with talking on the phone. I had a limit on talking on the phone, because Justin and I did live in the same house, I would at times sneak, and use my mom's cell phone when I could. We were more friends than anything, Justin did notice the change, I was growing distant from him, he became hurt and jealous, but I was not bothered. The life I formed was more interesting than the one I had with him, I was experiencing life, I was 17. I thought about the relationship and Justin being so commented to making things work for the sake of our child I took for granted, thinking I was missing out on something better. I went on a Tennessee trip with a friend from school to see some guys we met on freaknik weekend; I stole the school letter head from the office and made a field trip permission slip for our parents to sign stating we were going on a college tour. When I came home from the weekend, Justin had tattooed my complete middle name on his chest big as day, explaining how he would never let go. Justin was nice, don't get me wrong I was dead wrong for what I had been doing, but he wasn't moving enough for me, Justin was almost 18 and still had not had or tried to get a job to help me with Micah. He was an at-home-father, it was just a turn off, I played both roles and one. At one point I even took a position at the daycare that Micah attended just to cut the weekly expense, doing whatever helped. I ran game on the young dudes and some old ones to get extra money if the chance presented itself. In the mist of all this Mason and I continued to build our relationship without having sex, we had not got to that point. We talked, laughed, and smoked majority of the time, it had to have been four month into the friendship before I confessed to Mason about Justin. Mason was cool about it, but it was things that still concerned him, he asked me, "are you still sleeping with Justin" and didn't wait for the answer before he could tell me, "if you are you needed to stop." I listened and respected him; it seemed after that conversation we were around each other more. Even after school, he would get a friend to take me to pick Micah up, when I wasn't working, and take me to drop him off with Justin. I would take Micah in the house, leave right back out to go with Mason riding, smoking and chilling until we had to turn it in for the night. Justin started doing weird stuff at school to get noticed, like helping his friends fight and coming to school drunk. I was the least entertained, I was keeping up with Mason; he was dropping out of school for good. Mason didn't have the interest anymore; he was into making money more than anything. Mason not being in school made me not want to be in school either, we really wanted to be together more at that point, and he said he was going to see to it that we were together at all cost. I believed him because of the fact he was sleepless over the living arrangements I was currently in, right after spring he let me know that we could move in his mom's property that she had in College Park. I was down with no hesitation, with no concern about what anyone thought or what my mom would say, she was doing her thing anyway, I would be out of her hair.

Me and my boys

Moving into the house I felt new just like everything around me. The subdivision wasn't even complete; it may have had six or seven houses including ours. Explaining the details about everything to my mom, she never bothered to come by to at least see where I was. The house was initially for Masons' sister, but she had abandoned it running around doing drugs from what I heard. It was a chance his sister would come back we were told, but wasn't focused on that; it was just a sense of freedom to have our own. I hadn't met Mason's mother yet, but spoken to her plenty of times on the phone giving her my word I would keep up with the property. Mason never really told me the details about their relationship, I just knew she was a DEA Agent, lived in New Jersey, and that we would visit one day. She wanted the house we were living in to be for her daughter, because of the close relationship they had, in hopes that she would straighten out her life. Mason explained that he was trying to rebuild a relationship with his mom; Mason and I taking care of the house would create a starting point for them to rebuild. I never really cared about the relationship he did not have with his mom, I was happy to have escaped my living arrangements where I was. I could tell Justin was still in state of shock when I would come by to drop Micah off or pick him up. My mom was caught up in her life with another guy who was a real loser, so I kept moving forward. Justin would cry expressing how he couldn't believe that I was with a lame like Mason. Bringing up that Mason still liked a young lady named Spring, a female I popped up on at her school and almost got locked up getting her straight about the connection Mason and I had between her changing classes. That was just the first time, again, at a party at the Country Club that always held teenage parties. I think Justin was saying whatever he could to deter me. My vision was too blurry from the shine of the newness. Things that Justin said I knew were out of hurt. Justin had too much time to think unemployed not able to found a job, but I was working, at the local CVS (my fifth job by 17) and supporting Micah. Nothing had changed with Justin; part of me was still hurt that we had broking up officially, however, I wasn't going to do anything to risk the freedom I had with Mason, we were really happy. I waited 10 months before having sex with Mason I think it helped develop the friendship we had in the beginning. Mason never admitted it, but I know I was his first. He fooled around; but had never been all the way with anyone. It seemed like a month after we finally had sex the house living arrangements was presented to me. While picking up Micah one afternoon from Justin's, he expressed how much he missed us, it was so emotional. I had sex with him that day out of sympathy, it was like we were still together, and it was like I felt bad for what I did to his feelings. I had produced so much with Mason at that point; I knew I was wrong thinking about it on the ride home, and promising myself it would never happen again. I felt so guilty I couldn't even look Mason in the face when I got home; I just smoked myself to sleep that night. I did my best to stay away from coming inside to pick Micah up after that, I would just honk the horn, and wait on him to come out with Micah. Things started settling down, and we began to have a good routine going that was working for us in a cooperative way. Mason and I were saving money to start decorating the house how I wanted. One night when we were sleeping, his sister came home in the middle of the night. She looked sick and weak; her skin had dark blotches reminding me of a drugged or homeless person. Mason and his sister hadn't seen one another in years; I could tell he was embarrassed that she looked the way she did. He remembered good things about her like how she always protected him, as well as being smart, attractive and very athletic. He told me about the rumor through the family about the drug abuse completely true, and seeing that it was, we didn't know the level it had taken her too. Mason told me the peace we were having would shortly come to an end, and it was true. I noticed his sister buying Ensure milkshakes, she had an odor that was different like a detoxifying smell, but I never feed into it. She was in her mid twenties, so I look at her like one of us and nothing less only wanting to treat her like family. Mason told me not to trust her or get too attached. He told me she was a snake, a brown nose to their mom, but I thought he was just paranoid. Mason's mom would call us asking about her and calling her asking about us. Weeks went by time; I got comfortable, and rolled up a blunt in front of her. Thinking we all had some type of habit, so who could be critical. Well, little did I know rolling and smoking that blunt in front of her turned into the worst day? She went back to their mom and told her we were running a drug cartel. Mason was hot, that's the first time his temperament was displayed in front of me. Mason cursed his mom out like he didn't know her, and the aunt as well for not allowing Micah in the daycare any more. Mason's aunt ran an in-home daycare and started watching Micah. Micah was a typical little boy, but very well mannered, I did what I did still having time to talk and show Micah right from wrong. The expense of child was reasonable, even though it was Mason's family I still paid his aunt something every week out of appreciation; it was her means of living. Mason's mom asked us to move out of the house asap, I was in state of shock how things changed with the information she knew about her daughter. I let Mason know that everything was up to him to take care of because I had no support going backward. I informed my mom of what happened and she told me to withstand the best way I could, she was moving from out of the house with Sophia, and breaking up with the guy she was dating. Mason made arrangements for us to stay with his father, it wasn't going to be that bad because his dad was a postal worker who worked graveyard and slept all day. He had been very nice to me before, when I would visit when Mason and I were just friends. Mason let me know that we would move within a six month time frame, wanting to save more money. I personally thought we had enough saved, Mason was into making sure we were secure, not wanting for us to struggle with Micah being young and on our own. I noticed my cycle hadn't come on that month; I instantly thought Justin could be a possible person in this pregnancy, knowing I was already, and still feeling guilty. I didn't mention anything to Mason, but I did take Justin and I last ordeal into consideration. I let Justin know it was a possibility between him and Mason, just in case. Justin was so upset he said he didn't want to speak to me again. I was just being safe, not knowing what could have happened from what we done, and I didn't have the dates to remember, life was moving fast around that time. I could only imagine how Mason would have responded, if he knew something occurred between Justin and me. When everything was confirmed that I was having a baby, it got to Mason's mom, she regretted putting us out of the house, and started trying to reach out again. Mason mentioned something like his mom was trying to come around to see if she could help, so she wouldn't have to pay that last year of payments. It kind of went over my head then, but it explained how Mason dressed so nice in school. Mason's dad didn't have anything to say that favored her and made comments that she was dying of cancer. After the divorce between the two, she put her career first priority over taking care of Mason. She really never wanted Mason around because she didn't want to deal with the dad. Out of everything I heard, I was most taken that the dad took her to court for child support and got full custody as well. That said more than enough and I knew it was something more to the story. I stayed clear of it, I was not messing up what I had going on, my living options were limited. Mason told me after what his mom did to us he wasn't going to communicate with her anymore or anytime soon. It was different being pregnant on this time around because I had a supportive partner sharing the experience with me. I applied for stamps, healthcare and put Micah in pre-k program in Fayetteville.

Justin agreed to help pay for pre-k, it was like $18 a week, but his level of hate toward what I did to him and what I was doing with Mason intervened. Justin started ignoring my call when I was calling to inquire about the weekly payments due for Micah's school. It went on for four or five months until Mason was over me being concerned about it and thought we should do something else about it. Mason took me to the child support office, encouraging me to put Justin on child support, so the calling and begging another man to help with his responsibility would stop. I wasn't worried about Justin allowing Micah to visit because of the action; he wasn't allowing him to visit anyway. Mason just didn't want me stressing about anything being pregnant, I was just perplexed about Justin's behavior toward Micah the two had such a good bond. I called Justin before I went to submit the papers to the office to ask him for his address, telling him what I needed it for, he responded as if he didn't care at all. I progressed on after that day, I had another life to worry about. I went back to school trying to continue my education as much as I could before the baby came. It was tough, but I hung in there. Mason's attitude started becoming unpredictable, he just wasn't happy when I came out the house; it was like he made my mornings the worst before taking me to school. My peers could not believe how our relationship had grown, they remembered him from the year before and were shocked that we were living together and having a baby. Being a small body frame moving around in school, the activeness took a toll on me where the doctor asked me to slow down, but I couldn't listen to that. I didn't tell the doctor I was working at Publix some evenings after school, the doctor would have enforced bed rest. I was doing want I could to help save toward the move, living with his dad was cool, but it wasn't the freedom we first had. Mason's childish attitude showed more than I ever knew it could. I noticed Mason getting comfortable with us staying with his dad and not paying bills, so he had more money to put into his car. That was not the original plan we had, so when I started confronting the issue he became violent toward on me. Mason becoming violent toward me wasn't like Farrah

Facet in Burning Bed; it was more of torture tactics. For a minute I thought he was mad at me not being his friend anymore like, I was before I got pregnant. I had to become more motherly having my second child being 18. Mason would go into these rampages dragging me out of the house, strip my clothes off, leaving me outside naked. The events would happen while I was pregnant I kept it to myself trying to keep what we were building going, but I was in a bad place physically, emotionally for me and Micah. I became bitter with myself having the feeling that I made a bad decision having unprotected sex, but I dealt with things knowing I was away from the living arrangements with Sophia and Justin. Along with the abuse the drama that came in our direction from Justin confirmed to me that Mason was not going to be my long term partner. Justin started dating a young lady that was trying to make her baby daddy jealous by dating Justin. The two had sex together; the guy discovered what happened and did a drive by shooting, trying to scare Justin away from dealing with the young lady. To make Justin mad the guy wanted to find Justin's baby mom and make a pass on her, which was me. He was bold enough to come up to the shop where Mason worked to ask him about me. Mason stood up for all 5'4 of his rights, went and got strapped. He was going to shoot who ever was coming for the second round of questions and really wanted to target Justin for some reason. I can remember coming down the street coming to a traffic light, Mason having Micah and I duck thinking he saw Justin riding in the area. I believe Mason was still mad at Justin for trying to grab him out of the car one day when he came by to pick me up at the house when I was staying with him. I felt bad for Micah; hearing beef between Mason and his dad. The little boy loved his dad, but respected Mason, Mason provided, it was obvious Micah liked what he did from a material standpoint. Mason gave us the best holiday's, birthday's, taking him to movies, and letting Micah ride places with him, while Justin was playing the "miss me" game. Mason also took care of Micah's childcare while Justin was not able; it was those things that let me know what type of father Mason was going to be for his own son. He was concerned about the welfare of Micah, even in his bad attitude. I remember Mason kicking me out the house one night, throwing my clothes all over the lawn, and leaving Micah sleep. Out of fear of him maybe hurting my son, I wasn't trying to leave Micah in the house; he had to come outside with me. Mason kicked him out too, screaming, "take him with you then" both of us were on the curb at three in the morning. He let us in when he decided he wasn't mad anymore, Mason was embarrassed about his actions when Micah looked at him, that's when things got worse. I stopped going to school a month before the baby came with only a credit and a half left, it turned out to be too much pressure balancing home and school. Mason didn't mind with our arguing escapades at night, me up all night crying, my eyes were too puffy in the mornings. I had already been questioned by one of my peers before if everything at home was ok that previous night he threw a full plastic cup of water on me, just releasing anger. I thought of leaving him once I had the baby and it started coming to my mind more frequently. Right before holidays would come the torture intensified. Then the day of the holiday everything would be fine. It became a habit that I got use to; with me never knowing when he would snap I made sure I stayed quiet, out of his way until he wanted me. He didn't care what he did to me he still expected sex every night which gave me a confusing feeling about our relationship; I figured that things would get better after the baby. I was comfortable with Mason taking care of me and my son blinding myself, saying that the drama wouldn't last always. Trying to maintain the relationship with Mason I would leave Micah home with Mason's dad. Until one day I noticed Micah slapping Mason's dad on the butt like twice and start laughing, Mason's dad tried to spank him to tell him not to do that, Micah looked confused, as if it may have been acceptable to do before. I grabbed Micah pulling him from out of the room with Mason's dad and from then started really monitoring their relationship. Micah never mentioned anything happening, but that doesn't mean nothing ever happened. Til this day I have wondered if my son was shameful, scared, or embarrassed to say Mason's dad played with him inappropriately. Mark Mason Byrd was born after eight hours of labor. I knew I was going to need with Micah so, I sent a message through my mom to Justin and his mom, I thought it would be a good time to see if Justin would step in. I knew it was going to be different dealing with Justin again, I progressed emotionally from that point it was just strictly business between Justin and me, not much to talk about. Mason had gotten fired from the tint shop that he had been working for almost two years having a dispute and now had to find another job. In support I rode around with him filling out applications and even went as far as taking the drug test for him, after he got hired at a warehouse. Mason's income changed drastically from what they were before, we stop hustling the weed for the safety of the boys. I became a stay home mom, Mason made sure I had everything I needed for Mark, but shortly began to feel jealous about the attention I was giving Mark, and Micah making sure he had a certain amount of attention with the new baby around. I was so attached to my boys. Micah began going to Justin on weekends which was very helpful. Mason thought soon as I had the baby it was back to party me that was hardly the case. Mason started taking the relationship between me and the baby personal. At six weeks, I went to see my mom, and Mason dropped us off. The fact that I was leaving I guess for a couple of hours just made him mad. He kicked me out of the car, without the baby knowing I was breastfeeding him, took off, and stayed gone for like three hours. I'm calling him like crazy, the baby screaming in the background, it was the first time he had showed out on me and I had witnesses. My mom had to call and talk him into bringing the baby back; she even started checking on me more often after that day. He started arguments with not just me, but his dad too. They would have fights tearing up the house; at that point I knew a change was near. Micah would be so scared just staring at the two of them; it was no place for the children or me to be. I was completely over him when Mason eased my clothes out the closet one day and was outside burning them. Watching me try on my clothes from losing my baby weight just made him lose his mind. He expected me to stay in baggy clothes I can image; it had been over a year since I looked like a girl. It was time for me to start back dressing like me again. Well, all that was down the drain Mason burned everything that looked like a girl. It was time to get some type of plan together; his dad would even wonder what came over him, not being able to control the situation. My mom had to come over there with a bat and stand up for me after I started losing an extreme amount of weight breast feeding. I wasn't eating how I should have because I didn't have an appetite; my nerves were bad dealing with Mason. The doctor stopped me from breast feeding thinking the baby was taken too much from me, but that was hardly the case. My mom and I got together along with Sophia deciding I would work in the salon; I did a little bookkeeping from home when I was pregnant. I would take the position that Sophia had, administrating the front half of the business for self independence. The word had got back to Justin that I was in an abusive relationship and trying to change the relationship status, which he really had no concern about. He had every reason not to be; the relationship was something I choose to be involved in. He did however start taken more time with Micah and even started helping with his school expenses. It wasn't like I wanted Justin to be concerned for me, but at least more concerned with what his son was around. By the time Mark was more than six months Mason's showing out had gotten worst. The only break I gotten was when I had to go five weekends in jail for driving under a suspended license. I ran into Mason's sister who had to serve weekends as well, she would come in high looking like a zombie, sleeping all weekend with an odor that would knock you off your feet. It had been almost two years since she saw me not identifying who I was; I was thinking she was probably too high. Mason was humiliated when I told him about her along with him seeing how bad she looked for his self, when he came to get me on Sundays. Once my weekends were up it was back to the same in and out drama. I did noticed however when I was gone he had time to miss me, the relationship was better in that period. I started thinking we really needed to separate, but I was scared to say anything. Mason's mind started really drifting away by the time I started at my mom shop his events were crazy. Fighting with his dad, packing the car up with our things knowing we had nowhere to go, kicking me out the car on the way to work, making me walk the rest of the way, coming up to the flea market starting fights with me in the parking lot snatching my jewelry off. I started looking at him like the enemy seriously, he jumped on me and his dad was standing right there. I called the police and his dad told him he didn't see anything. Sophia was the only one who was available to come get me; by the time she came I tried to get my stuff out the house and the boys in the car. I had to fight Mason the entire time; I was embarrassed, nonetheless, she was glad to see me fighting back. The boys and I went to my mom's place to stay, I was over the drama, the relationship, and it was time for me to do for myself and the boys.

Moving allowed me to feel liberated, I knew I would still have to deal with Mason for the sake of Mark, but that was it. I was very disappointed that I was almost 20 with two baby daddies and I hadn't finished high school. Mason was taking it decent that we weren't together; because he was confident I just needed time away, thinking it wasn't going to be long and I would be back. Working with my mom, the business was growing she was creating a reputation for one of the businesses that made money in the flea market. The salon was selling retail makeup; most popular was the brush on brow, and had a waiting list for services that ran over an hour. I could leave the boys with my mom who was home in the evening dead tired from work, having an opportunity to go places. It had been close to four years since I had been out in the night life of anywhere social. I ran into this guy named Sean I remembered from Therrell High who was in my chemistry class that I never liked, yet noticed. This was the first person I dated since Mason and I separated two months prior. The relationship we embarked on was just what I needed, we weren't taking anything too series just having fun. Mason thought getting a newer Cadillac would be enough to win me back. I wouldn't admit it to him, but that wasn't it, the last honest comment I had toward Mason, resulted in breaking my mom's window in her apartment having a temper tantrum. Sean was doing things just as I needed and the way I liked, Mason could not keep up. I tried to have a family day with Mason and the boys, the day ended with me being lugged out the car and spit on in front of the boys, we barely made it home that day. I was ready for Mason to continue on, so he could make some else's life hell. Things at the salon were doing great retail was moving, the clients started trusting what I suggested for them, making me more of a assist to the business than I had expected. With my freedom I dressed in a way that made me feel good, and noticed that my appearance helped in sales. My mom moved in the suburbs into a house three bedrooms and two baths, my sister got her room, and the boys and I had a room to share. It was a very nice property two car garage, private fenced in backyard, with a wooded patio. Just what she deserved for working so hard, the salon had been open four years by then, and making almost 85k a year. We were very comfortable; she had accepted the fact that I smoked weed and drink alcohol, so I was comfortable being me. Sean and I still were growing our relationship; it had been like eight months. It wasn't until we moved into the house he started coming over and around the boys. Mason hated the fact that things around me were changing in my life, I was serene and living day after day without him. Well, on that note my phone rings at two in the morning, Mason is calling me collect from jail, he was involved in an armed robbery situation. A police chase, the car was wrecked, and he blamed me for everything happening because I had not come back to be with him. It was no way that was going to happen regardless of what was going on, with Mason being locked up I knew continual peace was one thing I could have, not that he was locked up. I don't wish that on my worst enemy, but he was out of my way no drama any time soon. Three months after we moved in the house my mom let her boyfriend move in, I didn't like it but what was I to do. I paid the utilities and all my mom had to focus on was the rent, I would have thought the system we had been working well enough for her. I knew it was a matter of time before we would have problems with our history, I felt like a man always came between our relationship. Justin started dating a young lady right before Mason and I split up. Sophia told my mom that the young Lady was controlling and that she had insecurities that were noticeable. I would hear stories about incidents between the two, but what was I to say, I had stories with Mason that was no better. I did know that I was mentioned to the young lady negatively because one afternoon, I spoke to her picking up Micah and she tooted her nose up at me, I ignored it, in faith that we will become cool one day for Micah's sake. Her name was Christy she had beautiful long hair, didn't draw attention automatically, but that was right up Justin's alley it wasn't too much for him. It was a girl named Shawn, Sophia would brag to me about that was very pretty. I could tell that would have pleased her better in Justin's choice, she would have liked anyone that could out shine me. I tried not to feed too much into his relationship, just being happy for him in what he was doing. At the time I was only concerned with making sure my children had the life, I wanted for them. My children had gotten accustom to having a big Xmas living with Mason, it was the first year I would have the responsibility on my own, I was up for the challenge. When Justin and Mason's dad came to drop off their gifts to the boys they were surprised at what I had done, the day turned out beautiful for the boys and they loved it. I can only image how the details went back to Mason, which was the least of my worries; his son had the holiday he always saw.

Things started taking a turn when I started back hanging with a girl I known since 10th grade. I had initially met her when I was visiting my mom during spring break; we always tried to stay in touch but were never too successful throughout my drama with Mason. We went to Daytona Beach that spring break it was my first vacation of any sort, and while we were there I took note of her spending habits, it made me question where she worked. She wasn't so quick to share, but told me anyway, she was stripping' in this small club downtown a few nights out of the week. When we got back from the trip, I asked her to turn me on, I was thinking I could float two jobs and really have my boys set, and the saving and waiting game would not be so long of a process. I knew the relationship with Sean would not last, I knew I would not be able to strip and maintain a faithful relationship. I was going to be around too many men, I was going to be realistic and honest with myself first, then Sean. There was no way I was going to walk in the club dance all night half-naked, nothing happen between myself and another man, something was bound to occur. Sean displayed that he cared that was one thing I did know for a fact. It had been almost a year with Sean; I didn't want my conscience to get the best of me. I figured maybe I would do enough for him to just break up with me. That's what I did, staying out and partying on my free time from work, never making time for us to do anything together anymore. He got mad, confused about my actions and did just as I thought, broke up with me. When he called to check on me a month or so later, he was so disappointed to hear what I was doing. He was never into strip clubs telling that he would snatch me out of it if he walked in seeing me. With the strip club being in the inner city, I never worried about Mason coming to it, after he was released from jail. I worried about the drama coming to me outside of the club from him. I knew it was close or in route once word got back to him, and it did. My old neighbor was that vessel, a female that lived in the same subdivision when I was living with Mason. She saw me in there working one night; watching me make money. I would rent cars to get around in and to also keep my mom from finding out what I was doing. In regardless to what I did at night, I made sure the boys were in school the next morning on time and dressed very handsomely. That was what she noticed most in my routine. Along with me being ready to go to the salon when it was time every morning, hiding every movement of my night life in my face, and in the way I carried myself. Mason would ask me if I worked at the club and I would never answer him, if that's what he heard from the old neighbor go with that and make your decision. One afternoon I got the boys early having some errands to run for the salon and he followed me. Starting an argument and trying to run me off the highway with the boys in the car. It was crazy; he bumped the rear of the rental trying to make the car spin (something he had watched from an episode of Cops) the children were crying, it was back to the commotion. I managed to call the police while on the interstate, telling them what we were experiencing. The call got to an officer that was close by, and he trailed me, scaring Mason away. The incident drew me to the decision of getting a restraining order in place; just trying to press forward from the spectacles, not nearly being as patient in dealing with Mason as I once was. Justin started calling, confessing past emotions, telling me Christy was pregnant. I was happy for them, but thought he was shady talking dirty to me; I pulled his card one night going over to his place he was still living with his mom and had sex with him for black mail purposes. That was the last time I had slept with him, it was horrible to be honest. Justin told me he was use to Christy sucking him off. Apologizing for not being completely erect, telling me how he would think of me some time when they were together. I asked him how she responded to my name tattoo on his chest, he tried to cover it up with a black panther, but it didn't help. He laughed and said, "The panther symbolized you," and I knew Justin was on some real b/s. He wasn't my problem to deal with; I honestly just wanted to see where his heart was about her. I knew I would always have something over him, but keeping it real I really didn't want to mess up what he had going on, I was proud of him. He was working and being more responsible than what he was in the past. I left there that night knowing I nutted in his mouth, and she would taste me the next day. The club money was coming in like a flood, everything and anything my boys needed and wanted they had or got. I meet a guy named Ismael who turned out to be a kingpin in the streets, but low key. We gradually started dating; I didn't expect too much to come out of what the relationship, I worked in the club. Ismael slowly introduced who he was to me, I remember when I decided to get my tongue pierced, and he took me to get ice cream. When he went to pay he pulled out at least $1200 to $1500 it was honestly embarrassing, the ice cream was only like seven dollars. I explained the drama that I had with Mason, because Ismael started coming over more often. I thought it was a good idea with Mason calling my phone like he lost his mind or something. I was so embarrassed when I was listening to the words I was saying trying to explain everything. I wanted to keep Ismael's interest in me for as long as it would last, keeping in mind the first rule that was explained to me from an older stripper, "personal relationships are out the window." The veteran went on to tell me, "regardless what a man tells you and explains how much he likes you, he is going to always feel a certain way about how you met." Working in the club, I adopted the pretty girl attitude along with developing that trifling mind state. I looked at a man only for what he wanted to see of me and what I could get from him in return. All I saw was money and taking care of my children, not having love for a man or anything outside of what I had to do for my family. I took everything into consideration, but watched how Ismael hung around like he liked me; he stayed close to whatever scene I was on and I did not mind. Mason decided to make more trips over to my mom's to find out what I was doing. He came over one afternoon to talk which lead to drama, bo-guarding his way in my mom's house calling himself taking Mark away from me. My mom didn't care for physical violence and was trying to calm the situation down before it lead in that direction. I was drama ready, just sick of his behavior, so I locked him in the house. I met him at the same door he came in and while he was holding Mark with one hand, I had the opportunity to punch him in his face several times. He was trying to open the door, keep a hand on the baby, and protect his face from my punches at the same time. My mom jumped in between us and caught some licks too, which made me slow down to the realization that I was hurting her. Mason managed his way out the door and ran to his car with Mark. I started crying while my mom was holding me telling me to let him go. I didn't understand why she was saying that, thinking she was being weak, and I was losing my baby. After I calmed downed, I started thinking he doesn't have anything for Mark, and he will end up dropping him back off in a couple of days. Mason wasn't working and didn't have the resources to buy Mark things he needed and had too much pride to ask his dad for what the baby needed, not wanting to explain how he got him over there. Ismael came over to comfort me while I was still upset, crying uncontrollably. Ismael asked me if I wanted him to make the situation disappear, he was really over the weak man tactics from Mason. Mason, not knowing how to handle his emotions and express his pain like an adult. Doing things to me to entail me in his emotional ride, it sounded like something that would have made me smile, but I couldn't live with the thought of having Mark's dad murdered in the back on my mind. I wanted him away from us, but not in a terrible way like that. Mason bought Mark back after like two days with the same clothes on, when he figured out I wasn't paying him any attention, calling and crying to get Mark back, it made him think twice. The situation only made me despise Mason more, everything in my life was cool except when it came to dealing with Mason. Just when I thought Mason could not do anything else to make me nauseated, he embarrassed the life out of me. Ismael was pulling up with another one of his friends to my mom's place and Mason had my old Publix uniform shirt hung in the yard, on the baby shower sign, with words written in ketchup that was to mimic blood that said, "R.I.P 2001 (the upcoming year)." Ismael was dropping me off from bonding me out of jail for a DUI; one that I caught on my way to his place after the club the night before. It was most embarrassing, I had the restraining order reinforced at that point, allowing the law deal with Mason, hoping that made him calm down for a while. Only six months into the nightlife before my mom learned, she was very disappointed in me stripping. The night I caught the D.U.I, I was in her car, the car was impounded and all my work clothes were in the trunk. She went to the shop telling all her clients, it also got around to the people who worked in the flea market. She fired me from the salon without telling me, she just left me one morning, going in early. When I tried to call her to find out why, she left me, she told me I had a job already, so there was my first source of income. Getting out of my mom's place became my top priority after her discovery; she was making all types of comments about the club, talking down to me, but cashing in all my dollar bills for the use of salon. The news about the club travelled far all the way to my grandmother and other relatives in Florida. My uncle once in a phone conversation asked me why I have been cursing my mom out, which had me at a complete loss. While she was sitting right there, I asked her, "why did you tell him that," she just stared at me. I guess that was her way of painting the worst picture she could have the entire situation, I spoke my mind in my dialogue toward her, but never cursed her out, being disrespectful.

I decided to give the club scene a six month time frame, stacking all I could, and stopping. Changing clubs would help increase the income, the club I was in was a smaller setting compared to the other clubs in Atlanta. I could make up for the money I lost at the salon x2 and I was now able to work longer hours. I developed an extremely high tolerance for alcohol which was not working for me. I missed numerous opportunities with this bad habit; one I most regret was the Snoop Dog video shoot. I was thinking I had to really be more focus in the new setting and get a grip on the reputation I had of being a bad chick. It worked for me at times the guys liked me more because of the respect I was getting from other women, the time I grabbed Ismeal's gun shouting at his friend made me really stand out over the rest. I was ready to take the popularity to a larger scene getting more money. Everybody at the new club was on some type of alternative drug; it was so much competition I felt like a tadpole in an ocean. The nickname energizer bunny was what they called me because I never stopped working once I touched the floor; along with Ms. Pacman because once I touched the floor I was getting the money that came my way. My stage show became one to see, I kept the name Honeybun from what I was called at the other club and it fit. I didn't know how to perform half the tricks as most strippers, but I was very seductive in the way I moved and my wardrobe was one of a kind every time. Some of my old clients followed me to the new club which was helpful in building clientele. I started really hitting the pavement working, with a heartless approach, but that was the only way I saw results with the only focus of moving out of my mother's house. What Ismael didn't know didn't hurt him, when he was around he got his respect and that should have been his only concern. I had three other men I was dealing with, but Ismael was the only one I was having sex with on a regular. I just knew it was a limit to where I could go with him and my financial business was the line I stopped at. Ismael was content with me working in the club, so he was no one I thought about in a long tern aspect of my life. If he loved me like he said, his approach would have been different asking me things like what was it going to take to get me in a better situation. He had the means in making it happen, it was not for me to initiate the gesture to him, so I didn't. We had the talk before me expressing to him how I didn't like working in the clubs, but that was my source of getting income. I liked Ismael, but he was still someone I met in the club dancing, I would have thought differently if we would have met under other circumstances. Once I told him the area in which, I was moving to, the drive became too extensive for him and we slowly and surely ended what relationship we had. I didn't tell my mom I was moving until it was time, I continued to let her talk about me and say things like, "You just putting myself out there, You making me look bad, You don't have goals in mind and its all fun and games for you." My actions were going to be my words for her to see, not just hear. I got a connection at a new complex from a client of my mom's; I saved enough for three months worth of bills, and moved. This was my first place on my own Micah's School was directly across the street and Mark's daycare was before you got to the apartment across from the shopping plaza. I knew I had to look for work knowing that the money I saved from the club would run out, so I got a job at Walmart in the bakery dept working graveyard shift. Some nights the boys had to stay home alone and other nights when my little sister was available, she would sleep over to watch them. The hours were around the boys sleeping schedule so it was convenient when they had to be alone. My Walmart check was little money compared to what I was making at the club, but helped me progress in thinking with a more stable mind and learn to appreciate things more. The process didn't make it far before I started thinking it just wasn't enough, onto the thought, I wanted more. The guy I started talking to before I moved named Keith suggested I flip my money in the streets for financial cushion. I would not have to do any work or anything, but what he didn't know was I was going to keep my eyes on things. I had children to provide for; I wanted to see how he operated before I got involved. One night on my way to work I made homemade lasagna for the boys and went to check on the operation. He was on the strip off Old National in one of the hottest hotels there known for drugs and prostitution. I'm running in to see how everything was set up and hopefully talk about what numbers were coming back to me. A play came to the door; he served him, the man left, but then knocked again as if he had forgotten something and when the door became opened four big College Park policemen came in like a hurricane. I was lost for words; Keith had two guns in the room under the mattress, an oz of coke, 20-30 ecstasy pills, and a nickel bag of weed. Keith kept asking the police to let me go, telling them I had nothing to do with what was going on there. When everything was happening all I could think about was me being pregnant, I had never mentioned that to Keith, because he and I had a sexual experience that started off protected, but didn't end that way, the condom broke. I didn't know how to explain to him before he started asking if I could get pregnant, knowing that I had already had the feeling before our experience happened. College Park transferred us to Clayton County, where I took the pregnancy test in Intake, and yes I was pregnant. The catch was it was not Keith's baby, it was Ismael's, I didn't mention it right away to Keith and had no plans on mentioning it, because I was not having anyone's baby. The hotel room Keith's was working out of was being watched, the police knew I had nothing to do with the situation. I was just caught up in the wrong place, at the wrong time. When I called my mom she was livid, the first thing she asked was why, was I on the other side of town. With the calls being recorded, I told her I was sleeping with the guy for money on my way to work. I had money on me when they arrested me for money orders to pay bills for that month. After the first month, we were still seating there with no court date, I started to worry. My mom arranged for the boys to go to their dad's on the weekend, and moving my furniture back home. Keith and I were in jail with no bond, while the D.A waited for one of us to confess to the charges, more so Keith than me. Our charges were possession with intent to distribute five counts. The D.A was offering me five years serve one when we finally got a court appearance. Keith was explaining to me when we could see each other for a quick second in the court appearance that the D.A was hoping I turned on him. Honestly, it wasn't a Bad idea at that point, it was over 45 days, I just needed Keith to be a man about the situation. I understood he didn't want to go back to prison having been before and that was his business just like everything in that room. The D.A. wanted Keith to accept the charges, but what had me baffled he made the remark, "they would give you less time than I because you have no criminal background with drugs." I started reading Psalms 37 and 91; these were two that my grandmother encouraged me to read all the time. Once I concentrated on those I then started reading more of the bible, my grandmother would accepted my calls at least once a week to make sure I was still mentally together. She was disappointed I was in there for sleeping with a man and got caught up with him with drugs in a hotel room that was the story she had at the time. I told myself I would explain things when I got out, I couldn't direct my attention on what the rumor was at that moment. I started reflecting on everything that was happening and came to the conclusion maybe it was time for me to really think about some of my past actions. I never said anything like, "I going to stop smoking, I'm going to go to church and become holy," I would have been just lying to myself. I just wanted to become a better person that made good concrete decisions. Keith was in my rear view after this was over; I needed help from God for sure to figure a way out of the situation. I had been locked up for almost two months, before the letter came from David Robinson, my dad. He was writing me from a Florida prison, keeping his ear on the streets he found out I was in jail, and they offered me time. He conveyed many his thoughts in explaining what I should do to get out after I was honest with him in my letters not holding anything back from him, giving details about how I was pregnant, and the baby wasn't the person I was locked up with, it was someone else's. I told my dad I didn't want to have anyone else's kids and if I got out in time I was going to the clinic. David clearly told me it would be something I would have to answer to God for and that was between him and me. My dad and I started establishing a relationship through paper from prison to jail. We covered everything from how to handle my case to personal situations from the past between the two of us. Forgiving him for what I experienced as a child helped me in that tough moment and I felt better about what I was facing in the moment. I took it as a test from God, the words from my dad was what I needed to push me through that tough time. I confessed to Keith's dad (who would visit me for Keith's sake to see how I was holding up) I was pregnant. My dad explained to me, "What sane man wants his baby being carried in jail?" After Keith got word I was pregnant, I started telling Keith what he wanted to hear in letters we would write each other (he did have sense enough to have money put on my books to get things I needed) even though I had other plans. Like my dad said, "use the circumstance to your advantage."

Mason started visiting me feeling bad for the condition I was in once the time got a little lengthy. It hurt him dearly to be talking to me through a glass window, I confessed to him about being pregnant and told him it was Ismael's (not mentioning Keith at all) and how I wasn't trying to keep it. I was completely shocked that he was so forgiving as well as confessing he still wanted a relationship with me after everything he knew. I let him know I would re-establish the relationship as long as he kept his hands to himself. I think what got me was the fact Mason was there as emotional support, it indicated that he genuinely cared, and he may have been a different type of man for even coming to visit me. When we got to trial Keith got 5 years, serve 2 confessing everything was his and I was released. When I was released, Mason came with Mark in the back seat to pick me up, he had gotten so big and my stomach had a small bump to it. I could tell Mason felt uncomfortable, but he dealt with it. He took me to get some food, dropped Mark and I to my mom's house. The break between Ismael and me was too much to come back around explaining a baby, I called him over once I got settled one night to rekindle, wanting to have that touch from him while carrying his child. I held in my stomach the whole time, I could tell Ismael noticed something was different, but he was too caught up in the moment. I was afraid of his reaction if I would have confessed, so I left it alone and decided to deal with it the best way I could. I really didn't know how many weeks I was exactly, but knew time was running out. It was one place that I could get the service up to 24 weeks. I called Sean for help with the financing of the procedure, informing him of everything that had occurred, and he was shocked. Sean looked at me differently, but still had love for my character, so between him and Mason I was getting the procedure done. Keith had his dad calling checking on me, I thought it would have been a good time to get some money from him to support me after things were over and that's what I did. After a two day procedure I was back to myself, I thought about how Ismael would have handled me, finding out what I was doing with his baby, I am most sure he would have lost it. Showing appreciation in the weirdness way I moved back in with Mason for a brief moment. I was living with him when the passing of the man I respected as my grandfather happened in Florida. After the burial service and I came home my thoughts about what, I was doing had heightened. I don't think I made the best decision moving backward, not that we were fighting like we were, but it was the same mental abuse as before. I understood Mason better this time around having more experience under my wing but, it was just some things I was not tolerating in his attitude toward me. I had not been interested in sex at all since my abortion procedure, so Mason and I had not been intimate since we were back together this time around. One night Mason came in drunk verbalizing what he thought about Ismael and things that had occurred during our time apart. Why, I had no idea, words got exchanged, and then he started bringing up the fact that I wasn't sleeping with him. Mason approached me wanting sex, the more I said no, the more it made him mad, and want to take it. Mason took sex from me that night, pushing him away didn't work, he stayed on me until he finished. Sweating over me and breathing with an exhaustion sound from me trying to fight him off. It was something I would have never thought in a million years would have happened. Did I think that was the level of pain he had from our relationship ending the first time, yes? Did I deserve it, maybe to a certain extent (referring to the pain, not the incident)? The incident hurt me so bad; I couldn't look at him the next day. Mason displayed no remorse and at that point I was convinced that Mason had a sick mind and needed help, mentally. It wasn't a week later before I was moved out with not another thought of looking back in that direction. When I got to my mom's I went to the bookstore and got a GED book. Thirty days later with the help of Sean taking me to and from to the testing site I was took my GED test. I got a job at Burger King in the meantime, 60 days from taking the test; I got my results stating I passed my test. The first time around, I was a GED graduate, and proud of myself! At that point I had more documented education than both my mom and dad, neither one of my parents completed high school or even tried to get their GED's that was something that I broke from my history it made me think that my kids would do better, because I was doing better. The feeling of accomplishing something really took a toll on me. All the things I had ever heard about myself from Sophia and her family growing up, along with certain things from my own family, I knew at that point none of it was true. It gave me more of an urge to do more for my boys that was done for me by my mom and dad. I always been on top of Micah and his school engagements, I would even go as far as participating in field day events, graduation dates during pre-k and kindergarten. I made sure Micah saw me illustrating interest in his education to help him in his confidence with learning. I dressed Micah to the extent his appearance got him in the school's fashion show. Mark had been doing great at the daycare and was getting prepared for pre-k the following school year. He was developing very fast watching and taking notes of his big brother's life, he picked up things really quick. Mark had a personality that you could not help, but to love, getting your attention instantly. Micah was more laid back, very charming when he opened up to you. The boys were a delight showing me that I was a mother and I had every reason to be full of pride about it, in regard to the age of 22.

I shortly moved out of my mom's place to the Atlanta/Cobb area, Micah attended the same elementary school as I once attended when I first moved here with my mom, Teasley Elementary. Mark was in pre-k in a great daycare, I was very pleased about the decisions I was forming for my children. I started selling pills in the nightlife to make due, not being able to find a job in the area I was in. I was not waiting on anyone to provide for me and my children. I tricked a guy into co-signing on a car for me to move around in and did what I had to do to keep it. One afternoon I was at the local Walmart and met a guy named Tristan. He followed me threw the store, asking me if I needed any help with anything. He went into explaining how he just moved to Atlanta from Jacksonville and had been in the city for a couple of months. We lived almost 15 minutes away from one another; we exchanged numbers and continued to talk. Tristan was selling weed at the same time which was convenient for me, because I was smoking like a chimney. I never told him what I did for income and he never bothered to ask, he would always want me over, and he was just pleasant to be around. Tristan kind of reminded me of Sean, but more relaxed, Sean had more personality even though he sometimes stuttered like me. Sean was also more talkative than Tristan; Tristan made me feel like he was hiding or even ashamed of something. Tristan stayed in and out of town going to Jacksonville, but after a month he moved his old living room furniture into my place. Ordering new furniture for himself and not wanting to discard what he had, it was in still good condition. He would ask me to move in with him and would not hesitate to ask me if me and my boys needed anything. He even offered to pay my rent; I was weighed down at how much interest Tristan had in me and how much time we were spending together. Tristan would watch the boys when I told him I had errands to run, explaining to him I could move faster if they stayed home. One morning I came outside to start the car, and it was gone, apparently the guy that was paying the note and co-signed for me, stop making the payments. Initially, I thought he took it, but no it was the finance company, after I called and inquired. My only responsibility was the insurance, which I was paying, I was so confused because I thought everything was fine. I guess the time I was spending with Tristan, it was noticeable that someone was in the picture, and the guy took a flight. I had a couple of deals to make that morning; I call Tristan and asked him if I could use his car for a couple of hours. He agreed and on the way to his place I explained what the agreement was with the car, he had been seeing me drive for two month by this time. I was honest and explained the story in detail he was shocked and kind of disappointed in me for not being smart enough to know that that wasn't going to last as long as I imagined. I took Tristan home, went back to the house, changed clothes, got my packs ready, and started my day. I was riding in the hood running my errands in Tristan's old school car that was fixed up nicely. Everyone really hated, they wanted to ride with me every stop I made. I said no, explaining how I had business to take care of and after I was hitting the mall, and heading home. After I made my money I hit the mall to see what was going on and when I came out the car was gone. Like missing, I looked up and down to make sure I hadn't parked it somewhere else and forgot (I was smoking all that day). Greenbriar Mall was known for car theft, but no way, I was thinking it had had happened to me. How in the world I lose two cars in one day and who was going to explain this to Tristan? He wouldn't have believed me; I could not believe me. I knew he was going to think I had something to do with this. When I called him his voice sounded like, he could strangle me through the line. I just knew he was going to beat me up when I saw him, I just knew it. I was so scared all I can think about was, "someone planned to do this to me." Tristan wanted to meet me at my place asap. I just knew he was going to do something to me; I called the guy I got my pills from, explained the story, he came and got me after I called the police and reported the incident. Word got through the hood quick from that one call, when my phone started ringing and everybody being high on ex pills you can only imagine what the stories resulted to. One person was like "you better get strapped that man ain't go play with you about his car." Now, none of these people knew Tristan from a can of paint, but honestly I thought the same thing. I started smoking and made the decision," they were right; "I needed to get strapped, just in case. The guy I was with called his team, telling them." it might be a problem when she get home, let's ride." That's what they did, now, the whole time I was out Tristan calling my phone like a stocker and very disturbed. He was already at my place, through the security gate, sitting in the parking lot waiting on me. When I pulled up that night and four dudes got out the car with me, Tristan was looking like WTH, but stayed focus on me. We went in, they started putting guns on the tables; Tristan just wanted to talk to me alone, I was scared and clearly expressed that to him. He kept asking me what happened and I was frustrated that I didn't really know. I told him, "I walked in and out the mall, and the car was gone." I just know he wouldn't have wanted to be with me anymore, I didn't want to be with me anymore at that moment, I was so upset with what happened to him while I was in his car. He told me he was still cool, but I thought he was just saying that because the guys were there. It had been one long day for me starting from that morning. He didn't deserve anything like that to have happened to him and for the unpleasant incident to come through me; I believed I needed to separate myself from him, so I broke off the relationship. He didn't want us to break up over it; he wanted us to work together, through it. He kept calling me for maybe a week after and when I kept saying the same thing he stopped calling. A month later I decided to go to school and take up a trade, wanting to come from out of the streets hustling. I was always interested in the medical field; I learned office and administration skills from working with my mom, so I chose to take up Medical Administrative Assistant.

Child Support

Three years had passed and plenty happened in between then, along with me completing my technical school being certified in Medical Administrative Assisting. My mom didn't bother to show up to my graduation; she was working at the shop. She never made arrangements in trying to make it, but I paid that little attention. She did at least organize with one of her clients for me to extern from school to an office she worked at that hired me permanently. A Radiologist office in Sandy Springs/Roswell, it was a good experience for me. I got laid off after about seven months and was referred to work in an In-Home-Patient Care Company doing Data Entry, enhancing my administrative skills. I quit that job to work for a mortgage company as a personal assistant to the owner of the company. The drama between Mason and me ended while I was school with him being arrested in Cobb County for interference in child custody. Mason had one of his friends follow his dad to the apartment I was living in at the time, finding out where I lived, and what I was doing. Mason was interested to see how I was operating, with me not having transportation I befriended my male neighbor, and he would give me rides to pick Mark up from school. I guess him seeing Mark and I riding in the car with another man even though it was incident, just took him over the edge. Mason embarrassed me that day trying and eventually taking Mark from where I was, carrying him by one leg and arm to his car parked on the other side of the building. Mason luckily locked himself out of his car, keeping him in the area long enough for the police to come help get Mark back to me. I didn't bother to check on Mason while he was locked up in Cobb County that was something he had to deal with. The boys started attending the same school which was completely suitable for me; I can see they enjoyed it more than I. The connection between us became my reason for living; we spent time together, we even took Karate for a while together, just the three of us. I was really coming into being a mother, the mother that I would have wanted for myself. When a challenge came up I was dealing with it more maturely, handling things like an adult. Thinking about only the long term aspect of my future, making sure my household was secure enough for the boys to have a better childhood. I was meeting my monthly bills on time and even paying off the debit that was on my credit report from out of my income taxes. My mom had unpaid accounts on my credit report that I was unaware of that hurt me dearly, I addressed it and continued my mission. Micah was coming into the age where he noticed aspects of his living situation, observing that I worked harder to display family without a father in the home. I had to work twice as hard to make that picture vivid for both of the boys as I thought about it every day. Justin would call when he wanted to get Micah, it was really no stress. Mr. Byrd would get Mark from time to time, being a way for Mason to see his son and I was just fine with that arrangement. I never put more into Justin and Mason's visits with their boys than they did, never denying them when they did want visitation. The boys needed and deserved that time with their fathers regardless of how I felt them or how they felt about me.

Sean was murdered by a boyfriend of a young Lady he met two weeks prior. When I went to the wake, I really couldn't just walk up to see him, so I sat a ways back and just cried, but then started listening to what was being said in the packed room. The guy shot Sean once in the chest and everyone around robbed him of everything he had on him. I was so shocked with the story and instantly stopped crying, walked up to the body, viewed him, paid respects, and kept it moving. I didn't bother to call his mom or answer when she called for the funeral the next day. Sad to say, but honestly I was bitter about how he pasted, especially when we were on the verge of getting back together. Sean was a chapter closed in my life in a very unfortunate way. I had since then met an older man named Aiden, our relationship started out nothing as I imagined it ended up becoming after almost three years. It was not a consistent three years, but we shared enough experiences within the time for us to make it a serious relationship and talk about moving into a house together. Mom moved the location of the salon three times into a property what she purchased for 317k, with my help working at the mortgage company putting the packing together. Sophia was still in the picture, but not as strong as before, she slowly started drifting into her own which was the best. I always thought it was a conflict of interest, my mom still hanging around, knowing they spoke negative about me, holding on to the things I was once doing as though the change was not easy to see. While working at the mortgage company I negotiated the boys, and I in a 4 bedroom 2 bath home in Gwinnett County with a basement that I put a 6 foot basketball goal in for Micah to practice basketball, a deck, and a fenced in backyard. I was allowing Erling, Justin's little brother come over from time to time, allowing Micah to have that male company every growing boy needs, it was his family, and at the time I thought it was best. I saw Erling like my little brother as well; I carried him around, and keep up with him then more than Justin. Erling was observing the operation of my household; I was a single mother with two boys, make a living more than Sophia was for him. Yes, it was hard, but I never let the struggle be the center of my attention, it was whatever it took to keep my children happy, which was my direct goal. When you have your tunnel vision beam on see and treat yourself, as well as things around you as if they are as you picture them in your mind. I thought about Erling reflecting on how when we were children and that fact that he was still enduring some of the same trials. We lived close to poor and had two strong, smart women in the household. When he was over to the house, I could tell he would be a little jealous or feel a certain way about what he saw. After you get older and reflect on how things were and the way, they could have been, it makes you a little annoyed. Ours moms had more of their minds in the wrong area, more concerned with being cute, getting high, and spending time with each other. Justin mom was lazy, but had a gift of gab; my mom was easily influenced and followed her lead a little more than she should have. Erling didn't understand how I could have the organization I had, coming from what he knew about me and how we were raised together at one point. Erling not knowing, which it was a great deal I saw on my own and the changes I promised myself I would make I incessantly worked to change as sometimes they did not happen in the first try. I didn't what I thought Erling's thoughts were to cloud my mind, as I was only concerned about the camaraderie for my son, picking Erling up from time to time. I was living off the last of the money from the mortgage company and waiting on my unemployment checks to start coming in from when I got laid off. I had time to get the boys in a great routine, the schedule was perfect. I was home 95% of the time and I can tell they appreciated the time, I could see what at-home-mom schedule was without the dad, unfortunately. I knew I could not live off the resources I had coming in for long, and it was time to make decisions on something different for my life. I enrolled in Esthetician School in Sandy Springs not wanting to work in the healthcare industry anymore. My mom was completely shocked in the beginning; she had little to say about the decision not knowing what type of outcome it would be. The administrative side of the salon I was good at, but I started thinking of getting into the service side, maybe one day being able to retire my mom. We all have our opinions of how our mom's should have been, but that was the person God choose and created as our earthly mom and you always want to see them relaxed and living a better life when they reach a certain age. Having that full understanding of the life you now must have to survive and make something for yourself and your children. I watched my mom perform services for over five to seven years, I don't think she ever knew I was taking in the concept of the creating a persons facial image without uttering a word to anyone; sometimes its best to keep your secrets a secret, until God is done fully developing them. Letting people know your secrets or interest sometime can hinder its growth, everybody is not into supporting growth or for another person to learn more or differently. I was happy to learn something that my mother knew because I admired her talent and business ethnics. I was proud of her and her undertakings in what she created in the salon. She started with nothing and was at a peak where she grossed over a 100k in a year off $5 eyebrow arching, $15 lashes and retailed her own makeup line. We once lived in a hotel room for a month my mom, me, my sister, Sophia, and her two boys, times were really hard. It was amazing watching her family finally putting everything she had into something constructive; my moms down fall were her so called friends, the hype men, and the people who were around her because she became popular. They wanted to control the situation as if it were their own, when you grow in the sight of people it can be very intimating to witness. Especially when they have been so busy watching you that they have not done anything for themselves, I think that's what Sophia realized that about herself and figured it was her time. I started going to school, continued to take care of my boys, keeping up with my house, and truthfully hustling at night working in a lingerie shop. Micah allowed Erling to influence him, listening to him say negative comments about me, judging who I was as a mother in his opinion. Moving like a machine I was thinking what I was doing would keep my boys happy and I would be paving a way for them to live a more comfortable future. The memories of the stages they would have witnessed would have showed them they can do anything they set their minds on. I had to clock in school at 8 no later than 8:10 to get my hours for the day, coming from the direction I was living in it was a challenge with traffic every morning. My kids had to be on the bus at 7:30, I had to leave the house by 7:15. The boys were instructed to leave out 15 minutes after me. I would get everything set for them as far as breakfast being made and made sure they were dressed before I left. All they had to do is lock the door, walk to the corner of the street, and catch the school bus; we stayed in a family community that was typically very safe. The parents in subdivision were very involved; most of them were out there with their children every morning. Micah let Erling talk him into thinking I was doing a horrible job and I should be reported to DFCS. I get a call from the school saying Micah has told them I leave them home alone all the time, and he was scared. I was saying to myself other than the new routine that was only in place for six weeks, the three nights a week I worked, and they were asleep never knowing about, so how were they home alone all the time. The school was sending an agent out to check my home out, wanting to see what the problem was, this was an unpleasing incident I thought I would have never been connected of. I have never in my entire life had DFCS in my home including childhood, where they probably should have been. I pondered that Erling was making this comparison between my household and his brother's. Creating this picture, making Micah feel uncomfortable about his living arrangements, just because no man was in the home. Erling illustrated to Micah that Justin's household was what he saw on the weekend's every day. Justin and his fiancé' had the perfect family appearance to Micah having that father figure in the home sharing the responsibility of the child and the household, while he saw me alone juggle all responsibility under the roof without complaint. Everyone knew things were hard on me, but I was going to manage or at least I had up until that point, why bring the burdens down on the children, what could they have done? Justin and his fiancé' treated Micah great on the weekends they decided to have him, and dogged what I was doing in that time frame. I remember mentioning how wrong it was to Sophia one day on one of our last conversation that left her speechless. Then I considered the attention Micah saw his brother getting from his dad that he wanted, Erling putting in his mind that he wasn't getting because he was with me, learning that information from a comment Micah spoken out of anger. The caseworker came out to my home and was highly impressed with what I was doing for myself and my boys. I had all my paperwork in order, I was active in their school with the teachers, never missed a parent-teacher conference, he was involved in school activities, my home was clean, they boys had their own rooms, and they were clean. I was on food stamps at the time, so the cabinets were stocked, I had a vehicle, and my bills were up to date. She apologized for me having to experience what I was, she got contacts to people close to me who could vouch for my character to better help my case that she explained would be open and shut. One of the contacts she called was Justin's mom, Sophia who had no option but to speak positive on my behalf, she knew how hard I was trying to make sure her grandchild was in the best condition possible. It was one thing I could say about her, she learned over time that I was the most concerned for my boys, their welfare, and I went overbroad to take care of them with any hustle I could handle. The severity of the stress from the DFCS visit happening (once you are in that system you have to be extremely careful, even if you are clear it's just wise to be careful) and me in school not knowing what was next I became very emotional. Micah's attitude was changing; he walked around with a chest full of pride about what he did with applauses coming from his uncle. Micah still had pressure from Erling in his ear who wanted to prove to his nephew that he was right in what he was saying to him. When I saw the negative influence, I should have stopped the visits, but then I was thinking about Micah, not wanted to display to him that I was entertaining the foolishness. I did more for my boys than their Sophia did for hers and that was where the problem lied with Erling's detest attitude toward me. I wasn't supposed to be the mother I was becoming it's like the enemy or devil wanting to slow your change or growth for the better in your life. One evening we were home and Micah had started treating his little brother unreasonably mean and I knew where that was coming from. Justin and his family never wanted my boys to be as close as they were, we did everything as one and I treated them as one. Micah was too young to see what was being done to him as I still allowed him to retain a relationship with his family. I never spoke negative to him about them, because that's his family and I knew that I would have to let him develop a relationship in his own understanding, he would one day decide what type of relationship he would have with them on his own. One day Micah's temperament reached the point of going off on Mark, and it was for a reason that I didn't think was necessary, so I got on his case about it. Micah snapped on me and told me, "I want to go stay with my dad" and those words killed me. I lost it, and jumped on him, whaling on him in anger, picking him up, threw him behind the bed, and continuously punched his arms, chest, and back. When I caught myself, I stopped, and I let him know I was going to make that happen for him, saying in a loud voice, "what you see on the weekend was not going to be what was really going on everyday."

My heart was so broken after all I was trying to do and did, I couldn't wrap his words around my mind, I wasn't thinking straight. I called Justin; let him know what was requested from his son, he said, "it's fine for him to come to live." I let him know that his son was reaching out to him and disrespecting my household in the process, Justin know how crazy I can get and disrespect was something I didn't respond well to. I think Justin understood that his son was going through a change and needed him; it was comprehensible from him once reaching out to his dad. I commended Justin because he didn't reject his son as his father had done him and we hung up with the agreement that it would begin the following school year. Christy, Justin's wife called shortly after crying, and asked me, "why are you doing this to me," I replied, "doing what?" I didn't understanding her calling me the last time we had spoken before Micah's birthday party at the skating rink was a year prior, when one day Christy called me saying, "Micah is with Justin." Christy put Justin out because he supposedly cheated on her, when he was on a job in New Orleans for two weeks. I was shocked she called telling me their personal business, but it was only to let me know my son was not there, which was logical. Christy dogged Justin in that conversation like she hadn't known him. Telling me about how everything in the house was in her name, he didn't have anything, and his credit was messed up, along with things Sophia mentioned about me. Illustrating to her that I was this crazy chick that would fight over Justin, I didn't want him to be with anybody, and every time he was with someone I would run them off. Now, Mason that was something different, I had done those types of things, Justin never. They sold Justin to her; by making her feel if she could get him, and keep him that would finally shut me down. Which explained why Christy initially never took to me, and maybe feeling like obtaining him was a challenge. They talked about me being this ghetto girl; it hurt me because when Sophia didn't have food to eat when we were staying in the Vinings, I would take her to the store with my food stamp card. I wasn't going to let my child's grandmother and uncle who I grew up with go hungry. I said this to Christy that day, never mentioning to her that Sophia talked to me about her family. I let Christy run her mouth more as she explained how Justin was scary as her brother played a trick on them acting as if he were a robber, turning off their lights, threaten he was coming in. Justin pushed her to the door to protect himself instead of it being the other way around. As we continued to talk, she wanted us to get the boys together to play sometimes and start talking more with each other. I took that with a grain of salt, the girl mugged me too many times, having unnecessary problems with me because of what she heard, never noticing my actions in determining if what she heard was true. Everything she heard, she never witnessed from me toward her or Justin, so that let me know that she wasn't a strong minded person or didn't have a mind of her own. Justin dropped Micah off with a friend he caught a ride with that night and I never mentioned the conversation Christy and I had, wavering that that was their business. Justin never interfered in any of my past relationships and I had to give him the same respect. No more than a month after Christy called me about Justin's incident, Justin called me to hang out apparently

Christy went to New Orleans. I was thinking to myself did the girl go check on the mistress that would have been sick, but it would not have surprised me. Justin and I went to Pinups Strip Club to meet one of his coworkers to play pool and have some drinks. It was a cool evening no horse play whatsoever just two old friends getting together, when I walked up and Justin introduced me to his coworker I hear the guy say, "wow,you messed up with that one" and Justin said, "yeah I know." I ignored it and continued to enjoy the evening. Justin had plenty to say about Christy that night as I just listened and remembered not to say too much. I had said enough in the conversation to her that he was still unaware of. Christy really never wanted Micah to live with them on a permanent bases, Micah coming over on the weekend was fine. Christy was more into having the family Justin and she created, not fully coming to grips that she married a man with a child prior to their relationship and when she married him that child was included.

If Micah was going to live with his dad Mark was going as well, even though Mark told me he didn't want to go, I could not have one without the other in my mind from the comfort of always seeing them together. To this day I regret the decision that I made because Mark kept saying he did not want to go. I called Mason telling him what Justin was doing for Micah and asked if he could do the same. Mason wasn't too involved in his response as Justin, but he did agree. I figured letting them live with their father's, I would have a year to fully comment to my new career, get in a stable position, the boys would come back, and it would be happier than ever after for us. I had never been without them, except for the 3 months I was in Clayton County in 2001. I was thinking I could accomplish more, have more time to work. I took a leave of absence from school to hustle full time, make sure the boys had everything they needed for the next school year, and with a summer to do it. After the decision was made I thought about when I took Micah to check out the Gwinnett YMCA. The basketball coach wanted him to play for the team and was going to work with me on the weekly rate since I was going to put Mark in also. I was thinking it could have been Micah's start on his dream of being a basketball player. The Christian summer camp I had them in that previous year was inspiring for Micah personally, but both were excited about going daily. I knew if I would have stopped what was already in place with him leaving to live with his dad resentment toward me would have grown. I have always stood by a little boy more so than girls needing to have that father/son relationship if it were accessible to him. I was going to Miami for Memorial Day weekend, and the kids were going to my moms. I traveled down to Miami alone and met up with some friends I knew down there. When I got there I discovered that this was going to be one fast weekend after, I was offered money to dance for some guys we met on the strip and that was where my hustle began. I went from dancing in a room for some guys on Memorial day to dancing in clubs having enough money to get my kids, bring them to Miami in celebration of Mark's birthday, and driving them to my granny in Tampa for them to stay there for the remainder of the summer. My granny was no fool she knew what was going on and made me aware of it. She also had enough trust in me to know I had a good reason, that's what made me love her so much. I would send her money every week through Western Union for the boys, working day and night in the Miami strip club scene. The clubs there started as early as noon and would be packed by 3 in the afternoon, so the money started coming in early in the day. Learning to walk around a get a dance in comparison to being requested some years back took some getting used to. A well-known rapper in Miami came in one afternoon with his friends and three girls. He requested me after my stage show, I was too nervous to ask him for a dance, to me the strip club it's a male's ego heaven. I was a very prideful woman at that time and it made me uncomfortable to ask for anything from anyone. I felt like if he requested me after my show when I walked over there he should have said something to me. I shouldn't have had to say anything to him; I was not asking or making the first move. I presumed he had enough company; I walked over, stood there for a second and walked back away. I had another man that asked me to dance for him, I was dancing directly in front of him and he watched me the whole time. The girls that he had over there were not getting the attention that I was, and they were right in front of the rapper, it was cute.

The man I danced for was an investor and offered to take me on a shopping spree when my shift was over, which was 4:30 5 that evening. I asked him what I had to do for that, and he was nice and said "nothing, just enjoy yourself." I was surprised not believing it, but like myself and a bunch of other women when we hear the word "shopping" it's on. We went to Bal Harbour, shopped, and had a beautiful dinner. That was really one of the first times I experienced that "fantasy date", beautiful atmosphere, shopping, and fine dining. I will never forget that day, modeling my clothes for him, him just wanting to see me smiling, and looking pretty. I detected the difference between street and corporate men making the conclusion that I like the corporate type better. Corporate men are not as pressed about sleeping with you they know it's going to happen; they want to show you want they have to offer, he was much older which may have helped too. I was going to Rolex Strip Club that night to work it wasn't something I wanted to do (quickly getting tired of the night life), but my boys were leaving. I was going to send them away with everything they would need, supplies lasting them a couple of months. I had my grannies words in my mind, "do whatever you need to do for these boys and bring your *** on back." I picked up a wax pot having to groom myself, so I started doing my brows and body waxing, the instructions and terminology that I used to hear my mother say I heard vividly. As I did my lashes that evening a girl asked me to help her with her lashes, and it did not stop with just her, before I knew it I was telling them how I knew how to do other things like body waxing and brows. I figured I could make extra money that way, maybe keeping my cloths on more. The stripping money is good, but I knew I had to keep my mind directed in where I was trying to go, I wasn't staying in Miami pass the summer. My craft was perfecting, it was much better than what happened one-time in the flea market cutting a girl in front of everybody. I was so embarrassed; the salon laughed, and told me to stick to the front desk. I took it lightly because I had the eye for it, just had to figure out the coordination between my eyes and hand. I feel my skills could flow more freely being that I was away and I had no other choice, but to make it happen. Funny what you would do when your back is against the wall or the pressure is on. I knew my time was running out when I started getting popular in the areas I was in, on top of the two incidents that happened within a week apart. I got robbed from a client I was with one night and my cloths got stolen out of my car. I was glad it was just the dry cleaning I picked up on my way to the ATM to make a deposit and not everything I had. The guy looked like he ran through the car is just how rapid everything happened. The summer was at an end, the decision I had made would be in effect, and one I had to face soon. I wasn't hustling when I got back home, Miami was enough for me to see and do for a while. On my drive to Tampa, then back to Atlanta I thought about the boys, the changes I took them through trying to provide for them, trying to discover who I was, and learning about life as a woman. Thinking I was always doing too much, I was living two lives and, I had to grasp the fact I was wrong in many of my choices. I began to think I wasn't the complete mom I knew I could be and what the boys deserved, I can say I tried though, unlike most I knew. I made choices early in life that made me grow up a little faster than most girls my age, not that I was the only teen mother, but I was concerned about my actions and things that I did. I never compared myself to the next knowing that we all are different in the way we operate even with the same circumstances. I thought with the boys gone I could clean up my mess and do things as desired, so when they came home they could have a better opportunity. I took it as a blessing for the boys to have the type of fathers they had, it was much about them I didn't care for, but when we reached out to them they responded.

Not too many females could say they could call and ask that from their children's fathers and they agree to allow the child to live with them. I was glad I never sowed the seed of drama in their personal lives, so it wouldn't back fire on me in time of need. We always had a cool relationship about the boys; it was only going to be for a year the time would go by so fast. Getting back into school I was at a focal point having one goal in mind getting back to the boys missing them from the time they got picked up from my mom's salon. Some people remembered me from my last attendance, the class I started with last time was graduating except for maybe two still making up clock hours. The class I was placed in everyone was already familiar with one another and had made friends; I would have to start over. In a section of the course you have the opportunity to double your clock hours for a week or two to help you make up hours you may have missed or to push you ahead in hours to finish early. I was taking advantage of the opportunity, sitting idle when my phone rung and it was Christy, calling to tell me about what Micah done with a little girl while they were gone out one even. Now, this was after I was served with the abandonment papers and had gone to court. Yes, Christy took it upon herself to go to Clayton County like two months after Micah got there and issue a warrant for my arrest for child abandonment. It stated, I said I would take care of him and I had not sent him anything at that point I figured she was speaking about money. Justin and I never spoke about me sending money regularly when we came to the agreement that Micah would live with him. I had always known Justin to look out for Micah while he was in his presence and if he didn't have it he would speak up, and Justin had not said anything. What Justin and his wife agreement were or if he even explained what we agreed to her was not on me. From her call that day after I asked Justin if Micah could come live, I knew we couldn't sit and talk things through like adults, so I didn't bother going over anything with her. I may have been immature, but I do not tongue wrestle. I thought when they came and picked Micah up from me with that huge U-Haul box of clothes, shoes, school supplies, and toys with the understanding that I was moving out of the house, getting a one bedroom apartment and starting over. It would have registered that I needed time to get on my feet, but if anything was needed I would have made a way to get what he needed. Justin knew I wasn't the type to let Micah go without, I never had been. I would think he would have explained that to his wife having a good line of communication with her. Maybe she didn't have it in her heart to extend the love and finances to Justin's child, she only had it to extend to him, I don't know. The entire time I had my children I never depended on what came from their contribution, I could not focus on it. The adjustment in their household had to take place with Micah coming to live, so I didn't bother to call and make things more difficult than they may have been. I later thought about it, maybe I should have called, even if Christy wasn't as comfortable with my presence as she should been. I didn't want it to be said I was trying to keep tabs on their household, something a woman with insecurities would come up with. I presume I was thinking too much about everyone else and that was my reason for not calling, when I should have been thinking about how my son was thinking being in a new household. I was still dealing with the feelings of betrayal to a degree from him trying not to display it. The story from Christy was they went out with some friends one night and they all left their children home different ages and sex. Micah showed his private part to the little girl trying to show her how big it was. I was thinking, "now that's good parenting," but all I could say was, "that was not a good idea and that's was how Justin and I start dating us being able to have sex at a young age because our mother's left us home alone going out, Justin should have told you that." She was quite not really able to say anything; it was something that they were to have to deal with in their household, like the table was turned. I just wanted her to know that that wasn't that perfect parenting decision that was (portrayed that they were) made on their parts. I thought about what I heard from Christy and wanted so bad to change what had taken place, but by then I was already on child support for both boys. Mason had gone down to the office and put me on child support for Mark too. I didn't expect it from him, but after it was done I wasn't shocked thinking about his father putting his mom on child support for him. It was a way to keep up with my income and make sure I was tied down somehow, Mason was about money and Mark was a good tool in getting more. What was going on took a toll on me emotionally, but I never spoke to anyone about it. I ignored court appearances with Justin being scared, confused, and angry at what they were doing. It was not like the boys were to stay permanently just one year. I just wanted to finish school and start working in the field to have more of a financial foundation to set. I would have never taken them through court appearance and warrants, I personally didn't have that much time on my hands, but I guess I should have. Christy was the mouth piece for Justin and Mason learned from his dad. I don't excuse Justin from the decision, but like Christy once informed me Justin has nothing in his name, everything is in her name, so he is more helmed to play by her rules in keeping his household in order. I remember when she put him out before he had to leave everything behind that had to be hard as a man not having anything to stand on, so I can't fault him if that's want it took. Women have to go through similar situations and worst to keep their household together with their husbands. I kind of knew those were his reasons leaving the courthouse the first time, answering the child abandonment, putting me on child support while I was a full time student and unemployed. I know with success nothing is giving and you have to deal with the obstacle to reach your goals, so I made up my mind I was up to take on the challenge and I was going to fight until the end. I'm not completely innocent I help feed the insecurity by not comforting it, not getting to the root of the problem, and putting everything completely on the table. Acknowledging that my character was being misrepresented and stopping it, I just let it continue to go on. I was in the beginning battle alone with no moral support and not knowing how to address the matter legally, Justin and Christy came in there with lawyers and Mason lawyer was always on standby, so I just tucked and kept moving on what I did know about, completing school.

I was very interested in what I was learning and always made good grades. I put my mind into the mode where I was challenging myself; I wanted to see just how far I could make it in this industry. I even looked into one of the best Theatrical Makeup Schools located in Ireland. I thought about the boys, relocating them with me cross seas, we would have to learn the language and culture, which would challenge us in every way, and take us out of our comfort zone completely. I was just thinking the fashion and makeup industry overseas is two years ahead of the states and I would come back having more skill and creativity than the rest of people here making my work more marketable. In school, when it was time for us to work on clients, I would always distant myself from my peers giving myself a chance to focus on the client and concentrate on my craft. I start hearing more how I had good hands from the clients, which was something that pushed me to do better. When the waxing instructor started getting me to do the majority of the waxing I knew, I had something worth putting time into sharpening. I watched a video from The Waxing Queen and a couple of other waxing experts to mimic and learn different techniques. Before I knew it my technique was not just noticeable to the instructors, it was noticeable with my classmates as well, and I started having repeat clients.

One of my classmates started working in a salon near the school named Raine's Brow Salon; I remembered seeing the salon years prior when I was working at the Radiologist's Office. She thought it would be a good idea for me to apply for the brow/lash position to work there while in school. Raine providing the services that I was strongest in would be favorable for everybody involved. I took her thought into consideration applying for the position, I went in for the interview, taking a model with me for Raine to see my application, and got the position on the spot. The income would help me tremendously with my current situation, not knowing how in the world I was going to start paying this child support before then. The little help from Aiden I was getting was helpful, I could have been getting more if I put in more time. I never put my mind into the relationship like I could have, not being sure it was the right one for me. I only saw the financial assistance from it and was more content with that aspect of it being truthful; he was 10 years my senior, my patience went so far. Once I got into the salon feel of things, I starting from making 15 to 20 dollars within a week to making close to enough to pay both of my child support orders, the people around me changed. The classmate that introduced me to the salon quit feeling out of place in contrast to the development of the bond me and the owner had.

I befriended a Lady who was new in my class name Gabrielle Blake; she took every school day like a fashion show. One morning during school hours when I was on laundry duty, she came in to help and get out the eye sight of the instructors. We got around in conversation about Miami, (by it being almost time for spring break) Gabrielle heard another classmate ask me, "are you going to take a road trip." Gabrielle asked me," have you worked in Atlanta before," having a suspicion that it was more than a spring break trip for me. I told her about the lingerie shop on Chesterbridge that I worked at for a while before the boys left. She laughed mentioning she worked there too, a couple of years before me, but what was crazy is when the conversation got into more detail the same people were there and the same things were still going on. She even knew the guy that owned the tour bus company that I was getting money from to pay the rent at the house for a couple of months (who I regretted losing contact with). By the time we knew it classes were changing, we exchanged numbers that afternoon and did the wait game to see which one of us was going to call whom first. We just basically talked in school when we saw each other for that week. It all changed one Friday night out with another classmate hanging out at a club, before we went in I got the call from my mom crying explaining that Tift (a Jamaican she married) had been shot in his head and died at her feet, so that put a whole heap on my mind walking in the door. It was a great deal to take in, I had sincere concern for my mom, but she was too far for me to break down about it in addition, I was high and about to go have fun. I thought to deal with it on the next day, I couldn't call her, and so I had to wait until she called me. When we got in the club a guy walked passed me, looked, leaned back checking out my butt, and asked me to follow him to VIP. I grabbed the hand of my classmate and off we were, bottles got involved along with loads of flirting, while we were up stairs looking down on the club I noticed Gabrielle and a couple of her friends. I called them upstairs and they joined us for the remainder of the evening, after that night Gabrielle and I was cool in and after school, we also started hanging out more. In the socializing I was doing, I kept my mind on establishing clients at the salon, so I knew regardless of what night I had the night before I had to be ready for work the next day. Raine was taking a liking to me, I remembered a huge amount of details from my mom's salon, I just had to get adjusted to Raine's operation. Once I got adjusted to Raine's operation I started putting my spin on things to make it a better fit for me and comfortable enough for me to release my talents. Raine noticed my work ethnics, how I was taking things serious, and the response I was getting from the clients. Aiden would give me pointers on things when we talked about business and I would listen to him, I had respect for him in business as he on his tenth year owning his own. We had a salon meeting one day and I brought some things to the table that Raine really valued, after that day she started marketing my services to her clients. Raine started considering me her right hand before two months were in, I would come on time and stay until the end. I liked how she maneuvered in her business, always thinking of ways to improve the clientele growth. She had an Asian Lady named Tai that would come in on Saturday morning and do the books, she noticed I was making more every week. Tai complimented me asking me, "stay around if you can deal with Raine and her ways, you are a light to the business." Little did Tai know I was not paying Raine or her ways any attention, I wanted to make a name for myself in the industry to have my own or take over my mom's salon and that was it? Everything else was bs, yes Raine had some ways about herself, but don't we all, the difference was Raine didn't hide hers. She had a reputation I soon discovered that at times she would not be in the salon on time, it would not be open at all, and she would look and act weird. I had not seen these activities for myself, they were things I heard from the clients that seemed blissful to have a person in the salon with a calm spirit servicing them. They explained how they were keen on coming because it was convenient and the longevity of knowing Raine; they also mentioned how the accuracy of her work was some timing. I took everything in and never said a word in response to them, I thought I would let my work ethnics speak for itself and build clientele solely off that. I started developing my skill more as I worked there, it was easier to display than when I tried to work after school with my mom. Her clients were so use to me being another way or more so hearing about me in another way, they could not take the new adjustments I had made. My mom really couldn't either, she would really make me feel uncomfortable working with her, my technique was different from hers I applied techniques that I learned from school and saw in videos. When I shared something with her she saw it as me trying to tell her what, she was doing was wrong which was not the case at all, I wasn't competing. The industry and techniques change every day, and in order to be a master you change or adjust to the change to stay in the cohesion of the industry. Why do you think they offer advancement classes after school? Roswell was a good area to establishing a name, the people there were about business and they carried themselves in a very polished manner, even if they were not as polished as the other they still carried themselves like such. The conversations were different and you learned something new every day from someone. Raine had a diverse clientele which was something else I like about her, she could put on that other face and pull it off well, she believed in having that professional appearance every day. Which was something else different from my mom, mom made money, but she never got dress to attract it. Her skill spoke for itself; I could see why she attracted certain type of people and why certain type of people shyed away or didn't take her as serious they could have no matter how good she was. Raine's salon started becoming very demanding of my time and school hours were interfering. I didn't want to start slacking off in school, I did want to graduate and have things in order more than my mother did. My mom dropped out of cosmetology school to work at my grandmother's salon, so I wanted to set a different stage for myself. I came up with an idea on Fridays to have some of my cool classmates clock me in, while I worked. They were down like four flat tires and it worked until an instructor got involved, caught me sneaking back on campus to get a special product I needed for a client. They gave me a warning, I took heed long enough for things to cool down, but then a situation came up at the salon where I was needed whole heartily.

Raine went on a relapse from smoking crack, I went to the salon one Friday morning and the phone rings, it is Raine she sounded dead to the world. She started telling me how she went out and was smoking crack in the crack house all night. She left her daughter some place and went to get her after she was done in the crack house early that morning and almost ran off the road. Police and emergency cruises were involved, she had to call her best friend to come get her, while Raine was telling me the story her best friend was calling on the other line. I could not believe what I was hearing, so I was ready to get it from another source. Her best friend starts telling me what Raine was telling me along with how she goes through this from time to time, now remind you this is just almost four months into me working at the salon. I was glad I had keys to get in and out; (Raine gave me a set to close up on Wednesday's when she left early for church service). The best friend asked me to support Raine during this time and do my best to hold the salon down. It was no problem on my end, I would never want to see the salon in which I was working in fall, over a problem that could be worked through, Raine had the place for like five of six years by this time. Now this would mean that I would have to skip school to open the salon on time (other than Friday's) and reschedule the appointments that Raine had. I looked at it as another way for me to now gain more clients. Gabrielle was floored about the news, it was like two months now in our relationship, and we were hanging tight, this had a bad taste in her mouth about Raine knowing she was jeopardizing so much. I stepped in and did me, explaining to the clients that Raine was out with illness and I did not know her expected day in returning, I was there to provide service if they liked, if not I can schedule them for the following week. My mom along with everybody else was surprised I was holding the salon down like I was and not trying to figure a way out leaving Raine looking bad. I even took the manicure appointments that came in, some clients allowed me to service them some didn't, but they all could tell that I was not running from the task. Tai came in to do the books and was shocked how everything was in order; I explained to her how I had to take the register home one evening. Raine called the salon asking when I was leaving and how much I made that day, she sounded like she was coming to get the money and smoke it up, I wasn't taking any chances. When I told Gabrielle, she laughed thinking I was out of my mind taking the register home with me, but why wouldn't I have, she wasn't about to smoke what I worked for. Raine's salon didn't have working Capitol, she would have had no way of paying my back, she called that night asking me," did you take the register home," and I politely said, "yes" and waited for her to say something about my action. I wanted to go off on her so bad about being irresponsible with this drug thing she was going through and whatever she said would have made me explode. I guess I feel that at a certain level of success I can't see myself stooping that low and risking everything I worked so hard to have to get high off any substance. Raine was a praying woman I knew she was going to make it through, but I believe I wanted her to be strong enough to fight that temptation and kill it. Tai was glad I did want I did, it had been like three days since, Raine was still recovering, and hadn't announced when she was returning. Clients mentioned she took absences like this before, just didn't have anyone to cover things while she was gone, stating it was good for her business I was there. By the salon being on the corner of a busy intersection, people would see if the sign were on, and the business was operating as it should, you would be surprised what people are observing. The extra money was good for me along with the experience; Tai called me a blessing for Raine and stated she should be grateful and pleased for what happened in her time of weakness. It wasn't until the following Wednesday that Raine returned to work, she was amazed how everything was clean and her books were in order, her personal working room went untouched and clients were booked for that week. I went back to class, soaking in all the compliments on doing my thing at the salon from my classmates that had to clock me in and out, while Raine was gone. I never told anyone but Gabrielle the real reason Raine was out, I just let everyone else know I had to cover the salon from open to close. I think I needed that incident to help push my confidence level up, I had some big shoes to fill coming in after my mom and I was nervous, the thought of not being as good was terrifying. The hours I stole that week the school took back which slowed me down from graduating with the same class as Gabrielle and everyone else, it was embarrassing, but I wasn't pressed. I was working before I was certified, getting paid before I was even in a senior position. The situation had its pros and cons and I took them both seriously.

The change in me

I finally got around to telling Gabrielle I was on child support she asked my why, I explained to her about the decision I made to enroll in school, the case worker visit, jumping on Micah because I was not understanding his change and where his mind was. Asking the father's if their boys could come live with them, showing her the letter of agreement with me and the father's (even though Mason had not had signed his agreement), I even informed her of who initiated each case of the child support enforcements that blew her mind. I gave Gabrielle the details on the conversation that took place once between Christy and me after the action was in place. Christy thought it was fair to put me on child support since I put Justin on child support, not clearly understanding what Justin wasn't doing that lead me to the result of putting him on child support. Whatever Justin and his family told Christy that was what she knew whether the information was right or wrong, Justin was the victim; I was painted as this crazy baby mama wigging out on him. I let Gabrielle know things were getting hard balancing it all and that was the best decision at that time I could make for them. Micah was beginning a stage where he wanted to know who his father was and establish more of a rapport; I did not want to become the bad guy in the situation not allowing him that chance. Explaining I was more wrong in the determination of my youngest son Mark, but I couldn't take care of one without the other so use to them together. Gabrielle had never heard of a women being on child support and I never put energy into the thought of really being on child support knowing it came from another place that wasn't based on the welfare of the boys. I thought sometimes maybe I ignored it until it put my circumstance with my child in the worst status. I was so mad about it in the inside thinking Justin and Mason should have had more admiration for the type of mother I was to their children. Gabrielle would ask if the salon money was taking care of the child support plus my living expenses, and it wasn't. The child support debt started accumulating from finally being in school the full hours (not sneaking to work at Raine's) and child support suspended my license. I still drove taking that chance staying on my routine not being able to afford to get off track. Gabrielle ask me if I would be willing to hustle in Atlanta again, we had a conversation speaking about Miami before and I was telling her I like hustling where I wasn't known keeping everything discrete. Which was a terrific idea, but something had to be done about what was in front of me at the time. Gabrielle brought some things to my attention about how the situation made me look from the outside looking in that I had never heard before. Gabrielle was the first person I had spoken to beyond my mom and Aiden about me being on child support. She said, "it makes you look like a bum chick, not taking care of your responsibilities. Two children, two different fathers, not married and had never been married, and wasn't in a stable relationship. The ghetto girl you no longer want to be is who you look like rather you like it or not." I took in what she said, it was the first time I heard it from a person from the outside looking in. Gabrielle suggested the least I could do was make money to camouflage all the drama, after hearing her out completely I thought she was right. She continued to say, "The other party is on a mission to destroy your character as you see yourself, I can only imagine how the wives look nothing like you and the husband's are not satisfied on their job as a man and a provider to even take putting you on child support into consideration." She also thought child support was being used to get back at me from the pain I put them through, leaving them. Gabrielle was employed with an online escort agency and had been since she moved back into her townhouse in Gwinnett. Gabrielle was finishing her education with the arrangements from a judge final ruling; she had with her ex husband who was ordered to pay alimony while she completed school. Gabrielle took him to court divorcing him because she discovered he was married to another woman in another state. Gabrielle thought I shouldn't give anyone anything bad to say about me and the only way in doing that was get my money up. Give them something else to talk about, let them see me on my grind, not pressed about what they are doing or saying. Gabrielle never understood Justin's wife taking the abandonment warrant out on me after Micah went to live with them. She clearly did not have respect for Justin as the man of their household and Mason was just following the family tradition his dad set so it seemed. I thought about everything she said and put my own thoughts into deciding what I needed to do. Giving up school and working for Raine's was not an option, I had short term goals for what I really wanted to do. I thought it was sensible to pay off the child support debt, unfortunately, I couldn't just blink it away, I had to do something about it. I had the boys just on the weekends when Justin and Mason would answer the phone not having any legal visitation in that moment, so I had time to grind a little bit. I was going to make every minute of my time to improve myself and my circumstances. Not knowing what I was getting myself into from a positive or negative standpoint but taking a chance hoping for the best outcome. Making the decision to work online was really scary all I could think about was, "what if any found out or who would find out." Gabrielle explained to me that the first couple of weeks I would do really well, because I was new. She was right within a couple of weeks I had my driving license back active. I made enough money to pay for my license and put back what I put in to get into the game. Once I cleared that debt I had more of a clear mind, I can imagine the look on the faces of the co-parents. Justin's wife was probably surprised and Mason just wanted the money he really didn't care. I became involved in a world that only a certain type of mind can understand, Gabrielle was a very proper Lady in this industry, she knew when and how to move being a part of it for so long. Gabrielle introduced me to restaurants I have never visited before, teaching me how to carry myself in a way that would grab any man's attention, but targeted toward the right type of man. Poise is the one single word to describe what she had. The more the money flowed the more I went into a trans, I was not thinking or concerned about nothing but what I had to do.

School, Raine's, hustling, and paying my child support was the only thing I was interested in. What Gabrielle was showing me was cool, but I didn't care about the luxuries initially. Feeling it was too much like a fairy tale and I was only having the encounters I was because I was selling my body. The more I got involved the more I started looking at men differently, 90% of the men that would call the agency were married it put my mind in a frame of men being distrustful. My approach toward the men when I worked was do you, give me mine, and keep it moving. I got to a point smiling was something I did leaving the scene, while I counted my money. Gabrielle was a different type of worker more personal, but that's what made her so good at what she did. Her behavior displayed she was glad they were dealing with her, I even saw her kiss them in the mouth when she met certain ones at times. Gabrielle didn't get how I was getting paid with such a standoffish approach, but like I discovered long ago, some men like the Lady that rejects them, the challenge. I was cool with the clients that didn't want sex and were married they just wanted conversation or company. Taking me to nice places for dinner and meeting them at the most extravagant hotels were cool, but even then I made sure I didn't reveal too much of who I was outside the agency. It was awkward to me when they would try to like me outside of what they would be paying for. Gabrielle didn't mind if they were not married she would think it was a possibility a relationship would take place. I never saw things that way they were confused men, and they were trying to take me along the confused ride. I learned something from every client they all were different, but I slowly gained a reputation of being hard to deal with. I wasn't as bubbly as the other girls in the agency and that didn't bother me because it wasn't anything I was trying to do long term. I had a time frame in mind, but I never mentioned that to Gabrielle she was happy to have a girlfriend that was involved in same thing as she, someone she could talk to about how she felt about things happening in her life. She had other girlfriends, one in particular that she known for over 8 years, but she wasn't with the same agency, a White girl named Willow who was more involved in the hustle than Gabrielle. Gabrielle introduced her on to the game as well when she was like 18 and this was the only job the girl ever had. Willow made great money compared to Gabrielle making good money, but personally she liked thugs, the robbing crew type of guys, and it was something Gabrielle never understood being a blonde with implants. We all would hang outgoing to clubs, buying out the bar, travelling, shopping, I had even invested in a timeshare property on our Universal Studio trip, thinking it could be something nice for the boys. The only thing I was missing was a nice or updated vehicle, Gabrielle had a nice car and Willow had three nice cars; I was the one still driving a '89 Acura Legend. A image for me I had to change one way or another, I bought a hot 2004 Escalade EXT for 15k from a guy I knew, which made me stand out everywhere we went. The boys dad was looking like what the hell is the girl doing, dropping them off on the weekends I would have them, with something new, and a fresh haircut. I would think about the holidays and the times we use to spend together getting cut back from the decision I went with when they were around me. When I was hustling before when I had them, I was more in a mother mode and could not hustle freely, working around the clock like I could this time. Having more money and missing them so much I spent an abundant amount of money on them, taking them places, and buying them things. I would picture us being together in that moment and how happy I would be able to make them having more finances to work with, but still knowing it was temporary, but on the other side of things I had to stay on the path I was on to make things better the right way. I was still working for Raine, in school, and had taking on trafficking for a friend of my moms along with hustling online. I stayed busy and liked the way life was moving despite how I was making it move. I got caught in the Escalade at a restaurant in Buckhead with Aiden and one of his friends. I got arrested that night; I qualified for first offenders not ever being arrested in Fulton County before. Aiden of course mentioned he knew the truck was hot, not wanting to say anything to me. I waited 30 days and got a Land Rover Freelander, a car note I really didn't want, still having the Acura in the parking lot, but having the pride of a fool not wanting to drive it anymore because it wasn't up to date. I sold the Acura just so I wouldn't be tempted to drive it or return the Land Rover. It was almost time for me to graduate from school when I started talking to Gabrielle about getting into business with me. After we came across a job at a pamper party for Justin's aunt that turn out to be great, a trial run to see how we would work together. Gabrielle bought all the equipment she needed to perform facials with and was really good at what she did; I performed the waxing and lash services. I wanted Gabrielle to become conscious that she was more than a call girl; but that was something she had to see for herself. Gabrielle had the esthetician license I needed to operate services at the shop, I could not pay of the school tuition when it was time for me to graduate, it was almost five grand. It would have taking me at least two months of saving to pay off the five grand and still meet my monthly obligations that I had at that time. It was irresponsible for me to take the hit knowing I could hustle up the money. I was getting tired of the men and the travelling taking risk; I was ready to change into to something I was more proud of. Having the credits and the education needed I thought I had enough to make it, thinking about all the successful makeup artist and people in the industry that don't have all their credentials from school. I pressed on building my clientele base at Raine's and the last month on the hustle. I decreased my hours with the web hustle making enough for my love ones to be taking care of. Raine had suspicion about what

I was doing outside the salon knowing I wasn't making the type of money I was spending, but just didn't know what I was doing because it never followed me. I lost a level of respect for Raine after coming back from her hang up and she talked about me to her clients, the comments made about me running her business better than her insulted her so much, and it should have, I would have felt the same way. She would tell the clients I wasn't the type of lady they thought I was I was a street chick and how she had to groom me, to get me where I was in the salon. I had to be doing extra activities like selling drugs to get the cars I had been driving and room to say that because I called out the day I was in jail for the Escalade. It was a mess, but I stayed in my element keeping my eye on what I had planned, remaining loyal, abiding by my regular schedule, coming in on time, and leaving late. I even continued to mop the floor every night before leaving, showing a humble side of me, keeping myself grounded from the other world I was living. Raine was involved in extracurricular as well; she was sleeping with this married man for years for extra money to cover the expenses of the shop. The shop wasn't covering its own expenses, Raine had a bad spending habit, and she wasn't good at budgeting. By her not taking time to learn what Tai was doing for her business, she would run into unnecessary problems, juggling the phone bill and her home expenses when Tai could not help. Raine business was Raine's business I never discussed her like she done me with the clients, one of us had to display good business etiquettes. I added to the problem being on my hustle and having a session with her and the married man one evening, the guy was into threesome's. The best friend she usually did things with was tried up with her husband that night. Raine confessed about liking me, she thought I was sexy and has been waiting on a chance like the one we were involved in to come up. What Raine didn't know is I didn't do girls sexually she was going to do her with her client and I was go do me with her client that was the night topped off with me leaving with my money in my hand. We made like $650 each that night and he let Raine know not to bring her best friend anymore.

He thought I would work out better, well, another surprise for Raine, I was not planning on having too many of those nights with them

Raine and I worked together; the Lady was my boss for Christ sake that was going to create an issue sooner than later. After she made that confession I knew our business relationship was going downhill from there, I felt uncomfortable being around her. Gabrielle was floored when I let her in on the information and the event that took place; she thought it was completely unprofessional for Raine to come at me like that. Gabrielle and I were really cool at this time we had a couple of session's together, nothing remotely close to pleasuring one another. She did her, I did me, client was pleased, and we got paid. I never could stoop to that level with another woman, it was just some sins I had to stay away from, I had enough to repent from as is, sleeping with married men. Raine's 7th year anniversary was here and Tai announced that she was leaving, moving out of state with her husband. It was commotion on the low about what had been going on between Raine and me apparently it was beef. The guy we had the session with wanted to ex her out and take Gabrielle and I instead after seeing us one evening out together. I never entertained it and ignored comments throwed at me. It was occasions in business Raine displayed being a coward and I helped her voice her opinion to people she didn't have the nerve to too many times. For her not to come directly to me and get things off her chest, but have everything to say to everybody else was not a surprise. Raine paid attention to the growth that was taking place in me with the business; shortly after my first year she started trying to figure out a way to lock me in working with her, close to the year and a half mark is when the submitting of the contracts began, which I did not agree with any of her terms. The terms were not reasonable, I submitted a response, but before I did I let Tai see it, she told me if Raine didn't accept it, leave. She didn't deserve to have me working with her and was trying to work me like a mule. Raine didn't accept the terms; I politely turned in a two week notice, just to remain business, professional, and not burn the bridge. Turning in that two week notice would mean my plans would move a little faster than I anticipated. I had not mentioned anything to clients within the year and a half I had been at the salon about any of my plans and now it was time to speak without causing too much turmoil. I had a location in mind that was not far from where Raine was, but out of competition range. It was going more into the Buckhead part on Roswell Rd, which I was expecting more clientele to add to the list I created with Raine. The clients that would call my phone or the salon to make sure I was there were around 40 ladies. Those were the clients interested in my services alone enough to get started with. I gave one of my clients from the online agency more of an opportunity to connect with me personally than I had with anyone else before, that client ended up being my investor for the salon. He gave me a list, instructing me how to establish credit for small businesses that I was ready to take advantage of without knowing. I set up the articles five months before the decision was made on moving. I was hoping to withstand with Raine another year to be more prepared for what I wanted to do. I added Gabrielle on the articles as an officer in anticipation she was coming abroad once the vision was vivid. My business did not have the season as my mom's business, so I changed her tax id number and ordered all my office equipment that I needed for the salon. I was educated enough to do my books and services for my salon and was grateful for having the knowledge I was not going to waste it. I got my cell phone service updated, opened a Dell account that got a laptop, and color laser printer. I also opened an OfficeMax credit card which helped me get a desktop computer and a Fax, copy, scan machine. I wanted these things to my access to be as creative as I could be, not limiting my business to no means not being able to advertising and promote. Everything came together on the front end of the salon, while I was not at Raine in those hours I checked in with the agency and got what came through, thinking of how I was going to put the service side of the salon together. Smoking helped me with my nerves; I got my call list together, with every client that was on my phone. I wasn't counting on everybody to follow me, but I knew most would. After getting the space renovated, business license, and flyers—I opened up my salon in July 2007, like 2 months after I left Raine. My clients were ready for me to become settled, I was doing house calls for a moment (this was around the time gas had been really high), so the expenses were accumulating. Between what I was making running errands, working on the web, providing services mobile and the money from the investor it was over $16,000 spent in the 500 sq ft space I was leasing, my hardest work ever. Twenty eight was not too late to start I was still very young in the industry, thinking about Rachel Zoe. Business started off doing very well; it took a great deal of getting use to. I was structured, but not as structured as I needed to be in business. It's easy to work for someone else's goal having the easier position compared to the owner, when you work for your own goals the spot light is directly on you, no one to look at or blame anything on. When you fail or succeed, it's you, everyone will see having different reactions and responses. I was still with one foot in the street and one foot in the change. Gabrielle was coming by and hanging out in shock that the salon I had been speaking about was in plain view. The things I would talk about while getting high and partying, I was doing. The chats we had were real to me and the things I spoke I put them in realty with no fear. Fear is what slow many people down, and it's the chance you take that God supports. I worked the minimum hours a day, leaving going to hang out, smoking, drinking, and just being the person I was instead of moving toward the person I wanted to be. Not noticing initially that it was a hindrance as much as I started to notice after a little time they were distractions. I had a great thing going and I wasn't respecting it. I was still playing with Aiden slightly getting anything I could out of him. He wanted us to get back together he wanted me to move in the new house with him and continue what we started. I just knew that relationship was based on a control factor that I had out grown. I had the taste of freedom it was too good to me, he was a nice man, but Aiden had past pain within himself that wasn't healed and was set in the way he saw life. When he finally saw the salon, he was so surprised the color scheme and the logo mirror on the wall hand painted he was so shocked. I was just looking at him like yeah you told me," I would be nothing without you." On my 27 birthday something I would never forget, I forgave him only through the trust I have in God, he has and will always bless a child that has their own. A couple of months had gone by, and it was fall, so the streets were not as hot. I collected the last of my trafficking money from the dread on our trip to Arizona and I was doing only 25 hours a week on the web. I reflected on everything I said about being tired and wanting to change, but I was depended when it came to that fast money, when it came down to it I wasn't completely ready for the change I strongly spoke about.

I got the call that my Granny was in the hospital and things changed from there, I flew in to Tampa immediately. She had never been admitted in the hospital before; she was in a diabetic coma. It was real at that point; my granny talked me through the completion of the salon and instructed things to me in how to operate. She encouraged me to move forward no matter what it took. She was one person I could say knew I had a good reason in decisions I made, even if others thought they were bad and my actions were not good. I got high as mars before I flew down, praying that would help me deal with what I had to face seeing. My cousin Farah who I once lived with came to get me, she knew how I was feeling and where I was emotionally once she saw me. When my family heard I was coming, they kind of cleared the way and let me come in myself knowing how close my granny and I were. It was one occasion I was going to display the temperament I was known to have at times not accepting the condition my granny was in. I went in to see her and could not believe what I saw, her lying in the bed with tubes in her, in a helpless state. Her vitals let me know she knew I was there, she moved a little, and I then started thanking her for her strength and praying over her. While she was lying there I promised her that I would change, I would be a better me. Life is about living and experiencing it to every level that opportunity allows. I expressed to her how I was learning to pray and trust God for his will being done in my life, and I was working on letting go, God doesn't need my help. Once we turn it over it's just that, not to say we sit back and just do nothing and wait, we carry on with our works and every day doings. I let her know that she was in the best hands ever that God had her. Closing the conversation I asked God to take the curse off our family and if I were the vessel to use me and chastise me how he saw fit. I was very open in that room I was thankful that I was named after such a good lady believing it was going to be my last time seeing her breathing, and it was.

I had a whole new outlook on my life it was like I woke up for the first time. Each week I got stronger, my creative side was peaking; my mind was moving to the point I started not being able to sleep well at night. I kept seeing my granny standing over me saying," I got my eye on you Paris," it was spooky. I would stay up all night and just think about different things, everything. I scheduled an appointment to see a therapist, because it was too much for me to deal with, losing her destroyed one side of me and birth another. The therapist helped me in many ways; he told me where my weaknesses were and what I needed to do about regaining myself. I started becoming distant from Gabrielle and the hustling I was doing stopped completely, I needed to do for myself and my children the right way, no more shortcuts. I started thinking I can become more than I was, I shook my way out of one arena into another; I just need to keep shaking. Since I am in this arena what am I going to do, I can take advantage of what I have or let it take advantage of me. The street money I was use to was not the money I would make honestly working at the shop. You have to push through even if it's coming in slow or fast that's your livelihood you are working for. The only person I have ever known to have it gravy (and that was even only for a moment) was my mom. She never ever had to call a client to remind a client of services she provided, she was really into her business and it flowed, some days not as busy but always flowing. I stopped hustling knowing I would be taking a chance, but I didn't want my granny to see just how dirty I was in getting my earnings. It's a difference between telling someone what you do and they see it firsthand, seeing every detail. I started looking on Craigslist for modeling positions, I found a couple of gigs that was paying, and I thought getting in that environment would be beneficial for the salon. I could promote the business to models that have to maintain a particular image every day. My first gig modeling was on a mix CD cover for a local DJ, it only paid $75, but it was something different from gaming somebody's husband or driving over the state line taking a penitentiary chance for someone sitting home relaxing or shopping. The gig after that didn't pay any, I was an extra in a movie "Mama I wanna sing" starring Ciara, I was an audience member. From there I got paid to be in an independent film called "Shake", and I played a stripper, it was weird I knew how to entertain, but when I had to play the role I got uncomfortable and the fact that it was those real die heart strippers there made me nervous. I was so pretty that day I got my makeup done by an artist name Day that now does Nikki Minaj. It was after that opportunity I decided to go with an agency to get into more of the industry life, I was making contacts slowly, but I knew I could go further. The salon was making slow money, I was still pushing to do everything legit, and get the boys on the weekends co-parents would answer the phone. I kept saying I need to get visitation orders, because they were getting on my nerves. We as adults should be able to work it out better, the boys knew about the salon, and would come to work with me when I had them. They were aware of the outside endeavors I was involved in as well, more than proud of their mother with the look I saw in their eyes. The agency had not booked me for the first 30 days which was not a bother; I was still doing my own research, and job hunting which I found myself in the office of the PZI Jean Company. They were having a New Year's Eve fashion show that paid $200 for the evening; we practiced for four days prior to the event having to learn a dance skit. Happy once again to display to the boys that I was doing different activities, modeling gigs became my hobby to an extent. The co-parents painted a different picture of me to the boys and I believe it was because the boys were going home bragging about what they saw and knew I was doing. The New Year's event was very successful, it was an experience I will never forget and enjoyed to the utmost. I had a major boost in my self esteem, I felt as if my inner beauty started unrevealing itself. I was very confident in my appearance, but in the inside at times I thought less than, knowing how I was raised, what I had done to get certain things I had in my life. I was once called a diamond in the ruff from a very successful man that couldn't take me too serious because I was sleeping with him for money, I would think about that from time to time as I worked of what I thought myself worth was. I was numb to men for a long time, Aiden was different, but then he even bought that thought back to me at times. The salon was making money, but not enough to cover its expenses. I was pulling it together as much as I could. The clientele I had was loyal and becoming stable to say the least, so I continued to be grateful but I didn't see the growth. The clientele I had was loyal and becoming stable to say the least, so I continued to be grateful but I didn't seeing the growth. My rent and utility bills at home was good, car note/insurance was up-to-date, the salon was a month behind on payments, child support was maybe almost three months behind of the full amount paid, but the boy's personal needs were met. I was spending time with the boys despite of everything that was going on and showed no lack of income in my presence or did I have it in my conversation when I spoke. A client that was an esthetician from California named Gracie was a client of mine that start coming to the salon more frequently. Gracie was working out of her townhome in Roswell; her townhome caught fire, putting her in a position where she had to find a space to work out of. She had a good clientele basic so bringing her on broad would not have been a bad idea; she worked with a few of Usher Raymond's staff, and writer Shawn Garrett was a good client of hers as well. She was best friends with mother of the twins from R&B group Jagged Edge, making her an asset to my establishment. The extra money would help catch me up more and keep me current with my lease. We made the agreement for her to work out of the salon and how much I expected monthly, changing our relationship from her being my client to us doing business together with one common goal. She really didn't know my business ethnics and the way I really operated outside of coming getting services, I was less smiles conducting business. I didn't want her to mistake the difference between the two, and take the fact that she was older than me, understanding that I was not going to bite my tongue and express any concerns of my business. The relationship last for a couple of months, before Gracie started feeling uneasy about working out a space from someone that was not as experienced as she. The comments started that finally led to her wanting to compete with me; I ignored every blow throwed knowing I was still going to collect a payment from her. I knew things were getting messy when she started talking to other salons in the area and the landlord to get the history on me while I had been in that space. To say the least the nearby salons did not have anything negative to say, but the landlord that was a story all by it's self. He was unprofessional in getting into detail about my rental history letting her know I was catching up on past due payments, which was all she needed to hear. While she was working on what was going to be the next transition in a section of my life, the owner from the bridal salon approaches me with an opportunity that was more than a miracle. He told me he had a client that was a wife of a celebrity that was interested in having lash extensions done, he recommended me for the job, but I had to be there that afternoon, and she was expecting my call within the hour. I was more excited to call the number than I was scared when Mrs. Pin answered the phone I introduced myself and did it without stuttering for once. She was looking forward to my call and was quick to ask me, "You know what you doing" and I responded, "Rarely do I lose clients as much as I gain them." She was surprised and thought fondly of my jazzy respond, she asked me if I could complete my day at the salon, come service her at her residence which was not a problem she gave me the address and I was on my way within a hour and a half time frame. When I hung up the phone, I felt like a transformation was taking place. I shared my joy and excitement with Gracie who was in a state of shock as I headed off. I remember thanking God on my way to service Mrs. Pin for getting me to this point in my life. My insides were all over the place as I arrived at the house and was entering the gate, I was cool on the outside I was confident my skills were worthy of being on this level of clientele. I felt like Beyonce when the curtain opens I was going to perform like it was my last performance ever. I was settled on making Mrs. Pin love me and request me again. Coming into the home, just making it to the bottom of the staircase I was thinking," man this is making it." I'm going to have something like this for me and my boys to take pleasure in and I'm not going to stop until it happens. The Spanish maid showed me upstairs where my client was residing. I was wondering how I would respond seeing Stevenson, him being the biggest celebrity I had ever met in my life at that point. Then I thought about the celebrities that I had been around before then that prepared me for the day I reached. I just kept telling myself to keep smiling, stay professional, and behave as if this goes on every day. When I got upstairs I wasn't expecting to be in their bathroom connected to their bedroom. This was the biggest and mesmerizing bathroom I had ever witness. It was every woman's dream from the décor, to the toiletries it was the heaven of bathrooms. Their sitting with the nail tech was the lady of the hour, an extremely polished woman very comfortable in her skin. We hugged and greeted each other as well as me and the nail tech before I began to set up my things. Mrs. Pin stated I was cute and informed Hillary the nail tech of our conversation on the phone and how she thought I was sassy and confident while they laughed together.

Mrs. Pin had a spirit that I needed around me daily, very outgoing personality. When I finished her that day, she was in awe's over my work. She bragged about how she had them done before, and they were nothing like what I did. She once lived in New York, she had a person there that she was about to fly in town to provide the service when her husband asked her to look for someone in Atlanta. She said that's when she mentioned something to bridal salon owner, who was doing her makeup at the time, who mentioned me, and she was glad he did. She ensured me that I would be hearing from her again, she paid me in big faces and I was out the door. I was so proud of myself it was amazing; I knew it was time to go deeper in perfecting my craft. Stevenson gave my work the nod of approval stating he liked what I had done, seeing him before I walked out the door (just as polished as I expected) being formally introduced by Mrs. Pin. I honestly was never a big fan, but I respected him in his longevity through his career, I thought his achievements were remarkable and could never go unnoticed. In the driveway Hillary gave me a smooch whispering in my ear," welcome to the family." I got in that truck and that's when all the nerves kicked in, I screamed like Queen Latifah in Set it off when she ran through that glass in that robbery scene. The first call made was to my mom, I had to tell her the great news. She was a dry excited it didn't sound like she shared the same joy, but she couldn't take anything away from me. I drove over in the hood to stop and get some weed from the man, stopped to the package store and got a bottle, and went home to reflect. Having the salon payments to catch up on and my child support obligations was the first thing I thought about as I got high, then thinking," this getting high has to stop." I was focused more on the positive, but the negative carried such a voice that I couldn't ignore. I knew what happened that day with me servicing Mrs. Pin was going to have a major effect on my career and I better start getting myself prepared. Surprisingly, Marissa Pin called me two more times after my first visit with her, before the week was out; one day was even on a Sunday. By that last visit she approached me about the semi permanent lashes. I had no clue about them at all, but I was going to keep her in the dark on that information. I suggested to her that it would be in her best interest to order her own kit, have me just come and apply them for her. I had to wait on what I made from Marissa to order my own kit. She agreed went right online and let me know when the package would be delivered. I really wasn't shocked she could order her kit in five minutes; she had things to her disposal. My concern was finding out and mastering the application process by the time this kit arrived. In the meantime I focused on what was going on with the salon and those circumstances were getting worst with a little help from Gracie. The owner of the building was starting to wear thin on my situation, already being behind on rent and then flooding a unit below me from a plumbing problem in my space that leaked one night during a storm. The renter of that unit expected the owner of the building to pay for damages done, which made the owner of the building upset with me coming from my unit. The predicament with the salon then became to a point, it was unworkable. I stayed focus on what came day-by-day, while I was going through that, I still was trying to keep up with the boys. My lease at the apartment was up and I couldn't halfway afford to look for another place, Kynton was moving in his dad's mother old house, and it was a room I could rent out. The rent there was over half of what I was paying for the whole apartment. Kynton a person who once worked for my mother, a good friend, the only person at that time I expressed everything too; he knew everything I was going through when I was going through it.

I didn't have anyone personally to vent to dating became a nightmare to think about getting involved in. I didn't do too much of it only when I wanted a nice evening to escape, I got it, and kept it moving. I got to a point where I looked at dating like I couldn't get into it, I had too much going on in my life to be involved, it was over whelming for me, so I could just imagine how another person would have thought getting involved learning everything I was experiencing between the salon and the children. A call from Marissa came in to help glam her daughter that was being nominated for homecoming, it was a surprise.

I thought I wouldn't be hearing from her until the kit came in, and she was ready for service. It was a good day that day, her daughter was there getting her hair and nails done as well. Time was of an essence, I had to apply her lashes while everything else was going on. Marissa's hair stylist at that time April put me up to the test, I passed with no doubt, a moment that reflected my future. When you are behind that curtain at a fashion show, things move fast just like we were that day and even faster. April, I could sense was a force, she was impressed with my work, we exchanged information, and agreed to work with each other again. When I was around them I felt a part of something special, I felt growth in my talent, it's the best to have that inspiration in your work environment. I was recovering from a hang over the night before and still had the same clothes on, but got my head together to make that visit, thanking God on the way to the appointment.

The owner of the building was threatening to file papers at the courthouse for the arrears of what was owned and that weighted heavy on me. We were in debate about the plumbing issue as he made a statement referring to me causing the damage to the unit beneath me. It stormed badly for like three days straight and flooded the gutter which flooded the pipe that was once sealed that was now opened. I paid him to open the pipe to connect to my sink; I had to have running water in the space for State Board. I was in a loss for words, I felt like if it were a problem it was there prior to me which was why it was sealed and he just didn't want to mention it. The owner was soft on me (I could tell by the way he responded to me), so I think he was just trying to fulfill my request. I expressed to him how the way he responded to me creeped me out, it was like his feelings were hurt. Gracie mentioned something on the lines of I should have worked him, flirt a little to stay on his soft side. Moving over to Kynton's dad's property was different, but I really didn't have many options. It was an older home not kept up with at all. It was nowhere to have company over or even to let anyone know that I lived there. I was very ashamed, but it was shelter taking

Aiden up on his offer to come live with him was out of the question. I hadn't even informed him of my situation or any of my changes that was taking place. I was hoping by the time my court appearance came up I would have everything owed. I tried to make the installments, but he was so livid he wanted the entire bill, what I owed him was nothing like what he had to replace to the space below that was damaged. I was busier than before, but I needed more, so I got back online looking for some modeling work. The money from Marissa was coming in and servicing Marissa with the semi-permanent lashes (that I learned to apply on site) boosted my income by 5%. The bridal salon owner approached me about working with his bridal company applying extended lashes after finding out I was applying Mrs. Pin's. He would add more to his makeup packages and ensuring I got my fee out of the deal. Well that would help me build my clientele and make a little more money to catch up my debt. The addition of the bridal owner's clientele was helping, but I started having a problem with the way he was paying me. The clients paid the owner a percentage upfront and they had two weeks after the date to have the remainder paid, which I thought was reasonable, but it was no discussion with me when I would get paid and that was the element of the situation which didn't suit me well. I didn't know if it were because he was upset that Marissa stop calling him and I was still on the scene or what, but it just became a trying situation that I could not endure under my current circumstances. I advanced on, thanking him for being the avenue that connected me to such a good client. I continued my duties between the salon and the boys, I hated that they had to see me at Kynton's place it was a real dump compared to where they lived with their dad's. It was embarrassing and made me look like I wasn't doing any of the things I was telling them or what they were seeing from the salon, like I wasn't doing anything with the money I was making. I stayed focus still remaining very proud of myself from where I once was. The papers were served from the courts to the salon and Gracie had the pleasure of removing them from off the door coming in before me one morning.

Which gave her every reason to display a new behavior toward me, yes, the rent was behind when she came on board. Did I expect to catch it up, yes? Do I think the plumbing situation took the circumstance to another level, yes? She came at me asking about the details of the numbers saying that she was going to get with her best friend to see if she would invest and pull me out of the hole. I remembered her best friend from years before at her grandson birthday party that Micah was invited too, she had the thought I could take it off what she gave me every month. That would have been a very good idea as I explained I had money toward it already. That was just talk to see just how far behind I was and how she could capitalize on the situation. Gracie approached the owner about leasing the space to her after I was removed, I discovered at a later date that Gracie explained to the owner that she had an investor, and she could pay him months in advance. That bothered me, but I never displayed it I then knew what her true intentions were. The only way her plans would fall in place were if I made out in court with everything that was owed to him. I came across a modeling gig with MillerLite that would put me right with my debts at the salon, but the shoot wasn't until after the court date. I continued with everything like nothing was going on, I was very afraid of what I was facing I felt like all my hard work was going to waste. I tried to stay hopeful, but realistically I was short $1200 by the time the date came the owner got to the point he was not even speaking. Whatever deal that was made with him and Gracie was in stone, and she was pissed off I was still collecting her money. Until the end of the result I was still going to, we had an agreement regardless of what I was facing. She felt like on that last month she was just going to walk in and out working without paying for her space, because I was in a position to lose everything. Court was devastating the judge ordered that all debts be paid or vacate the property within seven days. The partial payment amount I offered to the owner through the judge was not acceptable. He didn't agree when the judge asked him if he would consider. Leaving court I had so much on my mind, what my clients were going to do, what would they think. I worked in my salon all the way to the second of the last day. Gracie things were out before mine, I was sure she heard the information before I could tell her. I remained professional putting in a call to her after the court date; she was not bothered to return the call, as I left her a message for her to call me. I guess that was that, I never saw her again after. Kynton and I moved everything between his father's truck and my truck, we both being there from the beginning from when the space was nothing, to everything I put into it that someone else was going to be benefiting from was mind blogging. In the move I was thinking about the clients, I was going to lose and how the transition would hurt my business. I was four months away from being a year in the space and I was already moving not being able to show stability. Bringing clients to where I was residing was not anything to think about, it was not an environment they needed to see me living in. I had to work with the condition I was in until something else presented itself. Before two weeks was in another opportunity presented itself from a young lady I ran into at the courthouse going through the proceedings with the building owner at the salon. Elise, who once worked for my mom back in the day, she was being evicted from her apartment and going through transitions at home, putting everything in her business. She approached me with a roommate opportunity, it was a townhouse she was moving into that a guy she was dating had available. The property wasn't going to be ready for a month or so and I had time to consider. Between me making a final decision of moving again in less than two months, I enjoyed three days of being a model on the set for MillerLite. It gave me a chance not to dwell in the fact that I just lost my salon. I was providing mobile services again and did not get into informing the clients of the full details of what happen with myself and the space. When I went to service Marissa, I told her that the lady negotiated another deal close to my lease ending, because the owner wanted me to cover the damages made from the plumbing. It wasn't all the truth, but something like it, I had to explain why I wasn't in my owe space, especially when

Hillary wanted to come by and have another service done. Mrs. Pin asked me, "Where are you going to service your clients?" and I informed her I was moving to College Park and working from home in an extra room there. I guess my decision on moving with Elise was made from that statement. Elise had a space she was leasing to work out of; we did the same type of work. It was nothing like I had, but big enough for her to work. She had her space for a year, so my hats went off to her for her stability. I was thinking my vision must had been too big, thinking I could handle a space of that magnitude or maybe I came in too strong, putting all that money into it and not saving. When I first moved over there it was different, I started having flashbacks of my mom and Sophia the scene just start looking gay. Elise had an experience with another woman and that was her business, I knew to stay on my grind, stack my money, until it was time for me to make another move. The townhouse was brand new, somewhere to have client's come and not be embarrassed, and the travel was the only hang up it was 30-45 minutes away from the area I was once in. I tried to stay clear from Elise not to create too much of a bond only hanging out every once and a while. She didn't have a reliable car, so we pushed the Rover when we went places. We both had our fair share of personal visitors, but for me it was always beneficial company, a purpose to help with my cause. I really had no time for anything too personal, not that I picked up any of my old habits, I just looked at how I spent my time. I still had the loss of the salon in the back of my mind, and I wasn't entirely over everything. I came across a model gig in Miami that was auditioning for eye candy models that was tapping a pilot for a reality show; it had the concept of top model. When I submitted my pictures and resume' they were interested in having me try out. They asked me to get there any way possible, hell it was worth the try, what I had to lose? I travelled back and forth for maybe a month, gaining a cool relationship with the girls trying to get close in a reality show position. Between my travels I was caught off guard when Marissa called; she hadn't had services for maybe three or four weeks. She was getting prepared for an award show in Vegas, she was flying her hair stylist and nail tech along with their husbands. She stated she thought I had moved to Miami and I was down their modeling, as she remembered our last conversation. I didn't know how to take the comment as I thought maybe she missed me or I missed money. I figured maybe I need to stay on one career and stop jumping all over the place or stop telling people what I'm doing. When they call looking for me tell them, "I'm working out of town with another client." I was still applying lashes when Stevenson was ready; he nicely was trying to tell me to hurry up. She was telling me to take my time, it was a mess and we had been drinking Champagne on top of everything. I think by her not seeing me in a while, she just wanting time to talk to me more. We always had good conversations as I would find out something new about her every visit going through a bottle as we talked, going through half the bottle before one eye was done. By this time Marissa was wearing Mink Semi Permanent Lashes, known to be worn by all major Divas. An hour and a half service would take me sometimes three/four hours. Stevenson just came in that day and broke it down saying something along the lines of, "look the plane will be leaving in a certain time, I would like to get a little gambling in, make some money to pay for all this nice things you are doing for yourself and the things you want to do when you get there." Marissa mind state was the plane could leave when they were ready since they were flying private. That conversation showed me that their relationship was real, even though it was on a higher financial scale; they still exchanged words like every other couple. That's when I stopped talking and did my best to make sure they stayed on schedule. It had been a couple of weeks since I heard anything from Miami, when I did hear something it was from the coordinator, she was inviting me down to chill with her for another weekend. It was in this visit that the coordinator told me her and her partner was not moving forward on the project it was disappointing news, but a cool experience in visits. We torn the weekend apart as usual and flying home all I could think about was how people live in Miami and stay on point it was too much fun in the city.

Coming home Elise decided she wanted a truck like the one I had, but a different maker. She chose the Volvo type, and it was clean, never will I hate on that. How would she afford it being behind on her half of the rent where we were? My truck was over heating really bad and I had to be really careful driving it. Things were back to normal working out of the house for me which was doing decent. It was time for her to get her tag on her truck, she asked me if I were going to spot her, and she would give it back to me. That wasn't going to happen, we both had our own responsibilities and the only thing we meet up with monthly was the townhouse, and I was keeping it like that. I could tell she thought a certain way about it, but I had to stick to my guns. She did get a strip party together to raise the money and ask me to work it with her. Of course I was down for that, it was just dancing and beneficial for me. We came up a little and afterwards went to a sports bar; the owner was someone I dealt with a couple of months prior. I had not seen him since our last experience. I was very insecure about dealing with him in my in-between time; we didn't really have any money to spend that night at the bar. I called in a person that had been trying to reach me for some weeks, the guy that invested in the salon. When I called him he was already out and was excited to hear my voice, ready to come where ever I was that evening. When he arrived fun kicked in instantly, Elise tried to take over the conversation and was politely excused. He and I continued to talk and drink between the two of us; he just sent her a new drink when she got low. He began to tell me how he hated to have met me after the fact, after he was married; he said some things to me that I always thought he felt. When I told him about my living arrangements he asked me why, I didn't call him. The house in Douglasville was still available for me, but what he didn't know was the house was in Ismael's uncle subdivision and Ismael or family member would have saw me sooner or later. That's when things would have hit the fan; I would rather deal with what I was dealing with staying with Elise than anything with Ismael. It was a bunch of feelings expressed between him and me that evening, we were really good friends with one another. Other than him being married he was a great man in our experience with each other, he was a person I can truly say wanted me to have something for myself being that I was single. The tab came he covered it and we started wrapping up the night there, Elise was very jealous; because we rarely talked to her, we just kept sending her drinks. The owner walked past, hugged me, and asked me to talk to him when my conversation there was done, but that it never happened. The investor drove me back, because Elise was still flirting, I had reached me point. A couple of hours later she came in with her homeboy that had been over many of times before. He came with more alcohol, weed, and a couple of pills. We went up the street to another bar close, even though I had reached my point. I really had no business leaving, still partying, but I was thinking what the hell. We partied a little bit more; when we were at the bar she was dancing up on me it was innocent until she grabbed my toot toot. I knew from that moment it was time to go, we left, headed home, and her friend came in too. I went to the kitchen to get some water and empty the guts from my blunt I was about to roll. All I heard was," I always have wanted you," and her guy friend came putting his arm around me, telling me how cool I was. Then put me in a maneuver to where I could not move my arms freely, she came in on the scene trying to pull my pants down. We tussled and tussled until she could got my pants down and was trying to lick on me. She was wrestling with me pulling my legs open, by then we were on the ground, she was trying to lick whatever she could at that point even with my legs being crossed. I was very drunk trying to handle the situation, and it was hard trying to get loose. When I could get an arm out from him holding me down, I started pushing her head away. When I started getting my other arm lose my first clear chance, I punched her, we started fighting, the next thing I knew she went for her purse, and shot at the wall. I backed away from her, took my silk blouse off, drunk telling her, "I don't want any blood on my shirt." I remember the dude grabbing her and her saying, "I'll kill you." I went upstairs in my room locked, myself in it, and passed out. The next morning it was like a nightmare that was so vivid, I really couldn't believe what happened, but it did. I looked like it had happened, no shirt on, and my panties were down on one side. I got myself up and quickly jumped in the shower, feeling nauseated, when time I got out the shower, I looked around the couch was moved all around. Elise was coming in the door; she went straight to her room, not really being able to look at me in my face. We caught each other on the stair way a few minutes later; I just let her know I did not understand what happened or how it got to that extent. I still had love for her, but did not like her as a person for disrespecting my space like she did and my feels were hurt. I let her know the incident was something I would remember for the remainder of my life, but would not dwell on it though. We stayed out each other's way, but I knew I had to make a change and fast before something else came out the situation. My car needed to be put in the shop, child support paid and after that I needed to move and still made sure my obligations where I was met. I broke down and called Aiden, I knew he was too serious about me; it was only so much playing with his emotions I could do. I said whatever I had to and within 30 days I was back in my truck, caught up on child support a little and was closer to Marissa living in a loft in Roswell. I let her know I was closer and in telling her that it seemed as if she called me more often. One evening I ate dinner with her and Stevenson, he made comments about opinions he had about the relationship a man is to have with his woman. He even told me about his decisions in their personal relationship, keeping this very real. I had a beautiful time, the things discussed were genuine and it put my mind in the frame that I was right in the thoughts I had about the way I should be treated. I also thought about how I was treating myself, things within myself I had to change in order to have another person want to treat me how I see fit. I realized how much foolishness I had taken, holding on to people that

I needed to let go. People I should have let go to allow something better to could come in that I deserved with good intentions on helping me grow and develop into a better person. I thought about how much time I had wasted for so long and that's when I started really making the moves in my life count every time. I left there that night like 10:30 thanking God for that opportunity to have that one-on-one time with sound minded people. I didn't want it to be in vain, I was very grateful of the evening. I cried like a baby that night just thinking about everything, just mad at myself knowing I could have done better in my life. I could still make changes and make better use of my time while I was still living. I started thinking how I could have lost my life that night if Elise would have been the fool she wanted to be. Who knows? I had that go get'em spirit that needed to be channeled more toward what I really wanted out of this life. My truck started acting violently on me again, not even 30 days after getting out the shop. I had clients coming to the loft, but needed more income, I was over a client's house on her Internet and someone who was requesting me on Myspace asked me if I wanted a job. He was a promoter for a club on Roswell Rd and looking for an event planner from 9 to 5 Monday thru Friday. I had no skill in event planning what so ever, but knew I could do anything that was explained to me. I made contact and was working that following week. Even with my stuttering problem I met the task and got the job done, I helped with the Martini parties which were very popular every Friday. I ended up being very good at event planning, they moved me to the Blue Room from Taboo2 and when the Pearl opened they had me there before Blue Room closed. In between that time frame my sister came to stay with me, she had been bouncing around from my mom to her dad and everyone was tired of her not applying her self. She really adopted a mentality like she was from 4th Ward, she had more to look forward to than she displayed. I just wanted her to get a job and stack her bread. I gave her 30 days to find work and 90 days of stacking, she lasted 21 days with me. I later regretted how I threw her out while she was brushing her teeth one morning, before I went to work. I didn't give her time to put her clothes on, she got dressed from the clothes on the porch in her suitcase. The morning that happened I woke her up early wanting her to get a head start, she started poking around giving me attitude, and I lost it. The girl stood there thinking I was going to let her make a point brushing her teeth slow. I asked her to leave if she wasn't with the rules I set out, I didn't want to hit her, and she knew she was taking a risk of that happening moving slow. I cried on the way to work listening to Frankie Ski's morning show Inspirational Vitamin. He was speaking about how God places people and events in your life to test your patience, because you have the love that they need to get them through their trial. It was just hard to see her mistreating herself the way she was; my mom said she got off the bus with three big suitcases struggling. God was still dealing with me; I have always felt really bad about that morning, but I met well. I just didn't have time for the nonsense in that moment; I thought she was doing things unnecessarily. She had it too easy compared to my experiences, struggles that she witnessed firsthand. I was striving for change and didn't need any distractions; nothing was going to stop me. Work began getting interesting, I gained a reputation of making numbers. I was always very well dressed and kept things always on a business conversation wearing clothes from two to three years ago from that time. My coworkers entered me in a sun dress contest for $500 that I won. We celebrated by having a few rounds of Patron shots that got me so messed up that night, I missed my phone alarm to wake me up to service Marissa for a funeral. I was really hurt missing that appointment with her; it was my first time missing an appointment for her, I didn't know if that would have been my last time services her. I was taken back when she called me to take care of her before the Orpah Show. That's when I understood she was truly good with the service I provided to her, she gave me the look like, "now what happened to you" and made jokes about how she was blinking at the funeral. She had a great sense of humor, she asked me how everything was going and couldn't believe that I was working at the club. A couple more services came by before she approached me to work at the salon April (her hair stylist) was working at. She informed me it was something I needed I would be surrounded around women that could help me reach my peak. She further deliberated how with my look I would fit right in, "they are going to love you," she said with great joy. She explained how Sage the owner was a cute Lady who was well connected and her clientele would appreciate my work. She gave me the information, telling me to move into my career get from out the club, and work on my profession. I did express to her how the extra money was helpful with me getting my truck fixed at that time, but understood her completely as I thanked her. I always wanted to earn everything I got in this life and at that moment I realized things were going to come to me. I was establishing a relationship with the right people. Leaving there that day I was thinking I could hardly imagine who I would service at this salon; I knew I would run into Mia Miller again, the wife of a NBA basketball player. I liked her; she and Marissa had become really good friends. They had a great deal in common; both their husbands were named Stevenson which was a good start for them. She was another beautiful lady more grounded than I understood being a woman in her position for so long. I set the appointment up to meet with Sage the next day not wanting to do anything to embarrass Marissa. I understood she was new in town and was building her own reputation outside of her husband's name. I was proud to be a name she mentioned for lash services and needed to do what I could to hold on to it.

The Salons

Sage was the owner of the salon in Buckhead; she was very skillful with a distant person initially that carried herself classy and had an elegance that seemed very well thought into. You could tell she had been around elite and that she was elite. She has had a history of having a three month waiting list for hair services, so you know she was whipping some hair. I went to take a look at the salon and the space she had available, she explained to me that she has had young ladies there in the past doing the same services that never seem to make it. The last young lady moved back to Detroit, I didn't think it was because of the money, I did think however it was something else, but that wasn't my concern. I knew they would not have had my skill, I was very confident that they would be pleased in what I had to offer. I have always heard that my talents were on celebrity level and that I should service elite clientele. Sage had two employee's Ava her receptionist, Patricia her assistant, two hair stylist rented space from her, April that serviced Mrs. Pin's, and Piper who came in every six weeks from South Carolina. Patricia was from Bartow, Georgia and had been with Sage for like 5 years. I do believe her work ethnics was a good fit for Sage even though her personal image was not as flashy as some would expect, but neat. The salon was in the nestle of Buckhead where some of your most prestigious woman come. Your top lawyers, newscasters, athletics wife's, professors, professors wives, theater actresses, etc. Patricia's country personality was a very weird fit, but it worked. Ava was a cool lady, fashionable, very well-known in the social scene of

Atlanta from my understanding. Getting and keeping myself in a new frame of mind was something I was looking forward to, hoping to befriend her. I felt like I was in my right place, my time had finally arrived. I have always heard you can move faster in life around the right type of people and I was around the right type of people. I was inspired from every women walked in that door, they seem to be very cultured; I could learn how I should be from them. It made my mind think in advance about my career and not just working in the salon, I had a more evolving state of mind. I wanted to be like one of the women walking in, not just being around them, but be them. When you see one type of woman for so long you really don't think better quality women are out there. There are and if you have an opportunity to be in their company you embrace it and learn want you don't know, not by so much of asking questions, but by watching them as well. Their attitude and conversation were always pleasant, encouraging, and positive to listen to and take part with. I deserved to be where I was, I had always seen myself in my mind as being one of their type, but it was the influence of my surroundings that I would fall into, damaging my growth. I was 29 with no more excuses, this was a time that the old me had to completely died and the new me would be born and I wasn't going to let nothing stop me until I reached my full potential, personally, and professionally. Many women in the salon began to embraced me I believe because I was quite, I only spoke when I needed to, I always allowed them to lead in conversation, and I made sure my response was always neutral, still leaving room for them to continue in more conversation. Getting my foot in the door I knew showing dedication and commitment, I would be able to sell my talents, and all I needed was one chance. As I began to progress I had some haters that were supposed to be there and do what they do, and worked very hard to get my attention. One incident that sticks out to me the most, when my character was tested; I was accused of stealing from Ava's purse. I stood by the desk on a wall to talk with her and the clients from time to time, the seats were for the clients, so I would hold simple conversations with them to get around to asking if they needed a service or to introduce myself to those that didn't know me or what I did at the salon. Going behind the desk was something I would not and had not done; it was nothing back there for me and not a part of my job description. When the accusation came up I patiently waited to see what was going to be the outcome, initially it was said somebody stole the money then the story changed to I stole $200 out of Ava purse being accused indirectly. When it got that far I was asked not to stand by the desk anymore on the wall. It was one of the craziest things I had been involved in, and the topper was Sage holding a salon meeting about the incident, still not asking me directly just saying that the person was in the room, and needed to return the money by the next day. She also asked me if I had any comment about anything, I politely answered, "no." An incident person doesn't entertain comments made to them or about them. Ava was telling her long time girlfriends who received services from Sage about the situation and when I would walk in the room, she would stop talking. I thought that was disrespectful to me as a woman and certainly damaging to my business that I was trying to build in that establishment. I told myself I would not comment in it if it didn't come at me directly. When the money came up missing, I remembered saying to her, "you mighty calm for someone to have invaded your personal space," and continued to say, "I would have the front and back door locked, and it would be a search party going on just on the principle." She responded, "no it's ok." That let me know then she had coward in her and just wanted a show. I believed Ava pre-judged me because I did not come on strong in reference to what I had in my closet and how made up I can get. I had a laid back approach in the way I dressed when I first started, really not knowing how to dress, not knowing what to wear or what type of image to show to these strangers I had to slowly learn. My personal style is a dress to the feel of that day, if I wake up and I'm feeling sexy I dress that way, if I'm feeling laid back that's what the outfit is for that day. I think at that point I was hiding myself to make others comfortable ashamed to display my beauty. I always used my looks for what a man could give me, and because of that I did not have a sincere, secure identity of myself. Raine had us in uniforms at her salon when we worked, which I continued to wear at my salon, but this was a different place, they wanted you to show fashions. It was just weird for me always using my looks and fashion for what a man could give me, and because of that I did not have a sincere, real, secure identity of myself. I also assumed coming in as a reference from Marissa Pin would have sufficed, but not everyone was aware of my reference and the individuals to share that information cared not to. I later found out that Sage replaced the money, until this day I never explain to Ava my feelings toward the incident. I always believed Patricia took Ava's money out of her purse because of how she secretly co signed with Ava that I did it to everyone, being that it was easier to put things on me since I was new. I did speak to Sage about it after being part of the salon over a year and my statement had her speechless. I was thinking to myself during the accusations, "do they think Marissa would refer me here to pull stunts," it was embarrassing to her as well as me if she had known about what was happening. I would think Marissa had a good judgment of character, not counting how many times I had been in her home to service her personally. Outside of that I had enough to worry about honestly; Marissa was having a birthday party I was barely invited to. I was invited by text message three hours before I had to meet the ladies at the suite to team up with April and Hillary to get them ready. I was salty, because I assumed I would have had an invitation sent out with the rest of the staff. Marissa had my e-mail and contact in her roster; something told me however it was not Marissa's doing. In my assessment it was between Marissa's personal shopper Ulla and her assistant at the time Hope. I serviced Marissa, Mia, Ulla, and Hillary that evening, Ulla had a guy that she worked with at Phipps Plaza come in and provided makeup. After, the beans were spilled about what was going on, Marissa looked at me and asked me what I was wearing. Marissa gave me some bad pre-loved croc and suede thigh high Manolo

Blahnik boots in one of my visits one day. Sage thought it would be a good idea to wear them for her party after I asked her in privacy how should I feel about the short notice invite debating if I should go. I learned a long time ago when an older woman gives a younger woman something personal out of her closet they admire you. The only person I knew to wear Manolo's was Gabrielle and I knew how she got hers, so I was proud in the way I got mine, even if they were hand-me-downs. I told her, "I'm wearing a black cocktail mini dress and the boots" and that was all I said. She gave me a look like you bad chick, Marissa and I always agreed if we had nothing else to wear something black always work.

The boots were like a dark chocolate and I had a Louie bag to carry, so I was fine. I had to come up with something on the spot do to the short notice. Not to mention I had an hour before the party to get dress, so I didn't have much time to for myself. I had recently customized my wig, so my hair was nothing to worry about. I was wearing it something like Marissa's but a little longer with streaks. On my way there all I could think about was life is really changing and how I was blessed to embraces the change and not fight it. Stevenson completely had the house redecorated for Marissa's party, I knew they had arrived already the driver was picking them up at a certain time. Pulling up at the residence which was drop dead gorgeous, I just left her birthday card with a gift card attached to this bakery that bakes her favorite cookies in the truck until I serviced her again. Thinking she would have thought it was a good gesture, but thought it was petty and laughed at me. Walking up it was a man standing there with a list with names. He asked me my name I told him, it wasn't on the list. So I gave him my company name, it wasn't on the list. I had the weird look for only a slight second, when Marissa's son, J, came out with his date and was like Ms. Paris, you look good! The man let me in after seeing that and I walk in with him and his date with no problem. I felt like everyone was looking, I didn't know if the dress were too short, or my butt looked too big to be in it, but when I saw how tight other dresses were I felt better. The first part of the crew I saw was April, Hillary and Hope they were like you made it. When I continued to walk around, I spotted Marissa, Ulla, and Stevenson. Ulla spoke first hugging me like you made it in, her hug was surprising, because I knew she did care for me much. I took the hug from her as if she were saying, "You got in without being on the list, and okay I got respect." Speaking to Marissa and Stevenson, he had no idea it was me Marissa had to remind him of who I was and he looked like Wow, she has blossomed. I can admit I had a more polished look, I believe last time he saw me I had a curly weave pass my shoulder and before then I had a long 16'/18' blunt cut straight weave. I was always covered up, never dressed with makeup on, so I did look different. Marissa hugged me very happy to see I can get it together. The night went on, and it was something I had never experienced, everyone had their husbands or dates with them I came alone. I was thinking who in the hell would I have had to bring, the mix up at the door, I would not have wanted a witness to see that look on my face. I would rather have had a choice in sharing the story like I'm doing now, it was embarrassing. Then I got to thinking about Nene trying to get in Sheree party with Kim on an episode of Housewives of Atlanta and the incident I encountered. Ignoring the negative thoughts even though the incidents were similar I kept my mind on the party, listening to Stevenson tell everyone to mingle. Stevenson telling everyone to introduce themselves to people this could be your night to meet the right person, taking your career to the next level. He expressed how it was some really great people in the building, don't be shy, we were there for more than one reason. I said to myself now that's a businessman, it's always a moment for opportunity when you around individuals on that caliber. I was going to take heed to the suggestion, we started off at the bar drinking champagne, by then I was on my second glass and really wasn't interested in having another. I went to the bar with Hillary and her husband before we met the girls on the dance floor for a group dance. All I could think about was maybe my dress was too short to be dancing comfortably, I noticed men looking at my butt and the comment I got from Stevenson's bodyguard I was thinking, "stick with the two steps and smile." Looking at Marissa's birthday, the way she was enjoying her evening, and the way it drastically changed for her. I wondered one day would my life change in the same way. Not that I had to marry into my change, but change in from the aspect of my hard work having everything I want in my life at my feet. I don't think I am the only woman who would want that type of life for themselves and their family. I could just see the gratefulness that Marissa had about life in her face, along with her parents, who I rode the elevator with getting to the lower level of the house. My baby toe in the boots was killing me, so I took a small break off the dance floor with the girls, and watched everything from a distance. Five minutes after, Stevenson calls me over and wants to introduce me to his personal golf shopper. He was an older man in his early forty's, nice, but nowhere near my type. I was cool out of respect for Stevenson I was open to the introduction. On the way over Stevenson was telling me, "this is the type of man you need in your life," I danced with him while we small talked for a second. It was just that a second, as I went back to my seat to rest, Marissa came back from wardrobe change, she was on the dance floor by herself, and she called me out with her. I thought it would be fine to leave my bag on the seat I was in, I wasn't that far away from it, and when you got Boris Kujo, and Tim Joyer in the room you are not thinking about anyone stealing. Well, coming back to my seat my bag was gone; I was like, "ok you got to be kidding me." I asked the people in the area, "Did you see the Louie bag that was sitting her." A lady told me that the guy Hope was with took it, me being me I went straight to him. When I saw him the first thing, I asked for was, "where is my bag" nothing more nothing less. I ate at the dinner table with them and didn't converse there, so I didn't have conversation for either him or Hope. Hope gave that overbearing energy like I wasn't supposed to speak to him, so I didn't. While he was getting my bag he explained, "I wanted to put it up so it could be safe," then Hope walks up. I politely told her what I asked him as you could see the anger on her face as she approached; I knew it was time for me to go.

I been at the party for more than 2 hours by then, I thought it would be ladylike to leave by 11. Saying my goodbyes to everyone by the time I got to Hope, she didn't even look my way, I felt bad, but then again I didn't ask that man to touch my bag and I don't think the bag did, either. Before leaving I had a chance to speak with Stevenson's assistant briefly, who apologized like three times for not having me on the list. What was surprising is the situation had to have been discussed at the party, because I never said anything about it that evening to anyone. I responded in complimenting the night and how I was glad to have made it. So, I knew then it was a trick, and it didn't prosper, what god has for a person to see, they will see, and that was one example for me to believe that. Leaving I ran into the guy Stevenson introduced me to, he walk me to my truck when it came up from valet, we exchanged business cards, and agreed to speak with each other some time that week. We did, we talked for about three times on the phone never getting around to a date, and the conversations ended. I had my mind on the salon and getting more involved with my new surroundings. That night made me aware, I was being noticed; I needed to stay on my toes, because somebody was intimated of my presence. When you dealing with a group or clique it's hard to indicate whom, so I just need to be aware of what I said and did from then on. Getting back in the salon after the weekend, April was cool and we spoke a little more to each other. I felt good about being in there for the first time, it was known to the staff at the salon, I was a member of Marissa's team, and they accepted me more or at least that's how it looked.

The following couple of weeks it was Mia's birthday party, now I saw her at Marissa's party but our paths didn't cross. I was wondering how this invite was going to go, she was my outside appointment for the day, and called to make that appointment while April was servicing her at her place. It was my first time servicing Mia in her home; she was a little earthier compared to Marissa, like the money didn't change her as much. She had a very nice home as well, not as big as Marissa's but your mini mansion style of home. As I was servicing her, she asked me to come to her party, I was honored to be invited, and this time I had enough time to get something together to wear. She did tell me, "it wasn't not going to be as elegant as Marissa's, but still do you" and that was all needed to be said. I left there thinking, "maybe I should have a date," I didn't know who was invited and majority of everyone was in a relationship or married. I called a guy I had gone out with a couple of times, he was a decent looking man, his body extremely nice, I thought he would have made a good arm piece for the evening. I should have invited the guy Stevenson introduced me to if anyone, but I was not physically attracted to him at all and I didn't want to start anything with him knowing that. The guy I invited was a person I could easily brush off without thought. When I called him he was happy to hear from me, I hadn't talk to him in a week, but it was cool, he called earlier that day, asking me if I had time to get together. I let him know I needed him to look very nice, we were going to a client of mine's birthday party at a mini mansion. I figured once I saw him that evening, I would let him know who party it was, we agreed to meet at the mall, and he could ride with me. We met at the mall as planned, he looked nice, he was so surprised in my appearance, and he couldn't take his eyes off me the entire ride over. I felt fine going in the party accompanied; the only downside was it was not with a person I genuinely wanted to share the experience with. Everything looked very nice when we arrived and was walking in as then I informed my date that we were in Stevenson Miller's home and his wife was my client. He was completely surprised giving me a look like; he had to figure out who I was and who else I may have known with a client like that. I mingled throughout the evening, it wasn't as business associated as Marissa's party, you could tell in the conversations, these were people Mr. & Mrs. Miller had relationships with and were there to really celebrate Mia's day. My date was walking around taking pleasure in the atmosphere, it was funny, I had to remember he was there with me as I started drifting off into my own world. I barely was with him; I really didn't know how to introduce him we weren't a couple. Mia's brother was the deal in my sight, we kept giving each other the eye, and so obvious my date noticed me checking him out. Once he noticed he came over, kissed me on the lips, telling, "I just couldn't help myself." I was thinking I really want to slap him stupid, but as a man trying to get in, he was just trying to mark some type of ground. Before the evening was over I did have a chance to make myself in the presence of Mia's brother, not being able to resist being so attracted to him. I put my card in his pocket, standing very close to him when I did it, making sure only he could hear me say, "this card is not for business." I was mad, I came with a date at that point, and the champagne was making moves for me. I saw a guy pointing my actions out to my date, I knew right then it was time to go. Stevenson walked us out helping me in the truck making sure I could drive and I was. My date's car was at the mall, I didn't know him to that extent to drive my truck, I was ready for him to get away from me, and he could have taken a cab at that point. I knew I was wrong, but I just used him as an arm piece, I may be just should have told him that and things would have looked better from his sight instead of making it appearing as a real date. I thought about the night all evening after I dropped him off, I was mad at not being more on top of my actions with Mia's brother; I didn't need that to be a discussed in the circle.

The company I ordered my semi permanent lash extensions from 3D Beauty in California was having a competition on best photo with individuals and semi permanents lashes. Photos were to be submitted by November 5, so I was preparing for this when I was experiencing the Marissa/Mia events and the accusations of being a thief at the salon. Clientele was slowly growing for me at the salon and I knew this competition was one sure way to bring in more business. I thought I had to start getting public recognition for my work, it was one sure way the ladies in the salon would notice me more, and be more exceptive to my services. I organized the photo shoot and who I would need. I had the pictures visualized in my mind already; I thought it would be a great idea to use Hope, the assistant for Marissa; she had a universal look that would be good to use. The company being based in California, I knew what type of woman would catch their attention. When I mentioned the idea to April in the salon, she came at me like she was Hope's manager and ended my consideration basically telling me that Hope was her model and worked with her solely. I laughed as she walked off; because it was more than that, it was personal or a reason just to shut me down. My thought was confirmed when Hope mentioned to me, "I heard April shut you down, when you mentioned asking me to be your model for the shoot" on my visit to service Marissa. Moving on, I asked a model I worked with on the MillerLite shoot, which had a fabulous look to use as well as a long time client from Tridad. In the preparation I wanted to concentrate only on doing was the lashes so, I called in some help, a cool friend I went to Skincare School with that was the bomb in makeup named Vanessa and contacted a photographer I established a business relationship with. Paying everyone involved except the models who wanted copies of their pictures and to help me win as much as they could. I think it was the collaboration of believers that helped push things along so easy. I set the date, and the shoot would take place at my loft, after a week of getting my submission together, this is what I had:

Letter written with my submission:

> Lashes from my understanding are a tool to enhance natural beauty not to overwhelm it. I Paris am a second line family generation brow/lash specialist in Atlanta, Georgia. Being extremely fresh to the industry I made a healthy name for myself servicing elite clients in all areas where I am introduced as one of the best lash technicians in the business. Striving for excellent is a priority,

enhancing a person's natural beauty and creating a facial style that complements that individual is something dear to me. I want to commend and thank you for having this contest for technicians in this section in the industry. Welcome to my world "Your Best Face."

Credits:
CONTESTANT: Paris
yourbestface@yahoo.com or (404) 437 4211
MUA: Vanessa Edwards
PHOTOGRAPHER: Chase
FLARE EYELASH

MODEL: Avani Nanan

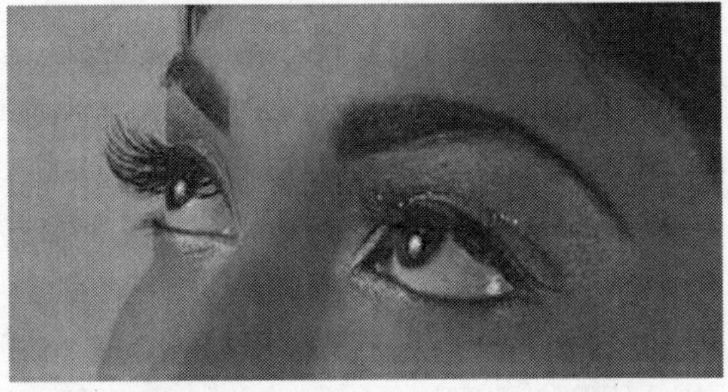

SEMI PERMANENT EYELASH MODEL: Yvonne West

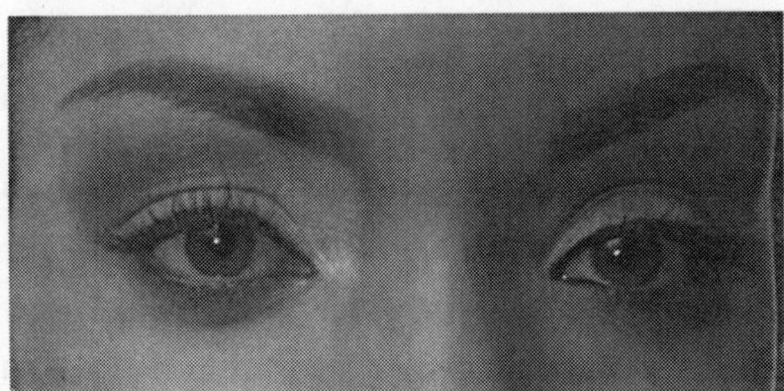

While waiting on the outcome of the competition to be announced, (which wasn't until after the New Year) I had my stylist for the past three years change my customized weave to a short look. I'd been in the salon three months and no one seen my real hair, after the accusation of my stealing the money was over, this was the next discussion. The salon wondered if I had hair and thought I would complement the salon better wearing my natural hair if I had any. Working in a salon it's second natural to let one of the techs do your hair. When some of the clients would compliment me on my hair and none of the stylist in the salon name mentioned, it aggravated them. I firmly believe that approach is everything in getting the response you get when asking a question to anybody about anything. The stylist talked about my hair and made me feel uncomfortable I wasn't wearing my real hair. I honestly think they were trying to be nosey, and my reason for saying that was Ava had an Indian Remy weave to her butt, and no one ever mentioned anything about her weave. I took into consideration that I was in transition, I would have to take some comments into thought, but the money incident made me look at them spitefully. I was still hurt and trying to get over everything. April wanted to get in my hair just as bad as the owner they just had different bad approaches in the situation. Out of respect I thought letting Sage groom my hair would help me maneuver in the salon better. I knew if I wanted to increase my clientele I had to change how I looked and dressed in the salon. Even thought I didn't like to feel like I had to impress people when I service them. I dressed for myself; I had a closet full of very nice attire, an outfit for any occasion. I just thought of it as if Mrs. Pin accepted my services into her home on many occasions without her continuing to using my services because of what I wore, but apparently the salon thought differently. I just thought it was all about the service I provided, the person that I was that Mrs. Pin believed others would appreciate, not what I wore or if they want my outfit that day. I worked better when I was dressed comfortable directing my full and complete attention on the client. My cute tights with a t-shirt on Saturday's was unacceptable, Sage mentioned it in a meeting and her statement was the," just got of bed look." Well, it just looked like I had to get out of my mind, learning to listen to the superiors in the industry of my immediate circle, taking heed to what was being said. It is all about learning and moving forward in your dreams, not allowing your ego or familiarity to stand in the way of what needs to be accomplished. Accepting constructive criticism and changing without conflict or rebelling. Sage had a best friend who has been recognized in Allure Magazine during her career, an extremely polished lady named Gina, well-known makeup/waxing expert in the area. She worked in the Salon around the corner and most of the clients that came to the salon went to her for waxing, makeup, and lash services. If I were in the salon, providing the same services and my services were just as good, I had to have that welcoming look the clients were accustomed to. Sage began tell her clients about what I did up stairs, a place in the salon that clients who had been coming there for years never knew she had. I had to compare prices with my competition, Gina who was charging 20% more than anyone I knew of in the game. What I had to offer was a great service to the clients, I gave my sincere opinion to everyone that I serviced, and most of them had very nice things to say about me. One day I was having a discussion about one of the cast members of the Housewives of Atlanta with some of the staff in the salon. The reality star owned a salon and had two locations; I was once referred to the star from a tranny that bought cocaine from my boy on the Southside. I was over there smoking weed and kicking it that day when my truck was giving me trouble. The tranny saw the work I did on myself and loved it, he/she told me I should call the star and ask if it were a position open for me to work at the salon. I had the number saved in my phone, but never used it. The star and Sage once work with each other in their past at Saks Fifth Avenue Salon. April use to work with them as well in the past; the star had a reputation for just clearly being a user and doing the worst to people in business. They were known for extravagant parties and being the life of them.

April sits next to me and says," if I want to make some money doing lashes that's the salon you should go to." Now the energy of that salon would be total opposite being that in was in more on the hood side of town where I grew up. I wanted to see if it were true, but I knew not to leave or mess up where I was. I called the star and set up a time to come in and interview, I had to have a model with me on the interview. I called Cody, a guy that I went to Skincare School that started off as a client then my best friend after time. I swept the star off their feet, they wanted to hire me, and did on the spot. I explained my position at the other salon and I let him know I would give them a call with my schedule. Now by this time taking the money out of the purse incident was still lingering in the salon was getting overwhelming to me with the whispering, but I was sticking it threw.

It was winter; I was using a friend's car for a moment before I had to result to the bus and train. I lived in Sandy Springs; I would have to travel between Sage's salon which was in Buckhead and the star's salon which was in Greenbriar while waiting to hear the results from the competition. I would get up two hours earlier than I had to be in the salon to catch the bus and walk maybe a block and a half to the salon, after working there in the morning I would pack my supplies to prepare to go to the other salon to work. I would ride the train on the other side of town to catch the bus to the other salon. I did this for about two to three months; people would commend me all the time because I showed no pride as I always arrived on time. People respect you when they see you won't let anything stop you, and you are converged on what you want out of the life you are trying to make. People from the salon in Buckhead would come to Greenbriar to get services when I wasn't there, which spoke volume. I put myself in high demand; they were missing me from one side of the city to the other. I clearly saw the class level in the two salons, appreciating my opportunity working in Sage's more than the other. I started in the star's salon with really no clientele, having to make a clientele over there, I stayed busy.

Passing out flyers in the front of the salon to draw people in, giving client's discounts for first time visits, knowing all I needed was one chance. I got to a point where I was making more than some stylist in the salon. The star's salon paid on a commission based, so I had to break pavement, I didn't really care for them taking commission, it reminded me of Raine's establishment. It was borderline rape if you ask me; the star was a pimp in the salon game. Three weeks before the results of the competition, I had a thought to use the salon paystubs to get a car, to find another place to work that was closer to the other in Buckhead, and where I lived. I was riding the train one evening, changing to the next train when my phone rang. It was 3-d Beauty congratulating me on my hard work and winning the competition. I broke down in my body; I fell on my knees and just cried for a minute. I got myself together, called everyone that was involved in helping me, thanked them, and let them know it was with their talents that it all worked out. I felt a sense of accomplishment, I was happy to have something to share with my boys when they came over on the next visit. When I told my mom she was happy, but didn't get into it a lot. She started talking about her accomplishments and the things that she was involved in. I brushed it off, staying in my happiness about winning; I knew I had to take advantage while it was hot. Make it out of a bigger story to get more identification and I had to come up with a way to do it once the word was out. I was cool with a guy that was an Athletic PR, thinking I could ask him questions, getting some direction on which way to let the news out publicly. I wanted to wait to ask him last after I put other things in place first, I knew he wouldn't know how to handle me winning, and wanting to do what I can to expose it. He really didn't support what I was doing; it wasn't as big as everyone else he was dealing with at the time, he was really connected in his field. I started with telling everyone at both salons, they were happy, and in shock. The Buckhead salon couldn't really believe it and felt like they underestimated me. You could tell they looked at me differently, Hope even came into the salon to get her lashes done for an event she was attending, it was the first time we had a real conversation. She had a regret type of energy on her that day, like she should have accepted the offer of being one of the models. The star's salon thought of me as value to their business, they started coming at me like they needed me to put in more hours than I was. Telling me when I wasn't there they were losing money, and it was costing them. I ignored them and stuck to the plan, I started looking for a car lot that would deal with my credit challenges. I was in a 2005 Dodge Stratus r/t within a two week time frame. Sage's salon was mentioning my services more after the word of my winning the competion got around, so more income was coming in from there. The star's salon was getting impatient that I had not yet decided to work with them for addition hours in the week. I got fired from the star's salon shortly after, through a phone conversation with the salon manager. They wanted to know when I was coming in; Sage's salon needed me to work longer than my set time because of the request for my services on that evening. I completely forgot to call that morning to the star's salon to let them know the changes that would take place for the day. Before I could call that afternoon, I got a call; apparently I had some clients requesting me there. In the time frame I was not normally there, so I was a little defensive in answering there questions. Not having patience with me they gave me the final ultimatum, if I wasn't coming in that day or later than the time, I could no longer work there. I answered them saying, "I'm not coming in." Sage's salon was where I charged full price, collected my money, and paid booth rent; the star's salon took commission from everything I did, I made more at Sage's. The manager put me on hold and came back on the phone explaining that it was getting to be too much with my scheduling and the star said don't worry about returning. I figured the star was still upset about not using the hell out of me on a taping of the Housewives of Atlanta. The star expected me to help with the makeup on the models and that was not a problem until we started talking about those lashes I won from the competition. The star wanted me to use my supplies without compensating me for the work that was going to be done that event. I got my new car that day and booked it, picked up my boys and went home to relax. When I came in to work the next day; they talked about how I disappointed the star like it was a sin. How everyone helped out, and they was proud of them, but still no one was compensated. One stylist turned out to be the savior for the evening along with a guy from the other location. It was weird it took the star a couple of days to speak to me again, after that event. I want recognition, but not at the cost of using my supplies that I can use to make me money. I saw the star after I was fired twice to service them before a couple of meeting they had in California, but no more after that. I could tell they were really disappointed I wasn't working in the salon anymore; they mentioned how everybody missed me. I had to do what was best for my career, with me winning this competition I wanted to make sure when my reputation was broadcast in the public eye I was in a good surrounding. The attachment of the star's salon reputation was not something I necessarily could have benefited from. Don't get me wrong I did enjoy times working under them, having the opportunity to service the wife of Joseph Lowery and Sheryl Lee Ralph, but it was more to accomplish. Sage's salon continually bragged about my winnings, they looked at it as if it blows into something big, I am a part of the salon. I was coming into belonging or deserving to be there and it started feeling good. The clients were very pleased, and the owner was proud of me. She asked me to hang the winning photos in the salon and menu of services to promote my business more. I thought in my mind," she starting to see me differently." I took the suggestion of a very influential client that thought it would be professional for me to start coming to work in a basic work attire that gave me a signature appearance. Taking the attention off my shape, which was something that was discussed a little more than I preferred. I guess it was my conscious using my body in the wrong way at a point in my life to survive and finally having the opportunity to correct the bad choice. It makes me uncomfortable for individuals to acknowledge my body when I want to expose my brain and talents for what they are worth.

The day I started wearing my signature, all black attire to work, and the client that suggested it was there, frozen. She said, "I have chills on my arms, I am very pleased in your growth" as she came up and gave me a big hug like a mother figure. Everyone in the salon that was there at the time was in disbelief; they could only smile with the thought of it being deserved. I had not even knocked down a full six months with the Sage's salon at this point.

The court battles

By spring time my image had change completely, I created my business cards that represented me in a manner in which I was I pleased. I was invited to be a sponsor for the National Coalitional of 100 Black Women, Inc Mecca Chapter. When I told Sage the news, she was said, "You making yourself around very well" and smiled; she was a sponsor for the event as well. I would be representing my business; my first time attending an affair of this magnitude. A long time client of Sage's and a new client of mine thought it would be a nice way to continue to expose my business to elite women and start establishing the business name in a larger arena. Along with that, Cody recommended me for the Rx for Brown Skin Event for the following month. I was on Craigslist looking for modeling gigs still hustling extra money as I was battling with child support payments. The co-parents started filing Child Abandonment warrants on me every 30 days I was late, keeping me in court more often. The parents were taking turns filing in the courts, on one occasion I was in there for Mark on Micah's birthday; I had to give Micah his birthday money for Mark. Then on another occasion I was in court for Micah when I had them for spring break with just the step mother that took the action out on her own. The money I had to spend time and do things with them, I had to turn it in to her, along with buying Micah clothes for the week. I called ahead before the court date and personally asked her to bring his clothes to the court appearance. She decided I needed to buy him clothes while he was with me for the week. I thought it was ignorant because whatever

I bought him I let him take it home, giving him the option of wearing it when he wanted to. I knew it was a reason I was getting the extra grief from the parents, my children were going home expressing their happiness for things taking place in my life at the time. When I figured out that was all it could have been, I decided not to let the enemy steal my joy. I would smile when I was screaming in the inside or even sad with disappointment that our relationship was still on such a ghetto level. We were too grown for the foolishness, I still had not displayed to either household that I was the person that was describe to them, so I was always confused on their behavior and response toward me. I ran across a gig that needed models for Slim from 112 new video. It was casted by a friend of mine Akene the Blackmack from the former Ryan Cameron Morning Show on Hot 97.5. I was selected and did an awesome job on the set; I sowed a seed there that got me a paid job later that year. The clients at the salon didn't know I was in the music video; I didn't want to set the vixen image with everything moving in a more positive direction. I did mention it to April and her response was "no not a video hoe" and I responded," yes ma'am." Keeping my mind off the drama that I was dealing with other parents, I threw my mind in work and what I can do to better in my business. I researched makeup books written by the top professionals in the industry, studying makeup and lash application techniques. I looked into adding more to myself for this industry and knowing that I had to further educate myself to be equipped. While I continued to build my clientele, I noticed that Sage and April's client were segregated from one another. Ladies that knew of each other or wanted to know each other, but didn't talk in the salon because of them thinking about how it would make the stylist feel. It was strange because April was threatened by Sage and displayed tension with a client about befriended one of Sage's client. I don't know if April thought the client would try to talk her client into switching over to Sage or what, it was just strange to see the division in the salon between clientele when the salon was only so big. I thought it was strange and came up with a cool idea to change or end the tension. I thought of having a pamper party/network event that would maybe change how the clients acted with each other.

"Getting into the Spring of things"

A Networking Pamper Party presented by ***Your Best Face.*** Your host Paris D. has created a networking pampering event specialized for woman in business. The circle is acknowledged as an archetype of wholeness and integration, with the center of a circle universally understood to symbolize Spirit—the Source. When a group of people come together in a circle, they are united. This unity becomes even more powerful when each person reaches out to touch a neighbor and clasps hand. This physical connection unites thought and action, mind and body, and spirit and form in a circle. Because a circle has no beginning and no end, the agreement to connect in a circle allows energy to circulate from one person to the next, rather than being dissipated into the environment.

Let's Network

This event will consist of 4 hours which will include: massage (30 minutes), facials (mini facials), manicure/pedicures, and ionic foot detoxifying, brow/lash services all while networking with business women. Catered lunch will be included in this package for $225 (+18% gratuity). 50% due by March 28, 2009 balance by April 10.

Sign up with Paris (404) 437-4211 Only Accepting 15 ladies until April 4.

Event will be held at ***The Salon*** located at 2965 Brickman Ct Atlanta, GA Sunday April 19, 2009 1-5 p.m.

This idea lead me to starting hosting pamper parties to generate extra income even outside of the salon. I had the support from my lead instructor from Skincare School, who was very skilled in exotic facial services. I can remember when I was promoting the event throughout the salon Mia faced dropped when she asked me, "Are you going to have some students from the school help you." I answered her in front of everyone like she asked me, "I have assistance from my instructor who will be providing chocolate and caviar facials." The question from Mia made me feel like my event was not being taking seriously, but I didn't let her comment or the way it made me feel deter what I was trying to do. I imagined what was talked about within the groups, with their sarcastic voices, "is she qualified to pull something like this off or who does she think she is to try to put something like this together?" I had a staff ready and in place for the go on the event that never took place, it was taking as a rookie event and dismissed without words. I was confused thinking my character was more trustworthy after winning the competition, but it deceptively wasn't. I knew of others outside of the salon who would be interested, so I pushed it in another direction. Presenting the company as professionally as I knew how at that point:

> Your Best Face is a premier beauty consultant corporation catering to the individual. Our goal is to assist you in customizing your ideal look. We don't strive for excellence we're committed to it. Your host Paris D. creates networking pamper events specialized to meet the needs of woman in business.

Packages come with 5 services starting from $200-$500 (plus 18% gratuity), catering and gift bags in clients color of choice. If you do not have a space for your event the company does have available space in Buckhead for $500 up to 4 hours. Services to choose from:

- Massage: 30, 60 minutes or hot stone

- Back Treatment
- Facials: mini, exotic (chocolate, chocolate cherry, caviar), or facial lift
- Manicure/Pedicure: regular or rose petals
- Ionic Foot detoxifying treatment
- Facial enhance: brow/lashes, makeup w/lashes, makeup w/o lashes
- WE ACCEPT PARTY SIZES FROM 5 LADIES TO 50

The salon staff and clientele did look at me differently after the deadline, knowing exactly where my mind reached about my business. It was something they had to accept however; I also was working on a patent for a lash I created. I started researching the different styles of lashes to make sure mine was not already patented. The furthest I had gotten with the project was submitting the idea, it was a process that financially I could not handle, along with the child support and my living/work expenses. I figured I would continue to work on my craft, stay on the side of life I could control, move forward, and let God deal with everything else. I started working on a eyelash portfolio that featured different styles of lashes. I thought submitting my portfolio to lash companies; my work would get noticed one way or another, and open another door for me. I needed more income out of this business, everything came in went right back out, I had to market myself to a higher level in the industry. Aiden was a person I could get to invest a little in my projects, of course nothing was going to be just giving to me without him getting anything in return. Our relationship had reached the point where we were basically over each other; it was the history that was keeping us even friends. I started thinking to myself a while ago with Aiden that I could have a better man, Aiden was a good person don't get me wrong, but stuck in one lane. He hung on to the hood environment because of his look I believe but was better than the hood environment; his personal lifestyle wasn't even like what people thought. Aiden lived in a private community; home was worth 350k and was still wearing his jeans hanging from his butt at close to 40. I was over it, I was looking for a person with less thug in them, I spoke how I felt, and thought directly to Aiden on many occasions. Getting money from out of him was getting harder than it was at one point in our history, it was aggravating, but I was going to try being desperate of seeing my goals accomplished which I had become passionate about. The exotic lashes I ordered were from a company in Utah called Premier Lash; I had been dealing with them servicing Marissa it was approaching a year. They had the best and most unique styles of feathered strip lashes. My model in my portfolio wearing their lash was posted on their websites Gallery section, something else added to my resume that slowly kept building.

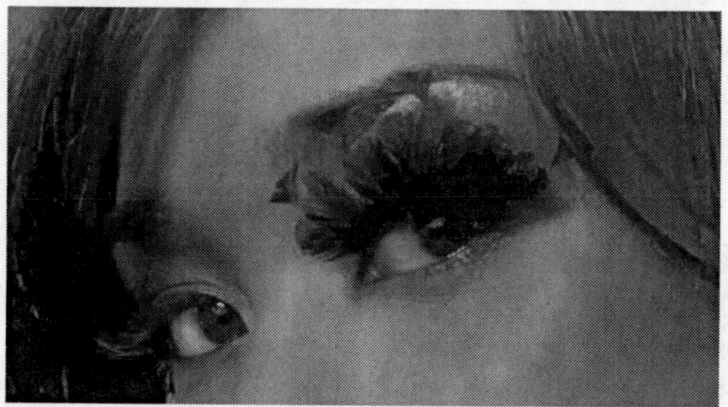

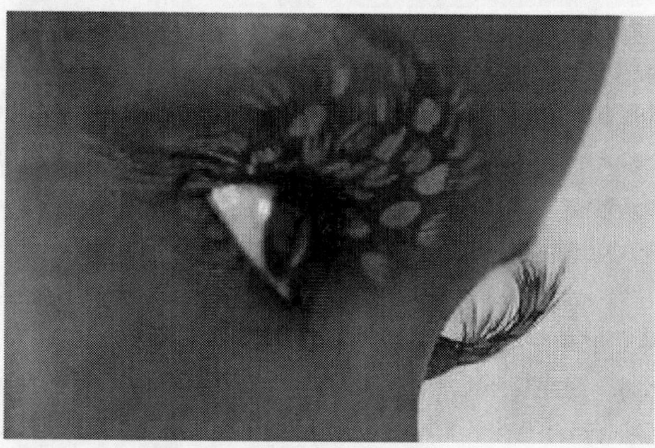

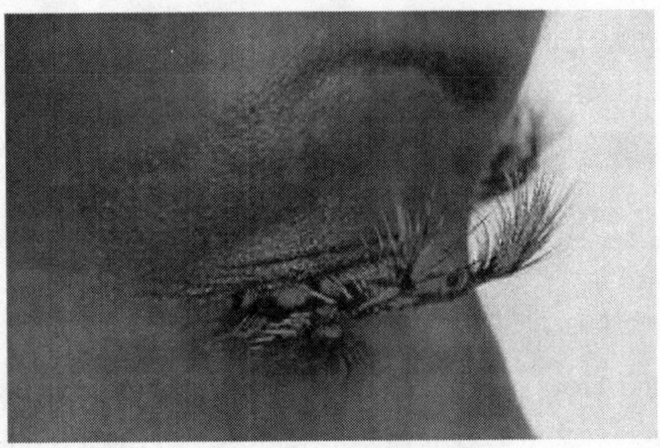

I was more than happy, I stayed in the loop with the owners of the company, and they loved my conversations about ways they should expand their business for the industry to utilize. I wanted to put myself in a position to where I was a pool of knowledge when it came to information about lashes. Having other areas of foolishness to deal with in my life; this area would be one with the most positivity. While all these good things were going on, I had become aware of why Micah was not playing football, his grades. I found the information out from a talk with Micah expressing his interest in playing ball and asking Justin the reason he wasn't. I was assuming Justin was on his grades and progress with the image he was portraying. Justin didn't frequently talk to me about anything that Micah was doing and was not doing at home or in school. I assume Justin was involved in Micah because of how much he was involved in his other children, being a little league coach I figured he would take his children grades serious. I decided on my off days to go up to Micah's school, get to the bottom of things, stay active until something changed for the better. I started off by scheduling a meeting with his teachers; this was the first time this had ever been done on Micah's behalf from anyone. I could not be mad at anyone I was a parent in the situation as well, they made me feel uncomfortable being distant with me and my pride didn't allow me to inquire as I should. The welfare of the child should have been understood and considered, which should have been us as the parents neutral place in the relationship. It was my understanding that he was not turning in his homework that lead me to believe he was not getting the extra help he needed home. When I had the boys, I believed in the homework being done as soon as they got their snack every day when they got home. I monitored them in making sure they were doing it to their understanding, and it was completed. I wanted them to know more than I did, I believe that I would have gotten further in my education in my younger years with that parental support and encouragement about my education. I decided I would come, seat in his classes, and supervise his progress. I did not want to cause any drama in the household toward Micah, so I figured a way to work around the situation to focus on solving the problem. Mark's conduct became a problem; I believe it was to get the extra attention Micah was getting at school. I received a call from his teacher about his behavior, something I never tolerated; they were respectable boys toward authority. I left the salon that morning, surprising him when I pulled him to the side while he was in lunch, reminded him of whom he was, and what I would not accept from him. His teacher committed on how Mark's other parents never came to the school on his behalf all school year. I could not be mad, because once again I was a parent of the child as well. Mason did not invite me in his educational life, because it would intimidate his step mother. Information I got directly from Mason one morning while we were waiting for child support modification. Mason took me to court to increase the child support amount and he stated that his wife was intimidated of my presence. She didn't trust us in any scene together; I really didn't entertain it because that was Mason saying things about me to keep her on her toes in their relationship. I had two children that needed attention in school, while the parents were only concerned about summoning me to court for child support every chance possible. I was at Micah school on one off day and Mark's school on the other off day, either side of the other parents had no knowledge that these activities were taking place. I never commented or spoken about anything that I was doing for the children in school to the co-parents, either did the children, just wanting to keep the peace. In a six week time frame both boys were on track, Micah grades had picked up, he was going to be eligible for sports the following year, and Mark's behavior was like I knew it could be. I would noticed in school events like field day or graduation day I was the only parent present for Mark, so things the teacher said I saw it for myself. I thought," why would a person be insecure about my presence involving my child knowing they were not truly concerned about my child," Mason's wife was a at home parent, so why wasn't she at least for the representation of the two at Mark's school functions? I enjoyed being active with them on the school time it brought back memories. I felt like I was closer to them, disregarding the picture that was being painted of me by the other parents. I thought after my lease was up in the loft I would file for change of custody, and try to get them back with me. Attending the Gala representing Your Best Face as a sponsor was a first for me and an event I took pleasure in being a part of. I was disappointed when I thought about Micah; I would have brought him as my date that evening to expose the experience to him being it was for teenage children. I left early than Sage, after I mingled a little and exchanged a couple of business cards, one I may add being an independent media consultant. He was an older gentleman that worked with many magazines in his history. It was time try to get public exposure for the winning of the competition through the connection; it was now time to put something into action. The client that connected me to the event put in a few extra words to push the idea in his direction to see if we could get a story drawn up. The gentleman was more into trying to date me than anything; I attended a couple of events with him in friendly manner. He wanted more and when I declined his offer that was all she wrote on pushing the idea to any magazine he was connected to. I tried to present the idea to the guy that was a PR as well; I did have a conference call interview to gather the information. After that I had to hear how paid clients were more for his time, and the story wasn't be big enough to push. I couldn't let any of that deter me from continuing to grow the name and expose the talent of the business. I worked and kept my head in the right direction, I received a call from a rapper I met on the Slim video set. He needed a makeup artist and models for a video he was shooting that also featured Eight Ball & MJG. He needed me to get him models and do the makeup for the shoot, which turned out to be a good payday when the day came. It was only a one day shoot, everything would be moving very fast, because Eightball & MJG time was being compensated as well. The shoot was set around a date I had the boys and I was excited, because they came to the set with me. The vibe between the boys and me, going to the set was like this was our everyday lifestyle. They were ready for me to be doing jobs like this more often. Aiden living in the area called me when he saw my car in the restaurant parking in the plaza on the way to his home. He was floored when I told him what I was doing; again he asked me if I would move "home" as he called it. One day of seeing my dream into reality with my children I moved forward on the changing the boys living arrangements and how I want them to change by the next school year. I paid for two changes of custody documents to be serviced at their addresses with these attachments to both:

To the parties involved:

My request is for the following reasons: Initially, when the decision of the child living with his father it was only agreed to for one year. The reason for that was too provided the time for completion of the mother's education. It's been a complicated time communicating with the other party unnecessary, I have never disrespect, threatened, or harassed the relationship, family, or the position of the party. I do believe it's a lot of insecurity and personal resentment toward my character for reasons unknown. It shows in how they handle business with me for my child, very unfortunate due to the fact because our unity surrounded around this child will boost his self esteem and invigorate him into being a remarkable being. I have educated myself to a personal level of satisfaction and do feel that it is time for this young man to come back to live with his mother.

This to Justin:

To the Judge involved in this Civil Case,

My name is Paris D. since the date of the Order; there has been a change in circumstances materially affecting the welfare of the minor as follows: The child needs the balance of both parents for emotional stability that he is not receiving. I take off my hat to his father for standing in taking responsibility for his son, at the age that the child is he needs that male figure, but I do feel that he is being very selfish and controlling toward the relationship that I want to maintain with my son. I have personal concerns about the fairness and how he is treated as the stepchild in the household that I want to expose for correction. Micah and I have a very good relationship is very aware to the father. I do admitted that if I were more educated in the legitimating and custody I would have requested the parenting plan added in the closing of the process so visitation would have been established initially, due to the fact that I could not make the last court appearance because of me taking my exit exams for school. I do accept fault in not standing on my obligations, especially if I know the father was going to take the judgment and handle the situation in such a poor manner. I as want to make it note to the courts that I am in arrears with child support and I am willing to discuss a payment plan to get back on track to get those payments current, not to say the payment is reasoning for my visitations being limited, but I do want to put all my fault out on the tables. Micah is loved by both parents and has every right in the world to experience that from both sides regardless of the relationship between the parents. Justin makes my son feel uncomfortable about his feelings toward me, which is mental negative treatment to the child and that can be analyzed as a personal opinion that he has toward me. We should have a good relationship due to the fact we never displayed in drama toward each other ever. I want to have everything understood and structured through the courts so there is no confusion or misunderstanding about me and my son spending time together. I have been patient, understanding, and compassionate toward the situation because it is a delicate and emotional issue. I am not into the fast talking or am I into tongue wrestling, but I do have things that I up eject to concerning the relationship, and the wellbeing of Micah R. D.-James. Thank you for your time and I do apologize for any inconvenience giving.

Good Parent, Paris D.

This to Mason:

To the Judge involved,

My Name is Paris D. and I am involved in Civil Action File No.2008DV125625. I am writing to explain in writing the outcome that I want to see out of my case with Mason Byrd.

Our son is involved between to loving parents and that can be a very healthy thing if it's structured correctly, but unfortunately it's not. I do not have anything negative toward Mason Byrd I take my hat off to him for coming in and accepting full responsibility for his son and with the age that the child is, he needs that leadership of the male parent. I do request that the relationship that I have with our son is equally respected in the same token and for the past 3 years it's has not or should I explain that it's controlled by if my child support is up to date. I do have the responsibility of that payment and I will admit that I have fell short for filling that every month. I do however believe that at no point should the child be place on the phone to ask me where the payment is. Since Mason Byrd has had the child, I have been a full time student, graduated, opened up a salon office suite and have had to close it until the economy picks back up again. I am aware of what a child needs in order to be taking care of, and this is not an excuse for me not paying my child support. I am in an agreement to set up a payment plan to catch up and I would as like to have The Parenting Plan viewed and included in what is agreed upon from this judgment. I do believe that we can work more together for the wellbeing of the child if it's structured through the courts. I wanted have things requested in writing only because Mason Byrd does have a bad habit of speaking over me. I do have 656 Catherine St Atlanta, Ga 30310 as my mailing address and I neutral meeting place for us only because in the past when I have the child I have had to have Mason Byrd arrested for violent activity toward me and I have had a restraining order place for a 6 month period, so with me experiencing that I do not feel safe with conducting my personal home as a meeting place for pickup/drop for the child. Not to say Mason Byrd is still in that mind state, but I do feel that works better for both of us. I do trust Mason Byrd with the wellbeing of or son Mark Byrd I do ask that he becomes more active in his love for sports and not Tae Kwon Do that his grandfather instructs that myself and both of my boys enrolled in 2003. Thank you for your time and I do apologize for any inconvenience giving. I'm not a fast talker, but I do have things I up eject to considering the relationship between me and my son Mark Mason Byrd. Thank You

Good Parent, Paris D.

I sent more information in Justin's documents, like every time I heard something or was called just to display the dysfunction he was experiencing, knowing that Justin would compare his household to the Cosby's in court. Listening to my grandmother who once told me when she was living and I would talk to her about what was going on, "write down everything" from what Micah would tell me or the incidents I went through with the other parents. I had over three pages of incidents to fight the case for the change to take place, along with a letter signed by Micah stating he wanted to move back with his mother. Micah being the age where he could decide was something to help in the decision toward the judge I was thinking. The court date was set for the same day, a month away from the date they were served. While that was going on I would concentrate on work and getting a larger apartment. I kind of knew that it was going to create an issue when the documents reached the other parents, I was also thinking the step mothers would not mind the boys coming back to live with me. All I ever heard from them was I wasn't taking care of my boys as if it were a lot of responsibility for them to deal with. They had three to four children in their households at the time; Micah was the babysitter in his home, so his presence was helpful if anything. I had one incident on the way to pick Micah up where I was happy that I decided put the custody change in. I called Christy to let her know I was in route to pick Micah up; I was leaving from the salon. She calls me back, asks me when was I going to send another payment in, I tried to ignore the question because I know misery loves company. I was in a happy place that day, not focused at all on the negative, I politely repeated," I am on my way" and I got off my phone. Now, it is more than a 35 minute ride from Piedmont to Union City we ended up exchanging words the entire time. I had to remind her of the conversation we had when she thought she was leaving Justin some years back, which was the first time I had repeated anything that was mentioned in that conversation. She was trying to become my best friend, and I had to ask her," would you be this spiteful toward me if we were in the same position." She could never answer it; she kept saying," You just don't get it." I wanted her to explain what I didn't get, by the time I reached the exit I asked her," come outside and explain it to me" as I hung up. Before this day I never showed her how angry she made me with her behavior, I knew that would have let her know she got to me and that's what she wanted. After all the years and incidents this was the first time, I was going to let her have it on sight, really not having anything to else to talk about at that point. I was out of my blouse, in my tee and barefoot when I pulled up, she never came outside or did she answer the phone, when I called, my son just came out and was ready for us to leave the property. I was so mad; pulling off, I went into a rage. My son, the person who never saw me lose my cool over anything that they had ever done to me could not believe I was reacting the way I was. I could not really focus driving on the way to pick up Mark, I was scaring Micah to the point he started crying, stating, "I never want to see you this upset, and it hurts me so much." It was not just the anger toward her it was the pressure of me continuing taking the steps of faith and not knowing exactly where I would end up. I had to pull over like four times, just to walk off to scream, cry to control from doing something that was going to put me in jail. When I got to Mark's place and his step mother came out she asked me what was wrong. My eyes were blood shot red; I was walking back and forward ready to just blow still trying to keep a level head at the same time. She had a look of fear saying things to calm me down like, "don't let nobody get to you, stay cool, everything go work out." I couldn't respond to her the way I really wanted to, I saw her at the time a little more sensible than Christy.

I thought that way because of a previous time when she took me to get Micah when my car was down, working at the star's salon. She was dropping Mark off to me, I asked her to come in, offering to do her eyebrows, trying to establish some sort of relationship between us, and that's when she expressed to me a few things that was going on in her household. I respected her when she took notice in Mark's behavior when he first moved in compared to what it changed to. She spoke about how well mannered he once was, responding to her better, and how he had lost that respect. She could tell I spend time with him, while I was doing her eyebrows, she poured out everything, things I didn't need to know about her, and Mason's relationship. Telling me how he gave her a STD while she was pregnant with their second child, he keeps a least six grand in the bank at all times, he disrespects, and has hit her in front of the children, and the only way he would married her was if she had moved back home when she had recently left him. Further telling me while I rode with her to pick up their daughter and meet Justin to pick up Micah, which Mason was arrested this particular time, getting charged with Family Battery. I thought that was a little unstable on her as a woman, she should have thought differently like it was not a stable place for her or her children. I thought about what I had experienced with Mason during our relationship and knew from that point that Mark was not in a stable place mentally. The outside of things looked nice, but Mason was still had that aggressive abusive behavior. Mark was witnessing too much and maybe that's why his response toward her changed over time. The girl mentioned how she was uncomfortable in going to church because when they were staying with his father, Mason jumped on her thinking a man in church was trying to talk to her. She stated the same thing I once did about Mr. Byrd, how he just as low down as Mason, she called the police that day, and Mr. Byrd said he didn't see anything. The same cycle was still going on just with a weaker player because I would have left Mason; she was younger, needier than I was, at a time for companionship. I thought between the two households it was enough going on, just different situations. I was more stable than I was before; I was thinking of the boys solely, and they should be showed something differently if the opportunity were there. I was thinking I was around good people; the environment was healthy for them. I managed to get over the night, calming down from wanting to break Christy's face with a brick, and getting back to working on the end result. That week I got an e-mail from one of the models I used on the competition about a company called KISS cosmetics needing a lash tech for the Bronner Bros Show. The try outs were being held by Danessa Myricks, she was a person I had on my list to follow her work and study her craft. It was a sure sign that God was guiding me further along the path. The try outs were the same day as the court dates for the boys, I knew I was going to be very busy, but determined to get everything done. Mason time was 9:00a.m, the tryouts were not until 1:00p.m and Justin's time was not until 3:30p.m. When the date came I was riding around the court building looking for parking, I noticed Justin walking to the building. I was thinking he was up to something; I just had no idea of what. He started texting with a grin when he saw me. I was not going to get caught up in the characters of the day, I had too many to deal with. When I got there Justin was there as moral support for Mason and his wife, I was surprised and knew that what Micah wrote in his letter to the judge was completely true. He stated in the letter that Mason was coming over discussing with his dad and step mom what they would say in court. When I first read it I was thinking, they would have the same story in the separate court appearances, but no these clowns were in it together coming to each other's court appearances. I came around the corner with a smile like I had always, with the most pleasant greeting I had in me despite the enter feelings of me wanting to slap everybody involved or shake them to good sense. Mason's attorney was an older man, it was his second, the first attorney Mason had knew I knew too much of Mason's history for him to battle with me like he was this perfect man. She remembered me from the past and felt very compassionate toward me for him behaving in the matter he was, knowing he was all about the money from the child support. The first attorney had been representing him since he was 16, so it was a heap of history there. The new attorney was green to the entire situation; Mason feed him a ghetto Black girl image of me as much as he could. In court that morning, the judge at the hearing asked both of us our true concerns me first and mine were. The guns in the house, the change in behavior from the child that was supported by the teachers at school in writing, several occasions of having to call the police to get the child on the weekends I was granted, along with what the step mother told me getting her eyebrows done. Then Mason his concerns were I was behind on child support payments and I needed to pay. The judge orders a social worker to come out to both of our homes, evaluate the situation, and give his recommendation of where the child should be in the custody change. I was cool with the decision which Mason was not and brought up the fact I was doing this because I didn't want to pay child support for the child. His attorney then spoke further about the arrears owed; I clearly was not in a position to pay them. I was barely managing the monthly payments for the two boys. Mason boldly asked the judge, "could you just lock her up; let her sit until she could pay the arrears owed and my attorney fees too." The judge quickly responded," no, I'm not going to grant that request," I think at that point the judge looked at Mason in a different way. It was too bitter and harsh how he was approaching the situation, you could see the anger in his face and hear it in his voice, and the situation was personal more than business. The judge scheduled the next court appearance and this would be after the visitation of the social worker and his report with opinion of the situation. I took it as a good move because the judge was considering what I mentioned. I was upset that I could not get the police call records of all the many times I had to call the police at his residence to get my visitations on my weekends with Mark. It would have helped me because the same officer would come out from the first call I had ever made, the officer informed me that he comes to the home all the time. The first time calling the officer out he described the step mom and informed me how she didn't like my son. I think me mentioning it to the judge along with showing him the letter from the teacher with her personal comments of the child's behavior difference between the three parents made his eyebrows stand. I also throw up the fact that Mason's mother did not agree with his actions of having me on child support and showed a money order that she sent to help me out in the payments. I stirred up some things in Mason that morning that he wasn't necessarily ready for, all he could say was I owed child support arrears and was trying to get out of them. I was thinking what was Mason, Justin and Christy meeting about, I had more visual evidence to explain my side. They had the attorney's with the legal terminology, but nothing visual to backup the claims they had on me being a bad parent to the child mentally or physically. Walking out the judged made a comment to Mason that he needed to keep his wife out of the situation and we need to do a better job at coming to an understanding. I was happy to hear that come from the judge; it made me believe the situation had start becoming easier to read. I wanted to slap Justin standing there talking to Mason's wife feeding her all his hurt, things that happened in our relationship from high school. I pressed on to the next appointment of the day which was at the Georgian Terrance Hotel for the lash tech position Bronner Bros weekend. Coming from the courthouse I was all over the place in my thoughts, I just prayed to God to direction my thoughts and help me with my emotions because the day was not over.

Willow and I met back up with each other from at least a two year absence, I let her know about the audition, and how it was an opportunity for her as well to take advantage of. I was patiently waiting on my turn, Willow; my model was running a couple of minutes behind going through some personal affairs with her living arrangements. I had to end up using the model I helped on the elevator with her makeup on my way up and blew Danessa away; she was asking me all types of questions while I worked. Questions like my time in application, how many people could I do in a day, and why did I stand in the back of them instead of the front like 90% of the techs in the industry. She let me know I had the position on site, she said she looked forward to working with me on the show. Willow didn't do so good on the modeling audition. I didn't know where her mind was, but it also let me see she had that call girl mentality still and I started thanking God in my mind for taking me through the times of change. She cried on the way down to the parking lot wanting so bad to get the position. Mad at herself for not being more prepared and focused, she had just got done with a call, and that was her reason for being late. Sad, but that was her situation I told her I would talk to her at the apartment that evening. I was letting Willow crash at my place while she was saving the money to get her own in the complex. I had been only there for a month it wasn't too far from the loft, newly renovated two bedroom two bath apartment. Willow was going to pay the rent for a month for staying there and working out of the second room when my boys were not there. Then move in the complex, so I can get the referral fee when she paid her second month's rent in her own apartment trying to do everything to continue to pay my monthly obligations. On the way to the second court appearance I thought about ways I could continue with the career I was on and pay off my debts with child support. The less they had to say in that area about me the better, I was good to the boys clothes, shoes, taking them places, haircuts, athletic investments, I provided what my children needed not wanting to see them go without. I was on Peachtree St in afternoon traffic, but I still had like 15 minutes to my understanding when the phone rings. It is Christy asking me, "are you coming to the appearance" and I was like, "yes it doesn't start until 3:30," she said, "no it was at 3." I was floored, I told her, "I'm on my way" and hung up. By the time I got there it was 3:35 Justin, Christy, Mason, Taylor, and Justin's attorney was walking away from the room together. As I walked past them by myself, I believed my insides were shrinking, I was walking alone and the enemy had teamed up. I knew I had the spirit of God, but no one knew he was with me but me. I would have like a visible being there as moral support, I felt like hitting the floor. I was hot, tired mentally, and emotionally, more than physically from running in the building. They walked pass me looking at me like that was easy and I was an idiot. I walked in the courtroom office where I was supposed to be, where they had just left from, for the judge to tell me she dismissed the case. The judge also explained I would have to do the procedure over; the first person I thought of was Micah. She gave me a copy of the dismissal before I walked away disappointed. The case with Micah, I was banking would have been easier because of the letter that he written. I knew it was going to be tension on him because in the discussion with Mason that morning he bring up Justin's case to that judge, letting the judge know I was going through it with another child I didn't want to pay for. I mentioned how both my boys wanted to come live with me Micah had written a statement expressing his feelings alongside with Mark. I knew Mason informed Justin of that information by then, and they were going to give Micah the business, but Justin had a strategy not to make himself look like the bad guy. He would have his little brother Erling get on Micah case, ruff him up a little, scaring him into thinking what they wanted him to think. I called Micah to explain what happened, that I missed the court appearance and why I was late. I felt like dirt when I told him because we were counting on a positive outcome, he indicated that Erling called already to curse him out about writing the letter, threatening to beat him up about it. Micah told me that he told Erling, "I'm not listening to you this time it's because of listening to you the first time I'm even over here coping with this." I expressed to Micah how sorry I was and how I was going to find a way to correct the mistake made that day, don't let what they were going to say or do to him dissuade him from that fact that I loved him, and the outcome was going to change. All I could think about but tried not to think about was what he was going to come into contact with for a little while from them seeing that he was over the abuse. I smoked my back out that night trying to forget the day of negatives, celebrating the positives. I wanted to forget the day in a complete whole because of the dishearten feelings I had about my son. I reflected on the meeting for the Bronner Bros show that was on the next evening as well as what I had to do at the salon the following day. I knew they would be flabbergasted I was working the Bronner Bros Show; knowing it would have been an opportunity for me to get more clients. My business was coming into one of the slow periods of the year, when parents are getting their children ready for school shopping for their needs, and not thinking about their personal grooming for a moment. I had placed the boy's clothes on layaway, getting their room together at the apartment after Willow steered clear, putting the image of them moving back into the universe.

I have always heard you have to walk in faith, holding on the dream or thought that God has placed on your mind about something. If you have the faith or belief, as small as the mustard seed that your thoughts and wishes will come to the present life. I also thought about me not having clothes over there for them, always sending them back with them, the last incident with the clothes was too much, and unnecessary. I started getting more into finding peace within to endure the personal things I was going through, Elizabeth Baptist Church was a church I have always heard good things about, the pastor was young, and the messages was always direct. I first attended a service in 2005 with a guy I was dating briefly for a time after I moved out the house in Gwinnett. I was very captured on the way the message was delivered, it was in a way that I understood, and nothing was sugar coated. The guy I was then dating ran down the aisle, wanting to accept Christ in his life, honestly I thought it was a way for him to get attention for himself, he was a drama king. Nothing he displayed before or even after that service stated his actions were sincere or that was just my take on things at that time. I do understand that nothing happens over night, but I do understand that a change does start to take place and in some cases things get worse before they get better. I didn't run after him or did we make the same decision together, I felt like I wasn't there spiritual. I wanted to be prepared for certain habits to be removed out of my life before I made the decision. I continued to attend on and off, every time I would attend the message was virtual, giving me an insight into what I needed to do or how I needed to handle a situation that was going on at the moment. What I was experiencing with the boys and their parents were a test to my spiritual growth, and it was going to be a testimony to others in another section of my life. I could not see it then or fully understand what it meant at the time, but I had faith that I was going to come out with full victory if I continued to hold on to my belief that God was in control. If I would just wait on the Lord and lean not on my own understanding of things going on, I would pull through. It was going to be hard for me because I relied on myself to make it or fix the things that came up in my life, for me to rely on God solely was going to be a challenging. I had to learn how to give God full and complete control over my life no matter how things look or how long it took to get it fixed or solved. It was only God that kept my mind stable when the incidents were taking place like when I was called the day before school started from Micah telling me he needed school clothes. Micah let me know that his brother and sister got school clothes, but he didn't, which I thought was unfair with them being all under the same roof. I had clothes for both of them on layaway; I still managed to get him something before he went to school the next morning. When I hung up with him that Sunday Micah or his household had no idea, I was going to drop the clothes off at the house 7:30a.m the next morning. I gotten him some things at the Fourth of July sale and just stored them in the closet, I went to the mall after the call and added items to what was home already. I was trying to save as much as I could taking advantage of the opportunity when Willow was there, but it wasn't going to be enough with surprises like that, the work of the enemy. I would read a scripture before I went into work, before any event I was going, to just to bring the presence of God into the situation helping me endure the people, and assignment of the day or event with a peaceful, clear frame of mind. The words I was reading started working on me slow, as I look back on the time. I was no saint, I still had a long way to go, I also had a song I listened to in my car all the time by Lil Wayne dedicated to Micheal Phelps that motivated me like the words I was reading in the bible (to let you what level I was at).

The Bronner Bros. weekend was here, I had the boys that same weekend, and so I had to ask my uncle who moved to Atlanta briefly to help out. Things had gotten a little more difficult for me as far as picking the boys up, Mason mentioned to the judge I was driving under a suspended license, so I stop letting them see me drive. My license had come suspended because of the Child Support arrears again, but I couldn't let that stop me from what I had to do. Everything is too spread out in the city for me to rely of the bus line; I would not get half of the things I was trying to accomplish done. I would leave the salon, park my car around the corner from my mom because the payment had become 60 days late by then, put gas in my uncle's car, and have him take me to get the boys on the weekends I had them. I would pay my uncle to feed them and take them places while I worked on the weekends until I got off. I had so much being thrown at me to slow me down, I knew and thought I was doing something that had meaning, and the devil or enemy didn't want to see me carry out. The Bronner Show was just what I needed, after coming from dealing with the boy's parents calling the police to check my uncle's license and registration on his car. Working, releasing my frustration doing something that was going to move my career forward and help me erase this mess I was in with my children. I made sure I beat my face down; I did my signature one eyelash look matching the color of the company's logo. When I came in to change, I turned so many heads; Vanessa the makeup artist I used for the competition was working event also she was a witness that I was the talk of the morning and that was just the beginning. When it was time to work the show, I turned into a machine; it was no time for play. I had not stuttered one-time, didn't have time to, I had product to sell along with myself to promote. The weekend ended too soon, I was complimented by Danessa with the statement," one of the best in the industry." She was so pleased with my work that weekend she invited me to a class she was teaching on lash application, it was a paid class, but I was asked to come take the class free. I felt special to walk in that room full of people, not see any other tech from the weekend and learn more about my craft. I was extremely quiet; I listened carefully and took as many notes as I could. Getting back to the salon, before I could tell them about the weekend they were telling me what they heard. Sage client was working that weekend explaining how it was a big production and I stayed business with a line so long. April had more than enough to say to me hearing how my weekend went, but I took her being nice with a grain of salt; she was jumping on the bandwagon because of the unexpected recognition. I had to remember April was the person that wished my client good luck before I serviced them a couple of weeks prior, making her feel uncomfortable before the service. I believed it was underlining, it could have deterred business from me, and I've always taken that as her trying to get me to leave the salon. Sage gave me a dress as a peace offering before April did the same, but I took it differently coming from Sage because our communication was getting better. When Sage needed help around the salon every now and again like making sure towels were stocked, and the bathroom was clean if she didn't have a receptionist or her assistant was out for the day. Sage hired Stephanie five to six months before things changed to clean up the salon administratively. Stephanie had a background of owning two very successful salons in Buckhead within the years. Stephanie had a realistic personality, a person you could talk to, she was into gossip, but that's one of the requirements of working in the salon. Stephanie had a way of seeing things in a helpful way with a little mess, but just enough mess to keep the balance; she didn't like the good girl role. Stephanie loved talking to me because what I had to talk about was honest and sincere. I can say freely the things I would tell her appeared in the physical. When Stephanie first started she was told by Sage that the salon was a mess and needed cleaning up. Well, honestly she wanted to make a good impression to Mackenzie (Stevenson Pin's daughter who came abroad), thinking she would draw this big crowd. Sage went into this stage in the beginning of trying to impress Mackenzie in my personal opinion, seeing Mackenzie as if she were her dad. Stephanie did straighten out the front and also put things in prospective about Patricia who didn't last too much longer after Stephanie started. For the longest Patricia talked about Sage to her clients, telling them the salons personal business, letting them know the true cost of the products, telling them how Sage was over charging them. Stealing products making sure she had everything she needed in hopes of deterring Sage clients from her so she could service. It was one good move getting Patricia out of the salon it was beginning to be too much.

Clayton County

Pushing my career forward I had three side jobs coming up in between the court appearances and my regular work schedule at the Sage's salon. The weekend had gone by and Justin made things very difficult for me to pick up Micah, it was his first to this degree. He put Micah in a bad position by having him come outside after the police was called to let me know himself he wanted to stay home that weekend. I knew it was Justin behind him because the child had tears in his eyes. I showed the officer the visitation documents from court and Justin let her know until we came from court Micah was not coming over. By the time we went to pick up Mark his step mother was on the phone with Micah's step mom and had already called the police to check the license status of my uncle again. The same officer came out, Mark came with me after my uncle's criminal history was exposed to Mason, and we had a quiet weekend without Micah. The nail tech in the salon at the time linked me to a vendor who had a booth in the lobby of a hotel for Gay Pride weekend that was coming up, it would have been the first time I worked gay pride this was not the main Gay Pride that's nationally known. In Atlanta they have a white Gay Pride weekend and a black Gay Pride weekend, the black weekend has more foolishness involved. That was another event for my business I was putting on the calendar not turning any money down. I was nervous about what the report from the social worker was going to say about my apartment. The social worker had come by, inspected the place which was not completely furnished; I explained I only been there for six weeks. I was the only one there majority of the time, so it was not shocked with food in the cabinets as if children were living there. He asked me questions about my concerns for my son and why the relationship between Mason and me dissolve. I was honest in all my answers not taking away anything positive or negative from Mason's character. After he left from my residence, he was going to Mason's, now what Mason had mustard up to say to the social worker about me I couldn't remotely put energy into it knowing he was going to play dirty. My next weekend picking up the boys was a mess with me over booking my clients; I had a bride to do, (one of Mackenzie's clients) and two other outside projects. I was so caught up in work it slipped my mind to get the boys, the bride was getting married the same time I had to get them. I was at the hotel doing the bride when I got the text message from Mason, "where you," I texted back," can I get them in the morning, I'm still at work." Surprised, he was cool and I called Justin asking the same; since they lived in the same area it made sense to pick them up at the same time. I could stay and work, but I felt bad because this was one of the reasons I was thinking about when they initially went to live with their dad, I knew it was going to be times when I had a more demanding schedule. I needed time to get this business in a position where it was making money that supported us and give them the time they deserved when it was there time.

I was approached by one of the Pin twins in being a character in a reality show that they were shooting a pilot for. I was asked to change my look to more of an international appearance that consisted of losing weight by, changing my diet, and exercising. It was explained I could be a character on the show that is at a vital state of taking her career to the next level. Makayla wanted to use the fact that I won the lash competition with an international distributor working through the changes of becoming marketable. It was some factors involved made the idea fishy but I was exclusively thinking about how this would help my business, pay off my child support debt, and give my children a better life. I befriended one of the studio technician's to keep a close eye on the progress. The twin's and I developed a very cool relationship; I was coming into their circle slowly, but surely, more slowly than surely though. I was working extremely hard to continue working on what was growing with them, because I knew that they had the connections to make it happen being who their father was. I had the feeling everything I had been working on was coming together, all I need was a real chance, showing my talents on television was it. While I was wrapping mind my around that part of my life sharing every detail with my boys when we talked on the weekends.

I got a text message from Taylor asking about the child support payment that I was to send in to them. Mason sent the contempt order to my job via Sheriff, for the second time in 45 days which was meant for embarrassment, they had my home address. The judge ordered me to pay a certain amount to Mason in our last court appearance; I had the receipt to prove the payment was made, so it was no stress. I texted Mason to let him know that the payment should be arriving soon and his wife texted me this:

> From: Mason wife Sent: Sep 16 11:16AMMsg: Girl u know u need stop u know half of that payment went to Justin

> From: Mason wife Sent: Sep 16 11:25AMMsg: Thats what u get for having kids here and there. Have a good day and god (2/2) bless u

Why was Taylor texting me getting involved, I don't know, but stand up for your man if that makes you feel secure. Personally, I would not involve myself being that it was so messy, and would have informed both parents how they need to conducted themselves better for their child.

My weekend was here and I had to take Micah to get his toe checked out, he hurt it playing ball at school. I had not been told until it was time to I picked him up for the weekend, which had me bothered, and when I got the text from the wife, it went as such:

> From: Me: Sep 18 5:36PM Msg: No rush sunshine just lettn u know im here <The God n Me>
>
> From: Justin Wife Sent: Sep 18 5:38PM Msg: Justin is going to meet u im at the salon
>
> From: Me: Sep 18 5:39PM Msg: Thats fine thank u enjoy your time there <The God n Me>
>
> From: Justin Wife Sent: Sep 18 5:46PM Msg: His DR office is south atlanta pedt. On hwy 85 by QT he needs 2 be there 8am (2/2) since he will be a walk n & they r going 2 make a copy of ur id in order 4 u 2 take him
>
> From: Me: Sep 18 5:47PM Msg: Thank u he will be there no worries <The God n Me>

She started telling me about how Micah joined church and had new member's classes on that weekend as well. Texting me about how he had gotten baptized, which was confirming that my son was respecting what I had done in my life growing, and developing a relationship with God not hiding it from them. The last weekend I had him I remembered showing both boys the DVD when I got baptized at my church, before I met the production engineer the twins were working with on their show, at a Comedy Show he was working one Saturday. Now she talking like she was there as a witness, come to find out Micah was going with his friends family to a branch of the same church I was a member of. When I found out that information I knew he didn't have new member's classes; it was Christy's way of making sure I was busy doing something other than work. The church I was a member educates the individual first and the baptism comes as a process during the progression of the class.

> From: Me: Sep 18 6:17PM Msg: We attend the same church just a different location i have the info but thank (2/2) u for being involved there will never be i n team<The God n Me>

The incident happened two days prior, if their schedules didn't allow them to take him, they could have called me, I would have made arrangements to get him seen, but that would have been too much like unity. Justin being a at home dad I really didn't see why Micah's toe wasn't already checked. I just knew I had to add this to my schedule, keeping it moving with no complaints. I woke up early, got Unc to meet me at the doctor's office, so I can check him in, and made sure he was straight, let Unc finish up, so he could take Mark to football once they were done there. I went to work; I had clients scheduled that morning. After getting the examination from the doctor I texted Christy and the dialog went like this:

> From: Me: Sep 19 9:04AM Msg: They wrappd his toe and he needs an x ray if u set it up i can help make sure(2/2) he gets there so u wont have take off have a great day <The God n Me>

> From: Justin Wife Sent: Sep 19 9:05AM Msg: Yeah he just called and told me thanks for taking him

Getting back to the salon I worked and prepared for the next morning. I was booked for a party of six; it consisted of the ladies taking pictures for their sorority sister's birthday. I had to be at the shoot at eight in the morning, when I pulled up I saw April unpacking her things. I was shocked, because I had no clue this chick was going to be there. April and I kept our relationship neutral for salon purposes, we had never been on an offsite job together, so I didn't know what to expect. April was doing the ladies hair; I was thinking this will be a different day. Now, by this time April had already informed the salon that she was leaving and opening her salon three minutes from Sage's. While I was working, we were all having girl talk, and April says to me," you know I will have a makeup bar at my spot, I would love you to come work there." I never answered and continued to work; I was in a comfortable place at Sage's when April approached me with this. Many different opportunities had come through that door from Sage's clientele, so I thought it would have been a slap to Sage's face if I moved with April. I then thought about how much money April has tried and screwed up for me in the past, to want to start putting money in my pocket now. I did take it as a complement that she recognized I was talent, however. After I got done there, I went home to be with the boys for the rest of our weekend. I got a call from Jeremy, the production engineer that I needed to be at the studio for physical training with Makayla. I called Unc to drop the boys off without me, so I can be there on schedule still hopeful that everything was still going with the show. I started communicating with Justin wife and it went:

> From: Me: Sep 20 5:45PM Msg: 610 <The God n Me>

Unc for some strange reason took Mark home first when he should have took Micah home first. The times were court order and I wanted to stay in my agreement as much as possible. Child support arrears was the only thing I was slipping on, I didn't need anything else.

> From: Justin Wife Sent: Sep 20 6:43PM Msg: Paris It's now 6:42pm you said you was going to have Micah here at 6:10pm

From: Me: Sep 20 6:44PM Msg: Call the number that just called u they should be closed he can get droppd(2/2) off at the house <The God n Me>

From: Me: Sep 20 6:53PM Msg: (1/3) Things are only what u make them out to be. I do apologize for them (2/3) running this far behind but things happen drama is something for unhappy people be (3/3) calm and look at things from a better view sunshine im not the enemy.

From: Justin Wife Sent: Sep 20 7:05PM Msg: Theres nothing unhappy about me I have my kids I take care of them (2/2) emotionally and financially i have a hubby of 10 yrs stable home n a great job the thing

From: Justin Wife Sent: Sep 20 7:05PMMsg: The thing that makes me unhappy is having to deal with u someone who doesn't (2/2) take care of their kids u drop them off over ur moms house n let ur uncle be their taxi cab

From: Justin WifeSent: Sep 20 7:05PMMsg: When r u going to be a mother and really take care of ur kids u havent paid (2/2) voluntary child support in over a year u introuduce ur kids 2 drugs per ur kids wow

Fwd:From: Justin WifeSent: Sep 20 7:06PMMsg: Due to the fact u r consistently late with ur kids n u didnt take him 2 the (2/2) drs office on sat. As usual me n Justin will take him to the DR and handle it

From: Me: Sep 20 7:14PMMsg: (1/7) Never calld u unhappy drama is for unhappy people think about before Justin got his son u had no drama from me and u never will i commend what u have (2/7) established for you self dont do drugs no time dont judge cause im not(3/7) the maker just live my life and making arrangements for myself while i have free (4/7) time n three years i havent wasted time doing the things i couldnt do due to the fact i had my children i did a great job with my boys and had them by (5/7) men that are willing to help raised them as they should they r the (6/7) other parent u carry on like a uneducated woman on what u did learn u r not applying it really shocks me. Be cool we got 3 more yrs to shared the welfare of a (7/7) child together. The energy from your workplace weighs on u. Try yoga <The God n Me>

From: Me: Sep 20 7:23PM Msg (1/2) Have a beautiful work week if u need me to help u with gettn him where he needs to (2/2) be for his toe im flexible <The God n Me>

From: Justin Wife Sent: Sep 20 7:23PM Msg: Paris I will pray for you due to my education background I know u have some (1/3) please let me know when you will arrive at the gas station (2/3) serious mental issues they u should get checked pls dont text me anymore if u need (3/3) please let me know when you will arrive at the gas station

I knew when Christy made the statement, "u didn't take him 2 the drs office," where she was in her thinking, I had a feeling she was playing my character for that was one reason alone, I sent certain texts to my email. Justin was so hands off the situation, it was easy to play me like I was asked to do for Micah, and I didn't, so she can have something else to talk about. I was having this conversation in the studio's gym getting heated, because I am still trying to understand why she has such a personal hate toward me. While I worked off my stress I was thinking how, she told me not to call their phones, how ignorant was that.

After some time and new information, I realized the reality show with the twins was not what it was said to be. I believe I was drawn in by Makayla to hide some personal business I discovered that was going on between her and the production engineer. I can be honest saying I had a feeling all along I was not in the project as explained, but I was going to take the chance just in case looking for some type of beak. Even if I were or was not in it, I wanted the girls to succeed in their endeavors, figuring I would get mine when it was my turn. Before, I rode to Tampa with Mackenzie for a weekend to visit a sister on my dad's side, while she visited a guy she was dating. I had a mediation appearance in Clayton County that was rescheduled for a later date with Justin and Christy about the child support arrears for Micah. I was completely convinced that I became a project for these individuals, they wanted to stretch me out, make sure they reminded me of who I was once was. They wanted to make sure they had enough pressure on me as possible about child support, and they were doing a great job. This was a letter I wrote to the court just to express how more of a personal appearance this was than business about the child. I did not know how to get this across to anyone to bring the real reasons out, so I always wrote the judge letters.

To the judge involved in Civil Action File #09/04CR3982-5

This case initially began in Clayton County with Application for Criminal Arrest Warrant for Child Abandonment from Christy James wife of Justin James almost 2 months after the agreement was made between Paris D. (mother) and Justin James (father) that Micah D. (child) would live with him for one school year while mother completed her school education. With both parties moving to Fulton County gave Christy James free will have taking me to Child Abandonment court there. We were just in Court June and also have an open case under Civil Action File # 2008DV256058. I was concerned about the Contempt brought back to Clayton in

July when for several years we have been in Fulton County. I do ask that this case in Clayton County be closed and transferred to Fulton County. I have attached documents to support the information just explained and also the personal attack toward my character as well. We are going through Custody Change and it has been a long journey to get my son back in my custody due to the greed of money and personal resentment. I try to stay involved with him as much as I can so these activities does not affect him terrible by being a volunteer at his school (sitting in his classes to see his weakness and asking his teachers for the extra credit assignments to help with low test scores, making sure he has school clothes, athletic physical for football, etc. My son's grades and self-esteem displays emotional abuse I feel from Christy James who is a professional Therapist at the county Jail. Thank You for your time and patience.

Paris D.

Getting over the disappointment with the show I was back to my focus, new member's class at church was over, having one more step to take before I was officially a member at Elizabeth Baptist. One aspect of my life that made me completely happy, in that area I felt no pain or stress with the help of attending service twice a week.

The court appearance arrived with the recommendations from the social worker. Reading the document before the hearing, I was astonished to discover that Mason had his father to vouch on his behalf on how bad of a person I was. Justin's opinions about my character were stated as well, but that was not a surprise to know like it was about Mason's dad. In the notes from the social worker Mason had to basically rescue Mark from a world of bad influence that was around me. Stripping in the club and taking ecstasy pills was the cause of us separating, I just would not stop. Mason's father added that I was smoking weed and I looked to Mason's mother as an idol who just so happily abandoned Mason when he was young as I did with Mark. Justin spoke about the incident in Gwinnett County when the case worker was sent out to the house, leaving out the outcome of that incident. I was surprised to see Mason's mom's statement on the document, she was a neutral opinion, but what she said didn't help me put her grandson in the best environment. She stated something on the lines of, I was not a responsible person. She had a comment about Mason as well saying he was revengeful and stingy. After reading her comment I called her in front of the case worker, he asked her, "who do you feel the child needed to be with" and she then stated, "Paris, his mother." I was upset because that was what should have been said when they spoke before, but she did not want her son to know she sided with me. My true character at that moment was stripped, but what was I to do with no moral support. The documents even spoke about Mark explaining that I was a nice mother to him, but his aunt as well as his grandmother smoke weed while he is around. Mason had four individuals siding with him in support of my character, which then, I knew I had not won Mark back into my home. Justin was at the court appearance once again to give Mason and Taylor moral support. I felt destroyed, they were waiting to see me break down, but I kept my head up. The judge continued the case, asking on our next visit that we submit our financial affidavit's because Mason was still requesting I pay the full amount in arrears owed. Mason wanted me to prove that I could not produce that full amount like I was claiming I couldn't. I was making as much of the monthly payments as I could, but he wanted all his money owed to him which is business even if it is out of spite. I left that day, everything went so crazy, it took everything in me not to break down in court, and I started regretting even more of the day I lost my patience with Micah three years ago. Before going into the salon to work I stop by the modeling agency to pay my balance of my website to the designer, still keeping faith in building my business. What I generated in my business took care of what I was doing for me and my boys; it was just a matter of generating more. Sage and Stephanie were waiting to hear how everything went in court this time around, they started inquiring about my emotional wellbeing knowing I was going to have a breakdown sooner or later taking so much and still moving forward everyday with my plan. I got there I explained to them I had to go back within another 30 days. Stephanie commended me on how I was doing such a great job handling everything, seeing how close the relationship was between the boys and me. I believe looking back if it wasn't for me adjusting to the suggestions that the Makayla presented speaking about the show changing my diet regime and having a workout regime. I would not have made it through those days in court with the co-parents like I had been doing.

I was invited to have dinner with the girls at the salon one evening. Stephanie was treating me; she got the whole gang together, a table of 10. We were having a cute evening laughing, chit chatting; Mackenzie and Makayla were the last to show. I had not seen Makayla in a couple of weeks, she had not seen my physical changes herself, she just heard about them from Mackenzie. Makayla sat by me, Mackenzie sat on the other end of the table, I felt pain from the other side were Mackenzie was that was so strong. My whole demeanor changed to the point Stephanie had to ask me," what was wrong;" I went into a trans so to speak. I snapped out of it and continued the evening; the twins were explaining how they had just come from their dads watching them shoot for a magazine cover. I stayed up that night praying about everything that was occurring in my life, the twins came to mind, and I just started texting them

> Fwd:From: Makayla Pin Sent: Oct 02 5:21AMMsg: (1/6) U guys r n my spirit early and i have to express as im talkn with god honestly dont look at me stranger lol marissa is a great Lady her and i have had (2/6) some very deep conversations and her energy is very well put together she traind herslf to sit n that position open

yourslf to her so she can had good (3/6) talks to the head she has his heart first cause come on now they saw each other living the way they r 20 years ago and i got that from the horses mouth (4/6) her as a lady thats awesome for us to still hold on so much they just had to experience things n order to get it right when its time thats god showing (5/6) that position u reach i am most over lookd cause i come at u from another approach your inner that matters a lot to me u two are built for something so (6/6) strong but once again have to jump the hurdle on healn the fact that u have to do something as one cause u r independent <The God n Me>

From: Mackenzie Pin Sent: Oct 02 7:28AM Msg: Thank you!! I will have to talk to you in person cause this was nothing but God

When I saw Mackenzie that morning at the salon, she was just like," Paris, I just could not stop crying." I was so embarrassed that I even went there with them, but it was how I felt. When we had a chance to talk later that day, she was explaining," we were not really invited to the shoot, Makayla didn't want to go, but went because I did." They were shooting a family picture for an upcoming issue of a magazine, and they were not asked to be in it. It really hurt her not being asked in on the shoot, but she was cool, she was shocked that I felt her pain. I cried telling her, "I felt what you were going through" knowing it was things in her past she was holding to, hurt from her dad and mom not continuing their marriage. Stevenson was not the man he is today, we all have a past, some have overcome some have not, but the twins knew the history to the point where the present was still overwhelming to them. I had a talk with both twins one-on-one, Mackenzie agreed to start making a better relationship with Marissa, and Makayla was in thought not really seeing the need. Makayla was trying to get in the industry through her dads manager, like he was going to over ride what Stevenson wanted for his own daughter's. When she spoke on the subject, I wanted to call her a fool, but I will let the outcome of the experience do that for me. Mackenzie told me days after that she called Marissa the morning she was flying out to Paris to wish her a safe flight; Marissa had to ask her "are you ok," because she was crying so hard. I felt good about exposing my intuition skills to the twins, especially Makayla.

BET Weekend was here I had to wake up and get to Nikki Minaj by 7:30, I got up a little earlier just to pray, get myself together, because I had to work at the salon afterward. I was coming through the lobby of Nikki's resident building and I look over, see a guy nothing major, but then something said "look again" it was Tristan who I dated in 2002. I said, "Tristan" as I walked up to him, and he said "yes." I was so happy to see him and him the same I can imagine. I gave him one of my business cards rushing off, telling him I was on my way to take care of a client, I never said who even after he did ask me," who are you here to see." I ask him," call me sometime, it is good to see you," I got in the elevator like dang, Tristan. He was one of the two I had screwed up on in my past dating history. If I could do things all over I would have tried to maintain some form of relationship, even if dating didn't work for us, he was a nice guy. It was good to service Nikki once again, I hadn't saw her since I did her lashes for the taping of the Cypher for the Hip Hop Awards that she was that evening attending. I had not talked to her since the text messages we exchanged, she was complaining about her lashes falling off:

> From: Me Sent: Sep 13 10:32PMMsg: (1/2) Sweat contains a level of salt that breaks down the chemical n any glue stream looses the consistency n the bond very sorry to hear but (2/2) sounds like u been workn your butt off <The God n Me>

> From: Nikki Minaj Sent: Sep 13 10:33PMMsg: No. I haven't been sweating. The lashes were not applied tightly.

From: Me Sent: Sep 13 10:35PMMsg: Wow first time i've heard that <The God n Me>

From: Nikki Minaj Sent: Sep 13 10:41PMMsg: I did about 15 shows in the last 2 weeks. Not one came off. With the same hair glue

From: Me Sent: Sep 13 11:04PMMsg: (1/3) The glue that i use is multipurpose lash glue from a company name kiss by Envy i dont use the hair glue on elite clients due to the fact its not a (2/3) professional use if u choose to receive services by me again you are more than welcome to bring the glue you want me to apply them with once again i (3/3) apologize for your experience good evening <The God n Me>

That was the first and only time Nikki and I had any disagreement about my service performance. The young Nikki had come from a long way not fully having a clue where she was going in her career at that time. I understood her mind state wholly being a person myself being used to one way of being treated or even treating my self, it's hard to see another way. The hair glue was taking out her lashes, causing them to thin and become difficult to work with, I wanted them to get as much air as possible for the growing process. I was working with a thin palette by her needing that dramatic attention on her eyes her application was heavier, so professional glue was very necessary. It was odd because at that time I had not even heard her rap or anything, it took me four months to finally ask her what she did to even know she was a rapper. I went to work that day and the day went on, I got email blast all the time about different events going on in the social life of the city. One in particular stood out about Mary Mac shoes, I remembered that name from a previous event I attended. I rsvp myself that night; I met the young lady that organized the event, Liz. She was hosting another event coming up; I knew if I stayed in contact with her I could get some more work for my resume. Liz and I talked about putting an event together for business to advertise my work, on a fashion show level, with an upcoming designer. We exchanged business cards, I contacted her the next day just to let her know, it was nice to meet her, as I starting then to build a rapport. That following week Tristan finally called, it was his birthday that next day, I remembered he was a Libra I just didn't remember the day. We talked on the phone for a moment and made plans to meet up that night for drinks, now I had not been in a bar in a while so this was going to different. When I picked Tristan up in front of the building, I could tell by how he was dressed that it was going to be a hood affair. I had not been to this particular place he wanted to go to in years, I didn't know if anything had changed, and getting there it had gotten worst, but I was still hanging. We caught up with each other very quickly; he was asking me about the kids. I let him know that they stayed with their dad feeling comfortable in telling him the drama involved in slight detail not wanting to spoil his day. He was surprised to know I was on child support, he didn't understand that part, but that's what it was. The evening was cool; I had my guard up wanting to keep my attention on the reality of my life. What I had going on, really not wanting to get involved in liking Tristan again. We had a great evening I sleep over at his place, but nothing happened sexually. I felt close to Tristan due to the fact that he knew me from once before, "you have changed so much since then," was his words. I could tell that he respected the new me that was still the same ol girl, we remembered certain things about each other that most people would have forgotten after seven years and many people between. I had the boys that weekend; it was honestly one of the coolest weekends in a long time, no drama getting them and no parental ignorance. They were maybe feeling bad about how they did me in court on our last appearance. That week in church the message was "Giving that pays Dividends," and on that day I had a blank check for one hundred dollars from a client for her deposit on her wedding makeup. I had court coming, yes, I could have paid more of my child support, but read Malachi 3: 7-15, Matthew 23:23, 1st Chronicles 16:2, and 2nd Chronicles 16:1,2 I felt like God was saying test me. I was expecting something great to happen in my life, because of all the pain I was experiencing fighting for the boys while building my business. I gave the check to the church and didn't think twice. I treated the boys to dinner at Applebee's after service and we headed home to relax before they had to go back home. Tristan came over that night; I was having a glass of wine, and watching TV. We started kissing before you know it we were having the best sex I had experienced since Ismael. He was very meticulous, he took his time giving me the feeling he was coming from a sincere a place. I was mad at myself being how I was really trying to stay focus on Christ, wavering about practicing celibacy before that incident. I went into the salon on a Tuesday which was a day earlier, when April was there, serviced a couple of clients, which was different because I usually start on Wednesday when Sage starts her work week. I get a text from Nikki Minaj asking me, "do you have someone to move this furniture, I am moving." I recall us having a talk one service day, and she was explaining she was moving, getting new furniture, and me needing furniture, I asked her to keep me in mind when she wanted to get rid of what she had. I was so happy she kept me in mind, but at the same time sad. It was the blessing I received for being faithful to the voice I heard in my mind at service the previous week; it just came after the social worker was over to interview me. The text had me all over the place, I texted back, "yes," and she went on to explain," it needs to be moved on Friday." I immediately thought of Tristan, I knew he would and could help, I called him, and he was willing. While I was at work, I explained to Tristan who apartment he was getting the furniture from, I paid for the U HAUL, and it was done. The furniture complimented my little place being that it was fairly new, I was very appreciative to no ends, I texted Nikki, and thanked her for being my angel. That weekend was a busy one with three outside clients to do as well as clients in the salon. I was glad to see business was steady, but I still needed more to pay off the entire debt for the child support arrears requested by both the boys co-parent. The closer of the weekend, I got an email from Liz; she was auditioning models for an upcoming fashion event she was hosting. I planned to attend to ask her if she had a makeup artist for the event. Getting there everything went as I thought, I became the makeup artist for Liz's fashion event. I was not getting paid for it, but it was a sure way to build my portfolio, and add the pictures to my website. I had to come from just being the eyebrow/lash tech to the makeup artist/facial stylist. I did my thing at the event; I performed makeup applications I saw in magazines with different lash styles. After the show they called the fashion designers, myself the makeup artist to the stage to introduce us to the crowd. One of the fashion designers was Rafael Cox from Project Runway season nine; it felt like I was there just in a smaller scene. It was very refreshing to get the recognition of my work for the evening with my company name advertised.

Weeks had gone by; it was time for me to go back to court with Mason to turn in our financial affidavits. The attorney was frustrated with me due to the fact I only had half of my documents picking up the wrong pack-it. The attorney asked the judge if I could be arrested for not providing the proper documents as instructed. The judge did not grant that wish and instead did a continuance on the case when he had an option to dismiss it. I believe it was the letter I emailed him the day before explaining more in detail on my behalf:

> This is Paris D. I am in the change of custody case with Mason Byrd. This is a hardship letter on behalf my case. Mason's mother does agree that both boys can back to live with me, but does not want Mason to know she said that due to the fact that their relationship is not healthy. My son does not want to come home without his older brother they are extremely close. We are a very tight family us three. I am fighting for custody of him as well I'm waiting to pay the $107 for filing and service fees through the courts to get the case started he is of age where he has made his decision

> and no one knows of this action. Mason Byrd and Justin James are attacking me to be cruel and spiteful its personal. Mason can afford the welfare of our son that is why I asked him to care for our son while I completed my career of choice. In 120 days he has paid 2 different attorneys Bailey Reid and the new one present Oct.8. We all have a past and I can truly say I have recovered from mine. When I found out that Mason was still the same but just good at hiding it from me being involved in a battery family violence & interference of child custody case this year I was disappointed and shocked. I thought he was over those abusive ways he just has the money to get out the trouble and make it go away Clayton County case 08cr13412b. He can behave in his life however he chooses but I want more for Mark Byrd. I have been employed at an very elite salon in Buckhead for over an year now they have tainted my image by calling a making apptmts to make sure that I am there when the sheriffs come to serve papers twice a month if not once for sure. My clients are leery of my personal dealings to the extent they are at my workplace. The owner doesn't trust for me to be in the salon on her off days to work for the unknown vengeance level from the other party. It's not helping my growing business. I do have an open house with Paces Academy on Nov.21. I am working with Linda Austin to get them enrolled by financial assistance so they can experience a better view academically. I do ask that a random drug test is ordered because I do not partake in activities of the sort and I don't want them to have time to prepare. I choose to send this email today so the case is fresh on your memory. If I were in this for any wrong pursuit why would I fight so hard alone with 2 sets of parents and their attorneys? See you Thursday 3:30p.m. Have a great week☺

The judge in so many words let me know that he commended me for my efforts in the battle alone, and he was going to give me time to get the help I needed to close the case out correctly. I was very happy that he did not dismiss my case continuing it for February 4, 2010. I continued back to work letting the girls know I didn't have court for another 3 months with Mason. Pressing forward I get a call from a young lady I met when I did the makeup for the video shoot previous month before. She was doing a calendar and needed my assistance, she wanted me to do the makeup, and needed help with her wardrobe this upcoming weekend. I also had to meet with Rafael Cox to discuss a Trunk Mix & Mingle at a boutique. They needed a makeup artist for a couple of models, all I was thinking about were pictures for my website, and more work on my resume. The calendar shoot was a paid gig, but the Trunk Mix & Mingle was not. I also had the boys on the weekend for the shoot, the meeting for the Mix & Mingle along with my schedule at the salon, but as usual I was going to work it out. Tristan and I was still spending time together, getting closer, going to church together and all. It felt good to have some kind of support system on my behalf, but I knew I could not rely too much on it, because he had conditions within himself he was working on. I slowly told him how my life was professionally, showing him my accomplishments on other websites as well as mine. I was moving away from being the cool ghetto girl that he once knew and stepping toward becoming a businesswoman. I got a call from a representative from AT&T I was eligible of getting a free business advertisement in the yellow pages for a year. I was thinking," it's really coming together," I was so relieved at every break through. My foundation was stabilizing all I needed to do is start building, with my children bearing in mind these transitions firsthand, they would know life can be more than regular. A mediocre life can be left behind if you press pass the naysayers, you can make substantial progress believing in yourself. Becoming completely satisfied with your life is your aim and nothing less. I remember crying alone that night just praising God, being grateful for the changing in my mind, my actions, and asking him to forgive me for taking so long to move toward correction. I started feeling weird, but nothing major until the morning I woke up like 4 a.m. and my lips was swollen. Tristan was with me and

I was so uncomfortable, I had to find out how to solve the problem. I was very vain in my appearance; my image was one of my advertising tools in making a way for my business. I woke Tristan up, we went to an all night pharmacy, I had been drinking this sugar free, all natural lemonade, and all I could tell the pharmacy guy was I had to have an allergenic reaction from it. He suggested Benadryl and carmax as a start until I can see my regular physician that I did not have. Heading back home I thanked Tristan for waking up with me, I was freaking out in discomfort. He was so cool and patient; he looks over at me and says even if you had to wake up with our baby I would do the same. It was so sweet, but I was like," ok, where did that come from." I always talked to some clients telling them I was going to have a little baby again one day, but I just never sketched it in stone. We still got up a couple of hours later from getting back for church service as I needed to refresh my mind to prepare for another week that was filled with the salon work, outside projects, and the boys. Mark had games the upcoming weeks as well, so I had to incorporate everything. Tristan was available to help me with the boys when the time came, making it easier for me to concentrate on clients I had scheduled. We attended bible study the week of this busy weekend coming up, the message was "How to get out the boat" covering Matthew 14: 22-33.

Pastor Oliver was speaking at another church; Tristan and I had a discussion about his position and what he was trying to do in his business. I had not been too critical of Tristan, because sometimes you have to stand back, and watch the actions to understand the problem. In order for me to give him the words, he needed to hear, I had to see where his weakness were. Some of the things I said to him were mentioned in service that evening, when I told him that you have to stay focus on the goal creating that mental picture of what you want to see fore past in actuality on the situation. That's what Jesus was saying to Paul keep your eyes on me and come walk with me, when Paul focused on the storm he started sinking. That night after service

I was still emotional feeling what the Pastor was saying. Tristan and I were not really speaking from the conversation we had prior to the service, with my cycle being late, and everything else I had going on I felt as if the walls were closing. I was coming to a conclusion we were spending too much time together, we needed some space. Helping him fix his phone and seeing a text message from another woman (that I later found out was old) didn't help the moment I was encountering, either. Tristan was very embarrassed that I saw what was said and had little words to speak toward me; he was quite the entire ride home. Icing on the cake was the misunderstanding that I would not have had brought him anything to eat when we stopped. Since I didn't offer, his pride didn't allow him to speak up, he became ashamed for not having money to buy either of us food. The incident like I explained to him was so pity, I was fully aware that Tristan was unemployed, why wouldn't I have paid for the food if he added his order. It was getting cold outside the season was changing all I wanted to do was go home. Tristan was stopping by his place to get some things from there, to come back to my place with me. I was not interested in having his company that evening, I asked him to take me home, he tells me I can either come up stairs or stay in the car. I was like oh ok; I stayed in the car, when Tristan closed that door, I got on my phone found a taxi company and was home in 12 minutes tops. We lived five minutes away from each other; the cab driver was in the area all ready. I was about to wrap my hair and get in the shower when Tristan called, "where are you," I responded, "home." He was so frustrated about me leaving like that, we hung up on a bad note, I cried before I went to sleep, thinking Tristan was being a clown; my emotions were all over the place. The next morning I got up as usual getting ready for work, got outside, and my car was gone. I was thinking, no not repo-ed, I wasn't making the full payments, trying to spread my resources in every area needed. I wasn't keeping a good line of communication with the finance company, because I thought sending something would be enough, better than nothing. I go to check my voice mail, I had a message, and it was the repo guy, telling me I could come get the stuff out of the car like one that morning. I was like hell naw; I got too much riding on this weekend, boys, salon, and projects. I got on the phone and called Tristan, he was close, and the only person I could explain this to, knowing he would understand. We did agree the night before that we had to stay in some type of contact until my cycle came on and we knew what was real. I called him, he was willing to help, forgive me leaving him like I did, I could have handled things better, but I didn't. I called around, trying to find where my belongings were, I located them, and Tristan drove me to get them out of my car. All I was thinking was what am I going to do while we rode, Tristan was telling me, "I'm here for you when you need me". He continued, "I'm not going to let you down, you I can trust me." I was thinking can I trust myself liking this man, his position is no better than mine; I had a habit of being selfish. I was developing that overly independent disease most women in Atlanta get when they have to depend on themselves 98% of the time. I scheduled my salon clients to come to my residence from the salon that weekend; I just will have to incorporate it around the shoot that was already taking place there. Tristan was going to help with the boys taking Mark to his game; it had to work out in that matter. The weekend came to a close with all of us going to service, Tristan dropping me off at the Boutique to discuss the next project, him dropping the boys off to my uncle to the boys home. I had more clients that night, so I had to get straight home after the boutique meeting. I hadn't had time to think, let alone talk about, what I was going to do after the weekend about transportation.

I knew I couldn't rely on Tristan completely, I moved around too much throughout the city. That Monday I figured it was time to take the test and see if I were pregnant or not. I took it that night and it came out positive, I just stared at the words, "pregnant" looking at the digital test. I was so throwed off the first thing I was thinking was what are my children going to say and what am I going to do about my business. Tristan wasn't financially stable for a baby, he didn't mine having one, but I didn't want to struggle with a man, hell I was struggling by myself that was enough for then. A woman that has had the same position can only imagine what I was thinking; I had so many thoughts going through my mind. Was Tristan going to be an at home dad, and I provide for the baby financially or he would run off on me out of fear, I was not going to raise this child alone. I then had to call him and get his view on things; I sent him the picture text of the test results. He called right back and said, "ok, you ready" I responded, "I have no other options," it was weird because we both knew that night we had sex I got pregnant. The first time we had had sex was the night, while we were engaged he asked me, "are you going to give me a boy," I said, "yes." I thought that was just deep sex talk at the moment not thinking it was really going to happen, even though it could have happened, which it did. We made plans to get the proof of pregnancy the next morning so, I can apply for Medicaid, neither one of us had health insurance. The health department I went to didn't accept walk-ins, I made an apptmt for the following week and a half from that day. I had court the next day in Clayton County for Micah, my nerves were on edge, because the last time I saw Clayton County Courthouse was 2001. That is just a county I don't deal with, at all, I told my mom, dad, and uncle about my pregnancy. Uncle said, "wtf," in the beginning, changed to, "this is what you need for the other father to see you in a relationship and happy." I really didn't have them in mind concerning my pregnancy, but that's just a man thinking like a man, worrying about another man, and what he thinks. I did think about the boys in what they were going to say and think because for so long I told them I wasn't going to have anyone babies it was always going to be the two of them from me.

My mom response was, "good luck," and I let her know I had court the next morning and got off the phone, disappointed in her response to the pregnancy. I knew she was probably saying to herself, "Why did she do that and slow herself down, Tristan ain't stable enough to provide for her, hell, she might not even like that man in another week." My mom knows me; I have to admit I had the reputation of passing men by if they were not what I wanted. I was looking for something in them that maybe I should have had in myself. I gotten so self absorbed that evening, I talked to Tristan about how he didn't have enough going on, how he was depending on what I was doing, and who I was around for his own personal benefit. Venting about how much pressure I was under dealing with people that wanted me to pay a full debt I had no means of paying, while I was trying to make a life for my family. The night before court I went to sleep reading my bible, dwelling on what I had gotten myself into with this relationship, and now having a baby on the way.

On Wednesday morning I woke up to face the day, Tristan slept on the couch that night. I was nervous about court in Clayton County, it is not the place to go to a court appearance of any kind with the understanding that Christy worked at the jail, and this was her territory. I read passages out of the book of Jeremiah that morning, listened to Darina Clark as I took my bath, and got dressed. I arrived at court by 8 a.m. to face the private action with Justin and Christy James concerning the child support arrears for Micah. Tristan drove me; I really didn't want him to get involved in my past drama, so I did not invite him in with me. I didn't even want to deal with it; he was involved as much as I wanted him just being around the boys. I feel like when you have a past drama issues that you are still in, it's out of respect for the other person that you deal with your business before introducing them completely, if you can help.

Tristan didn't have children, by us just getting back together even though were having a child, I respected him enough to not involve him too much or it could have been the embarrassment of what I was facing. He was aware, of everything from an overall picture, but not involving him physically or emotionally I just felt like that it was mixing too much too soon, not wanting to give him a reason to run away. He was supposed to drop me off at the salon that day, after I left court. I walked in court, like any other day, me against two parents, and their lawyer. Mason wasn't there; I was not surprised he has a heavy criminal record with Clayton County that goes all the way back to 1996. Mason fears Clayton, but I'm very sure he was waiting for the phone call to get the info of what happened that day. When they called the calendar we all answered, their attorney answering for them of course. Before court got started their attorney got up, walked to the judge, she said something to him, and the judge called my name. He said the words I was never thinking I would ever hear, sorry Ms. Paris you have a warrant for your arrest. My facial expression changed in sadness, my heart dropped. I started smiling in the inside questioning if the enemy were in heavy pursuit of what was about to happen in my career. They walked me to the back, placed the hand cuffs on my hands and shackles around my ankles. Before the sheriff closed the door for them to further proceed she said, "You missed court yesterday." They placed me in a holding cell, I laughed at first, and then I wept, trying to figure out how it got to this position. The events that I had planned, what I had accomplished thus far flashed before my eyes, was I not suppose to display any type of joy about my progress? When they called me back out to the courtroom, the enemy was in joy seeing me in hand cuffs, being in the worst position ever. Christy looked happy, Justin could not really look, he kept his head turned in a slat direction to where he could see but couldn't. The sheriff was about to stand me beside Justin, but looking in my eyes she sat me at a desk on front of a speaker. The judge began to allow the attorney to speak on Justin's behalf, she spoke on how much I owed on the arrears and stated Justin was asking for her fees to be added in as will, because he was currently unemployed. I was thinking to myself the old in between job stage for Justin, doing just enough, sitting back, and then my emotions went toward Christy. I was thinking that's why I'm in this situation; she was tired of carrying the full financial responsibility. I believe that if she entered into the relationship, knowing Justin had a previous child involve. She either should have stood up, knowing that her love for Justin was strong enough to still want a future with him. She should have been a better support system through thick and thin as her vows declared or said she didn't want extra responsibility in her life and moved on. She could not have thought just because she was in the picture everyone in his past would be erased, child included. I think I was an outlet for her to take the stress and pain of the relationship out on. She was mad at the fact Justin was the type of man to take the responsibility for his son and willing to take him in. She didn't want her man taking care of another woman's child that's the selfishness she had in her heart that she has to deal with, and it's honestly sad, because I never caused their relationship any drama. The judge asked me if the amount I owed was correct, I answered him by saying, "I believe so" only acknowledging the $2700 I was there for. The judge then said, "You will be released when you pay that fee in full," he banged his gavel, and I went back to the holding cell.

I was then taking down stairs to be processed in still wondering how in the world I had a warrant. The officer that took me down in the elevator wondered why I was even being processed in and what did I do to be charged with Contempt of court. I just shook my head just as clueless as he and asked him, "Can I have my pocket bible out of my purse." I put it in my front pocket because I knew I was going to have plenty of time to start reading and focusing on God discerning I would need him more than ever, not knowing how much time I would have. When I got to processing they allowed me to turn my phone on to get the numbers out before they took everything away. The processing officer asked me, "are you a case worker," because that's how big my files were between the two cases that I had with me.

I kept my records on me at all times going to court never knowing what all I would need. I turned on my phone to send Tristan a text message saying, "I'm locked up, call my mom 404-582-9874," I knew he was getting impatient still outside waiting for me. I got the numbers I needed for future calls and turned off my phone. I sat down with the nurse, she asked me about my health conditions, and my last menstrual cycle. I let her know I took a pregnancy test on Monday and it came out positive, she was like, "ahh!" The next nurse called me in, took my weight, height, and started my records. She told me looking at me from behind she said to herself, "that sister in good shape, she takes care of herself." I just looked at her and cried I told her," that was one of the reasons I'm in here." She asked me, "do you have God in your life," I replied, "yes." She then said, "you will be just fine." I got myself together because she was right I was going to be just fine. After that I went to another window where, they let me know how much my bond was and what I was charged for, the male clerk told me I had a hold for $4,632.97. I challenged the amount only knowing about the $2700 from what the judge mentioned upstairs in court. He read what was in the computer and even wrote it down for me, not really having time to go back and forth in debate. They let me make a call after that, but of course everything had to be collect. Thinking about my schedule that day I tried to call the salon to let them know I was not coming in that day and where I was, but there was no answer. I was so lost. The next steps, was for them to put me in a holding cell until they dressed me out and take me in orientation. I just sat there thinking, "WOW I am really in a bad place, and the enemy think it's over for me, they have not won, they only put themselves in an embarrassing position once this is over." I felt a chill over myself meaning every thought and believing it was true. I was going to sit on the right hand until my enemies became my foot stool, knowing in his right hand I would not be move out of his grace and mercy.

Redirected

In the first 72 hours of Clayton County, they put me in what is called an orientation pod. They pulled me in this prep room, let me know all the rules, and what they expect from me while I was there. They gave me my mat, which was hard as a rock and very heavy, a used wash cloth and dry towel, tooth brush, spork, a little coffee mug, and roll of toilet paper. They issued me to a room, and the party began, when I close that door behind me all I could say was here I go. I was on lock down for 66 hours for 72 hours only allowed out of my room to make a call and take a shower. It was so cold in the room, but that was to keep the germ count low like they may do in an office full of computers, but even colder. I got in my room and I was the third to join, I had to let the girls in there know I was pregnant so I got that bottom bunk I needed. I had a letter from the nurse upstairs stating that I was pregnant, no top bunks and special diet trays. I wasn't interested in the diet trays, the oven was broken from what I heard and everything was cold coming from the kitchen. I went in with this mindset that I was not going to let my surrounding and current circumstance destroy what I worked so hard to create in myself. I was going to stay focus on getting this problem resolved the best way possible. I felt as if the past and present had met each other and I was in the middle. One world wouldn't approve and the other world was applauding with a standing ovation, I had so much to think about. My first question was how I let this happen; I should have done whatever I had to do to pay it. I questioned my faith in God and in the changes I made for myself, did I make them too soon? I should have sold my body a little longer; trafficked drugs a couple of more times, or trick Aiden for a lump sum. Who was going to help me, I distant myself to gather who I was as a person, so I had no one really close enough to help. The changes I was making no one supported them anyway, so what was I going to say when I called. The people that knew I was on child support probably thought I was doing well in my career. They probably thought I could take care of my problems, and the image I demonstrated didn't help if they did think that way. I was so new to everybody; I was a person just beginning to love them self, the more I displayed that the more I was despised. It was my time to focus on God, everything that I had learned to that extent about prayer, and worship it was time to apply. I decided that I would only eat fruit, drink milk, and water. I would keep my head in the bible that I walked in the door with repeating the routine until my body couldn't take it anymore. I had negative energy around me and I knew that I would be facing a spiritual battle if I interacted, so I had to prepare a strategy that would work for me under my condition of pregnancy. I had women younger than me in my room; I would listen to their conversation to realize what was on their minds, and what they thought about themselves. I started thinking, "what can I do in this position that I'm in to help others come from out of the mental and emotional rut I was once in." I have been in that dark place, so I could relate having enough experience and knowledge to tell them certain things that could help better themselves. It would help me take my mind off the problem that I had and bring something positive in a negative place, I still will always believe changing for the better is the most positive thing a person can do initially and continually. I knew I didn't need a speech before I spoke to anyone I thought having a more relaxed approach would be best. Remembering a quote out of the bible that stated, "never to worry about what you will say, because within the hour I will give you the words to speak." By the time I made a call, it was the next day I thought I would try to call at least my mom, because earlier that day I was called out to sign my property out. I was thinking I was being released, but the correction officer let me know what was going on. My mom figured if Christy worked at the jail, my property with all my documents didn't need to be there, she knew I went to court that previous morning, I was sure Tristan talked to her, and let her know from the text I sent him. I had too many documents in the building, things that they didn't know about concerning my Micah, and I was known to keep these papers with me at all times. When I could reach my mom, after speaking to her, Tristan went directly to her place. I was so mad by the time I finished explaining everything I remember telling my mom I was so disappointed at myself and hated the attention that had been on me from Justin and Christy, I let the enemy see me go through my transition making the envy level higher. My mom went on to tell me about how she was working on some things, how she put a call into Aiden, and let him know the situation. I was thinking yeah right I wanted to see how that came out. My mother really didn't understand how I cut everybody off to the point they would laugh at me in this position for hurting them. She was even asking me for Ismael number, he called one night when I was with Tristan, but I ignored the call and I didn't have his number saved, so it was no way to contact him. Our last face-to-face conversation he was straightforward in telling me, "I miss the old Paris, I don't know who you are." I was hoping she remembered what happened last time I was in this position, she had to depend on him, and he gave her the run around. I was thinking I am really screwed, I have no one to help me bond out, so I just fell back patiently waiting to see how things panned out. I was coming from out of orientation that Saturday, but for some reason I came out late Friday night.

I was issued to pod four the first room down stairs 3401; I was in there with two more women. One lady that was a crack addict, with good sense, she was cool, and respectful toward me. A young girl that was a lesbian until her male lover came back from services, when I told them I was pregnant my nickname became baby mama. That's what they called me for the remainder of my time; I was quiet for the first couple of days. They asked me what was I doing in there, I told them I didn't want to talk about it, and that was that. I wasn't ready to expose my person business yet; I was really embarrassed that I was even in there for child support in comparison to the other charges I had heard. It wasn't like a misdemeanor, felony, or traffic violation, I was charged with not paying off my debts in full, and reinforce by my haters. I took time to feel my two roommates out by listening to their conversations when I wasn't reading. I didn't start really speaking to them until the second day, when the crack head started telling the scoop of the pod, and how things operated. I started asking questions, like visits and commissary orders; well she couldn't tell me about commissary, because she couldn't afford to order anything. She had a support info package that had information about churches, shelters, and food donation facilities that would help her with her new start once she was released. She started telling me how she wanted to change her surrounding when she got out, and she would be looking for a place to live. I spent like an hour and a half helping her with a plan to get her started, the other girl paid attention to almost everything I said, and did. She commented on my hair stating, "I can tell you do very good on the outside, your hair so trained." I started telling about the salon and how I believed that I was in there for the habits I started applying to myself, taking life more seriously, and putting God before me daily. Not letting where I came from, how I was raised, dictate what I was going to become and what I wanted to be in life. I didn't get as deep as I wanted to, but I started tapping into their minds about their own situation. Sometimes you don't have to say a whole lot to make a person start thinking differently. Monday morning came, it was time for me to start trying to make calls, I knew nothing could really get accomplished over the weekend, and I really wanted to know how everything was going on trying to get me out of jail. I was surprised with a visit before I could even make a phone call, I just knew it was a lawyer or mom coming to tell me what was up. It was Tristan, I was so shocked, like 10 o'clock in the morning, and he was just looking at me like what the hell. I could only stress to him how I tried to tell him how the fathers really had it out for me. I told him, "I'm in here for private actions, nothing the system did directly, so that can let you know I was doing something every month." I explained to him what happened that morning and he let me know my mom let him know she was trying to do what she could. He was so shocked how things turned around, we were just celebrating finding out I was pregnant. I let him know that they did start my prenatal, and they were looking out for the baby as much as they could. In a place like that it's only so much they can do, you wouldn't get the care you would normally get, but it will be something that you would appreciate under the circumstance. It least that's how I was thinking about the situation, he started telling me," I'm not in a financial position to help; I don't know what to do." I was aware of his position before I got in this situation, he promised that he would stick by my side regardless and that he did love me. It was words I needed to hear under the circumstances, but I questioned them. He was concerned about the baby, which was comprehensible, I assured him that nothing was going to happen to the baby; I was going to stay calm and in my room reading my bible. He didn't have money to put time on the phone for me to call, so once the visit was over I had to wait until the next week to talk with him, and find out the status of what I was facing. I explained to him," when the situation was over I was going to work twice as hard and nothing was going to break me from what I built at that time." Continued to say with passion," it was going to give me more drive, to keep pushing, I had to take my anger put it toward cleaning this mess up and that the state of affairs confirmed that I was really doing my thing. My past saw things they never wanted to see that they have always saw. I made my mind up to get as much positivity out of these conditions as possible, even if it had to be through helping people." Tristan's shortcomings were one's in time I wouldn't have dealt with, but it was his heart I looked at, needed, and wanted. He was a sincere man, that's mainly what I remembered about him from my past, and that's truly what I was missing in my life at the time we met back up. I was missing plenty after I look at things; I thought it might have been smart to start with the fundamental aspects. Love, sincerity, respect, honesty, and a sound mind. He lived with his mother, was still driving the same car he replaced the old school that got stolen from me, and even still had the same furniture he bought when I was with him, but he had a peace of mind. He had goals he wanted to achieve, a plan, and like with every plan you don't know every step until you began taking the first step forward. It's the energy around you that determines much of your progress; I saw my energy as complimentary. I looked at his stand stills like stability, seven years had pass by, and the only thing changed was his address. It was like he was waiting for me, so we can finish what was started at one point in life. Our visit was truly blessed, because we could talk in a more intimate way. Visitation is only for 30 minutes, we got like an hour, and we were laughing, because we knew we were over time, but we were going to wait until the officer called me down. When I got back to the room, I felt different, like it was going to be fine when my time in jail ended. I was just wondering when it was going to end, because still out of all that conversation a resolution wasn't mentioned. I still hadn't talked to the salon; I could only imagine what they were thinking, and what they were going to say. When I got in the room the girls asked me who came to see me, the crack head had never had a visit being there 45 days, and the other lady wasn't in there long enough. I told them who it was, they were so happy for me, and the fact that I had that support coming from him. I thought it was thoughtful of them to think about that. I was thinking about what I was going to do, the girls asked me, "is he going to help you get out." I didn't answer them, just went back to sleep, and when I woke up I continued to read. I remember reading a passage that quoted," if anyone should fast let him anoint his head with oil." I was thinking to myself I need that, Wednesday's was bible study in the facility, my roommate signed up for it, so when they opened the door I went out with her. In bible study after the reading and leisure segment, we partnered up, the teacher walk around us anointing our head with oil, while we prayed for each other. I was only seven days in by then, I felt like it was really met for me to be there at that moment. That night I was up with the girls, we were talking, and I just started venting about everything that was going on. The things that I did to the point of my getting in there with them, they were so shocked to know where my mind was really at. I got on to them about not caring for themselves better and how they have to make use of their time in jail, changing, and turning away from their old ways. Being proud of whom they were and the adjustments they made when they got to that point in making them. I was moved out of that room the next day, upstairs to room 3411 with an older white lady. The first day we didn't speak to each other, she knew I was pregnant and that was about it, I was on my last couple of days of fasting, my body could not take any more. I was called to have ultra sound, the exam showed I was about five weeks; the baby was like a dot. I couldn't wait until my next visit with Tristan to let him know I saw the seed, I was so happy I just laid there, and cried. I can remember a text from Mason's wife one day telling me, in a cynical tone, "you done had 10 abortions and that's the reason you haven't had any more children because you can't." It was surprising to know she knew more about my business than I did, especially my history. What she was saying I knew that wasn't true and I never defended what she was saying about me I just let her talk and be wrong. When you hear things sometimes that the enemy is saying about you, it can look as if what they are saying is true, but you hold on to what you know and believe. I had three abortions in my earlier years, and I always thought that maybe God wasn't going to give me another chance, but he did. I hadn't missing a period since my last abortion with unprotected sex between, I was slightly shocked that I was giving another seed; it was just in the wrong time frame for me, I thought. I went back in my cell very happy despite what I was experiencing; it was amazing to see what was going on inside me. The lady I was in the room with sleep a lot that was good for me, I needed time to read, and think about things. I started talking to the lady when she came in from the phone that evening, I was concerned for her, she was crying, and just really upset. I didn't want to see her like that and I didn't need that energy around me. I had a plan to get through my time and that was to stay in my room on free time, and stay focus on the words that I needed to work for me. The lady was in there for battery, she was on probation already, and she was trying to get out before her probation officer was notified. She admitted to having a problem with drinking, which she had had for years; she poured all her personal business to me. What was so crazy she had a lot of things that were similar to what I was going through. She shared how she was on child support and only had one child left to go; she explained her living arrangements with her partner. I then had to let her know I understood where she has been and where she was trying to go, because that's where I was currently. I than explained I was in there for child support and I just got back with a person I messed up with in my more ignorant days. She explained how she was in there a time before for child support, she offered the courts half of what she owed, and the courts took it with payment arrangements for the rest. I was glad to hear a way to start coming at this situation, because I didn't know where to start, especially when the number was so high. She had more of a history in Clayton County than I did; she told me how she was put on child support out of spite from her child's father after he remarried. The lady and I had like three days to spend together; we ended up being really cool. I prayed for her, she said, "I don't know how to pray" and I let her know," it's no right or wrong way in praying, praying is a personal conversation with you and God, speaking to him directly from your heart in all sincerity." She told me, "I'm shocked you are not freaking out about the position you are in, you are handling it well." She left on that Friday hugging me so tight, stating sincerely, "I don't want to leave you here." I had the room to myself for at least five days before I got visitors; I stayed in the room, prayed, and read. Tristan came to visit me in between that time frame, I told him all about the ultrasound I had, he was sad because he wasn't sharing that moment with me. I could get out of the room on bible study days and church evenings, really staying connected with God. The girls going out for free time would stop in my window to ask me, "are you coming out," they thought I was weird. I washed up in the sink in the room; because of the conversations I would hear about the girls looking in on people taking showers from upstairs which was just nasty in my mind to have to experience. I called the salon on the following week, I at least wanted them to know where I was, when I called I talked to Stephanie. They did know where I was, getting the hang ups on the voice mail, I was up stairs trying to call collect when I first got there. They were very concerned and thought it was completely crazy that the situation got to that point. They knew how much it was for me to get out calling up there, getting the details; I did let them know the numbers were not correct. Stephanie told me she was going to get with the salon to see what they could do as far as raising money to get me out. I was refreshed that they were concerned about me to that level and they accepted my call to speak to me about my personal business. I was really embarrassed that I was having this conversation from jail; it was a bunch of mess. I had an image at the salon of having everything under control regardless of what they knew; now it was looking like control was over me. I left the conversation with Stephanie where it was until further notice. I understand things take time, especially when it's no concern of theirs, it may take even more time. It was occasions when I thought about the messages from Stephanie who claimed she went to Cody's job and informed him, he told her he didn't want to be bothered. It was hurtful because he was one person I had known since Skincare School and I had built a close relationship with his close friend. In the years they were the two I considered friends and people, I would look to in times of trouble, even though I had never had to come to them for help to this magnitude. I couldn't put ample enough energy into who was doing what and who wasn't; I needed a flash light to see my way out, at that point being completely in the dark. I got visitors in my room like the next day, it was two black ladies, one older with dreads, and the other was younger. It had been 5 days of privacy and peace; I needed that to continue by all means, being in the room alone I gotten territorial. My first questions were in a very jazzy tone, "do y'all talk in the toilet and vents to the men upstairs," they said, "no." I let them know I was pregnant and needed the rest at night, it was enough listening to the others, and I just couldn't take it in the room with me. The older lady was very mean spirit, it was very strong in her presence, the other lady was very lost, and scared. They were in orientation together, I listened to their conversation sitting back getting a feel for their personalities, and I could tell they had not been exposed to quality of life. I notice the things that the older lady was telling the young lady, who was in there for stealing a perm kit out of Wal-mart. The lady had her feeling like it was no way out, like she was going to have a hard time getting out. I wasn't happy to see an older woman doing a young lady how she was, it was like because they came in at the same time one couldn't leave until the other left. I waited for their conversation to finish for the evening before I started talking to the young lady. I knew it wasn't going to be easy getting to her, because she was painting this picture like she was a dope boy's girlfriend, her man got all this keys of cocaine in Georgia, but couldn't come get her out on a $300 bond, because that's to risky for him. I guess her being in jail she had to have a street image, so she wouldn't look poor or not of value. I didn't see anything she was saying; furthermore I wasn't interested in that end of her affairs. I just wanted her to see things differently, so she could apply something else to her life. She was 19, wasn't into God or praying and her man was in his late 20s, she smoked, drink heavy alcohol, the norm in the street kids these days. I learned not to press the issue of change because it's not an instant process; change happens gradually with a constant reminder or with viewing the changes in the area. People fear it because it comes pressured and with more authority than needed. In some cases, not in all cases, people do have to go a lot harder than usual to convince them to change, they take it better. I first let her know in a firm voice; "whatever you are doing now should not be the same thing you are doing two or more years from now." I continued to say, "That as a lady you should display to your spouse that God is in your life on some level. Man has a respect and does fear God; it is the humbleness that comes over any man when the word is even mentioned in conversation. A man would look at you differently regardless how you were raised and what you do in your social life, when you displayed that love on some level." I had to find that out the hard way, I would have progressed faster if someone took time to explain things to me like that. I let her know," a human's sin is done daily on your journey to whining those old ways and habits away, but start taking the first couple of minutes of each day thanking God for what he has already done, thanking him for what he is about to do. Asking him to forgive you and work on you, guide you through your daily walk is the least you can do. I let her know it was the invitation that was needed; I also talked to her about making decisions earlier in her life, because minutes walk, hours run, and time flies." She cried telling me," something about the room when I walked in felt like I was in a good place, it was warm, and I knew everything was going to be ok for me." The next day after the lady drilled her again about how hard it was going to be for her, an hour later the young lady got a visit from her entire family. Her family expressed to her that they were there for her, how she would be leaving shortly, they were waiting for her father to send the money. The mother that she claimed wasn't going to look out for her, because she was disappointed in her actions was even at that visit, a correctional officer for City of Atlanta. The young lady came back in the room, hugged me so tight, and thanking me for talking with her. I noticed the older lady's face; she had a jealous and hateful look expressed. It felt so good to know someone else was getting good news, it made me forget about my own troubles, I forgot where I was for a moment that's how bliss the moment was. The young lady left the next day and all the things she heard from the older lady was like foreign language. I thought about the young lady, if she were going to apply at least one of my suggestions to her life in improving herself. I was glad our paths crossed despite the place, it all had a reason. Thirty days had been by I was still in the same position, since then the same lady was there, and we had another lady that had been there two after the young one who stole the perm went home. Being that I had not left yet I started thinking about if I were being punished by God for compromising by obedience. I told myself that I wouldn't have sex with anyone and follow his instructions the right way. I didn't do that, I think being in the situation with the co-parents of the boys and facing everything alone, I was looking for companionship, and since I was familiar with Tristan's character someone that knew me in another time of my life I thought it was ok to sleep with him. I also deliberated that maybe it was Tristan's attachment that brought everything out, I've hear sometimes things happen to you because of the people you are attached too. Not to say I was being responsible about trying to pay the entire debt off, it would not have gotten to where it was. They pressed the entire debt being paid because I exposed their flaws in taking care of my boys in the custody change letters, it made them mad, and that was the real reason the pressure came. My mind was all over the place I was just looking for the reason, I was in such a bad position, hurt because I had no one in my corner, when I wasn't that bad of a person. I don't think I was the only person thinking that where I was, they watched how I moved, and the things I said when I spoke while I was in jail, they thought the same. I can truly say I heard the voice of God clear in this time frame, clearer than ever before, things I could share with others I did without hesitation. Looking back on the way I was, to the person I became, was like an outer body experience, I thought about the type of woman I was to Aiden. Aiden was older, and it was my place as a woman to instill what I wanted out of that relationship. I could have had more out of it, I wasn't thinking with the right mind. I would give the young lady in the room advice on certain things I would have and should have done in that relationship to make the most of the situation. Aiden was in a position to purchase and did purchase the type of home I asked for when we were working on our relationship. I would have thought if he loved me to that extent he would have responded to me in a desperate time of needed, but he wasn't. I didn't blame him, the relationship was settled, and what I was going through was not any of his concern. I just thought the sympathy intensity would have been there for me because of the length and depth of what we once had. I guess that was his way of being vindictive about his loss of the relationship, the man did call on several occasion, asking for dates, wanting me to come over, and spend time with him. I thought I could have a little more out of a man in the four years of dealing with him. I guess thinking back I was suppose to make the most out of what I had in order to keep myself in a better status than what I was. I knew dealing with Aiden in the right manner I would at least had more financial support. Aiden would tell me from time to time," it ain't always what you want; it is what you have to do sometimes. You may not be with a person because you necessarily like to, it may be a better condition than what you would normally be in." It was one time I was wishing I would have took his advice on those comments, even if it wasn't the best advice, I just wanted out from where I was. I thought about Aiden from time to time, but at his age he could have been a little more polished than he was. I wanted and deserved a little more from a man 10 years my senior, he was still holding on to his past and old habits. I needed to keep my focus point on what was in front of me, child support, pregnancy, and jail. I continued to put my energy into those around me, I thought it would keep my frame of mind intact and afresh. Everything I learned from Elizabeth Baptist I shared with the ladies that came in the room, I slowly gained respect in the pod without notice. I prayed to God to give me the strength for endurance to handle the hand of cards that was dealt. I was completely and utterly thankful for the heart that was in Tristan's body, he was coming to visit every week, and getting more involved in a situation he had no ability to help me out of financially. I think the thought of seeing a person he knew change to a better person, in such an oppressive state was hard for him to witness. I can't say what he was thinking; I am just thankful whatever he was thinking the thought never made him change him being there for me. He would complimented my disposition often about how I was handling the element I was in; he thought I was doing well. I would explain to him I wasn't going to displease God in the mist of my tragedy by feeding the enemy my fear. I was looking and focusing on his word and promise solely that was all and everything I was expected to do. The more time went by the more confusing things got about my case; Tristan would come back with more information about what everybody on the outside wasn't doing to help. The most shocking news was that my mom was having a 50th birthday party, I asked Tristan to bring my mom to come see me. It was a couple of days before Christmas; she had not visited once, when she shared the news of her blowout. I just smiled in happiness for her on the outside and cried on the inside for another display of selected support. My mom had a way of giving me that confusing love; it had to be a time when it was convenient for her or when it didn't take a lot. It made me reflect on our last dispute, me confronting her about my sister's weed habits being spoke about in court. Me coming to get the boys from work one afternoon, her and her boyfriend at the time having weed out on the counter, while the boys walking around. I just made a comment that her and my sister should have more discreet for their habits in front of my boys, knowing I'm in a battle for custody change. Her defense to my suggestions was their names should not have been mentioned in my court battles. I just thought my mom out of all people knowing and seeing my growth would have put herself or our differences aside to do a little more to help. I was embarrassed as well because Tristan's family contributed money toward bonding me out and I had only met them three time's. The only contribution mom had done was the $30 she left on my books, when she came to get my property when I first got there. In the visit my mom went on and on from her having to move again, this time it was going to be with her boyfriend, to information the salon getting on her nerves calling asking her questions she could not answer, everything I didn't want to hear. Stephanie mentioned how my mom was hard to reach and didn't have a workable attitude with them on coming up with a solution. Looking at it from the way they were seeing it I would not have wanted to get involved, if a person's mother was not corresponding to their needs. Tristan had a look on his face like he could slap her, and I didn't blame him, when he came to pick her up that morning to come to my visit, she was just walking in the door from the night before. That's my mom! I was still happy to see her in regards of how I thought about our differences and her level of support. I prayed that night for forgiveness for me toward my mom, I was so angry with her, and I resented what she had not tried to do for me. I knew I had to love and honor her anyhow under the foundation God set no matter how hard it was going to be. When talking with the girls in the room, I would be ashamed to say what my mom had not done to help me out. The older lady that was in the room said in a nasty tone," you must not be the person you are portraying to be, if your mom is responding in the way she is, moms do anything do get their children out of jail, especially their girls." The comment hurt like hell, but it was met too, so I ignored it. Despite what some thought, I decided to be an example of handling longsuffering, one of the fruits of the spirit. I was going to display an attitude of how you should be when you are a abased position during life; it was a part of my testimony to the others that was keeping up with my story at that time. I noticed the change in how others were processing their case; they had more patience, they conversed about it in a different tone than the harsh tone I once heard. I think if it wasn't for what I witnessed in the previous two years of my life I could not expose the mannerism I did, when I did.

Spending Thanksgiving wasn't as hard as spending Christmas and New Year's in jail. By that time my emotions on what was going on in my life was numb, I lost my place, my image was slowly erasing from the career I built with the unexplainable absence, to say the most I didn't or could not image what my boys were thinking and what they were told from their parents. The positive news was I had a court date January 13, Tristan could keep his patience with my mom long enough to get a lawyer's information from someone she knew. I thought it was a good gesture coming from her at the time to say the least. The attorney was to come visit me the day before the court appearance, but never did. The objective of the court appearance was to notify the judge of the two cases for the same child, have one dropped, and get a purge reduction in place. Tristan had $1000.00 toward the purge reduction and paid the attorney $300 for the court appearance. I had one issue with the entire visit with the attorney, Tristan gave him my file, let him go through it, and keep the original documents. I would have never allowed him to keep the originals, but in the position I was in I couldn't be demanding. I was excited thinking I would get released from jail after the court appearance, I was sure the attorney could straighten out the confusion. The morning of court appearance I felt very light, I had assurance that it was over. I prayed that morning and stayed confident for my release that day. The guards putting me in the cell could not believe I was in there; they were even making positive comments about me going home that day. I saw my attorney minutes before my appearance in the attorney booth. He told me that he spoke with the child support attorney, he was going to speak to the judge asking him to accept the purge reduction, set new terms of monthly payments, and I would be released that evening. I was so relieved, he even had the documents all written up with the terms to present to the judge and have him sign the approval. The attorney wanted to speak with me after I was released in regards to straighten the child custody case that was in shambles. Leaving from the court area going back into the pod all I could do was thank God for the day. I let the girls know who was waiting on the news that an agreement was made and I would be released. I was going back to my room, to wait for them to call my name to tell me to pack it up, it had been two months and two days by then, and I was ready. I clearly would have to stay with Tristan and his parents, starting over from scratch with everything I worked for in the short time to build without street hustling. I always thought about if I tried to change myself and my life to soon, I just never remembered having these many issues when I was thinking from an emotional state of mind. It's like when I focused on doing things God's way a little bit everything wanted to happen that could happen. My name was called, they popped my door and the girls went crazy, my bunk mate carried my mat down stairs for me. When I got to the speaker to let the guard know, I was ready, she wondered what I was doing with my mat and things in hand, she stated in a bossy tone, "I never told you to pack it up, I just called your name." I looked startled, she told me, "You have a visitor;" I looked at the top of the visitor's booth and saw Tristan. I didn't know what was going on, I was thinking maybe it was such a long process to be released he was coming to see me before he saw me on the outside, he was just that wound up for us to finally be together. Tristan had a look on his face that was so poignant, I didn't want to sit down that's just how bad his facial expression was. He explained to me that I was not leaving that day; he had been downstairs talking his head off with the officers. Apparently, I was still being held for the other case with the same child. Yes, it was agreed I was to be released, but that was for one of the two cases. Now from my understanding that bit of information was being explained to the judge before they presented the terms of the reduction. Tristan was really proud of how I took the news; I had a child in my stomach to think about, breaking down was nothing I needed to do at the moment that was not going to get the problem solved any faster. The first step that needed to happen was contacting the attorney, get him on the job, it was nothing we could have done on our end, it was disappointing to hear the news, but I was already there. If they would have told me the news at the door when I was in the process of dressing out, this would have been another story. I had endured the winter months with no hot food, I felt like a little while longer would not have hurt me, even though the growth of the baby was a concern for me. When I got back to the pod everybody wanted to know what the deal was, I was still processing everything and was a loss for words. I didn't share the update with anyone but my bunkmate, I let everyone else mind just wonder. It took a couple of weeks to get the situation solved, the attorney let us know it was too much confusion, and he was no longer interested in representing me. The interesting part of one of the cases being dropped is Child Support dropping their case and awarded Justin's private case. That would mean we had to come up with $1700 more than what we had, Tristan was still holding on to the money orders. Tristan never paid the courts that day when they mentioned I was not going to be released. Tristan got a job through his step father, which came at such a good time. The plan now was to wait until he saved up the remainder of the money; I just had to be a little more patient. Tristan became a friend more than I ever expected, we talked at least four times a week on the phone. Every conversation was positive, speaking about our future together, putting aside the doubt we had, and the turmoil we were experiencing. It was all a test, if we passed the test, God was going to bless us to the point where our minds would completely forget the amount of pain we were currently enduring. I guessed being in a position where I built a halfway decent relationship with many people that had reputable reputations of being responsible, I was thinking they would have come through, and helped. It turned out that I only had this one person that I didn't believe was capable, stand on his own two feet, and came through. Tristan alone was helping me out in my problem, which made me grow not to just respect him, but love him as well. I tried to keep my mind on the positive aspects, God had giving me another chance to be a mother, and be a partner. Yes, I thought of it as a punishment for premarital sex, but is pregnancy a curse in the eyes of God? I would ask the young girls around me all the time, "What would you do if God gave you a chance to start over?" I would tell them in my case," I will take everything I have ever learned that I didn't apply the first time and apply, it the second time around, making every move count, and never looking behind me no matter the cost or who it was." It is written in the Bible that God takes away the first, to establish the second and if that were the situation I was experiencing, I was all in. I had to understand I was going to be walking toward a relationship I wasn't confident in and had doubt or that it was something even long term for us. I truly was in a situation where I had to trust God's direction, taking the first steps without seeing the next. A person that was looking at me, instead of my circumstances, was nothing I could believe without it being in my visual, and it was probably, because I was looking at his circumstance. Tristan and I continued our regular routine with visits and phone calls, up until I was released on March 5, 2010. Before, I was released I was served documents from Child Support Services from Mason Byrd at 2 o'clock one morning. My bunkmates were in shock when I was called out to sign for the documents, they could not believe I was encountering that under the conditions I was already in. The papers had my address as the jails; it was a mess, something else to worry about when I was released. I didn't get much sleep that night, and I was still thinking," why am I being attacked about this money to this level?" I think me overlooking the seriousness of what could happen focusing so much on my career is what got me in this position. At that point I washed my hands entirely on returning to the salon, I had too much of a mess to clean up. I thought about what I was going to say to Sage and this is what I came up with to send once I was free from jail:

> Sage's salon:
>
> This is my 30 day notice, terminating the lease made in agreement on 5/5/2009 between the salon and Paris D. From initial start date 09/12/2008 my booth rental was set as $175 per week. It was verbally changed to $100 for the month of August 2009 to assist me with financial challenges that I was facing personally. A new monthly rate was set to $135 weekly in September as a permanent weekly rate. I am aware that before the week of 11/11/09 two weeks of rental was due to the salon. I do agree that

it is still owed. I have been absent from the salon from 11/11/2009 to 3/5/2010 and if still charged for the weeks I have been absent it is totally understandable, it is business. I want to have a total of what is owed, so a payment arrangement can be made for the closure of my lease. I thank the salon for the past year of support, business, and personal relationship that has been established. I would never do anything to jeopardize the reputation that the salon has and do feel that the welfare of my personal issues are not like fond of what the salon represents. I would not want anyone to feel uncomfortable in or within my presence under working environments. I have no regrets in the decision I have choose, it has been very will thought out. I only want to leave on clear and fair terms as respect for myself and the salon. It has been a beautiful experience.

Your Best Face, Paris D.

I never sent the letter once I was free, but the way I believed about me returning in my new state was confirmed to be very much on target with how Sage believed from a conversation with Mackenzie Pin a year and a half later. My bunkmate was going to miss me like crazy, she was sentenced to prison for a year. Twenty-one, stealing a hotdog to feed her children, violated her first offenders probation; you would have never known that was the same young lady that walked in the door after us spending 3 months together. I wished her many blessings in her growth with God and her walk in life, as I had my own walk to finish.

Coming home I was very afraid of how my life was going to be. It was almost like I felt safer in Clayton Co. Tristan did everything he said he would and I was thankful of that. Riding in the car I could tell he was happy, but still had nervous energy too. We were living with his parents and that was different for me, but it was a place I could call home. I felt insecure about what his mom was going to think, but at the same time I couldn't worry about that, I had a plan that I had to get in production, and that was that. We stopped at IHOP and all I could think when I saw Tristan walking up with the food, "what was going to come out of this?" I was praying for the best, circumstances were more different than before. When we got to his place, I felt so weird like a stranger at home, Tristan's energy felt weird to me because he wasn't as compassionate as when he was on the phone and visits, it was like reality was vivid. I hugged his mom as she got out of bed to come she me, I was happy to see her again; I made sure I thanked her for everything that she helped Tristan with. Tristan took me to get my hair done and see my mom the next day. We closed out the weekend with church, and his mom made me a big welcome home dinner. Monday morning I was up at the food stamp office by 8 a.m. by 10 a.m. I was approved for assistance with food. All I could think about this professor at the salon was getting her legs waxed, telling me I was too smart to be just waxing that it should be something I did on the side until I got where I deserved to be. I hate I had to go through what I just endured to realize what she was saying. By experiencing what I did in Clayton County using my spiritual gifts, getting educated I could use my credentials and I could make an impact on lives seriously. I was very capable of more than creating outer beauty that was a plus, but inner wellbeing is what needs to be cared for first. I started looking at what online school would be good for me to attend, and what was needed for me to get started. By 3 that afternoon I made some calls and got some things in place. When I stopped for the day I was proud of the time and things, I had done. I felt sad about what all happened to me in the time frame, but I had to remain hubbed. The reality of me really about to have Tristan's baby was more defined, even scary. Things were very good that day, I could thank God first and Tristan second for not giving up on me like some did or would have. All I wanted to do was start showing Tristan appreciation for what he had done for me. I stressed to him how much I appreciated him for being committed to helping me and not flaking out, even if it were for the baby. I poured out my heart to him how disappointed I was in the actions of others and how I wouldn't have given up on a person that I knew was applying her best for the good of her future. I expressed to him how I thought since I was around a higher caliper of people they would do more, but how that wasn't the case. They saw something in me that people who have known me for years hadn't; I would think they would not have wanted to see me in a position that would ruin my hard work. I also thought about when I have ever heard a celebrity or famous person serve time they always come back better, but I was not at that peak of my career. I was still building in a section of building where I could not take an unexpected absence, what would my explanation be once I return? To my understanding it was a discussing helping me, during my dialogue with Stephanie while I was in jail she explained how they had a meeting about raising money for me and how the twins along with others said," they didn't have the resources to help." I had a very high level of respect for Tristan and his family, because he initially didn't have anything, but ended up doing almost everything. It's not easy handling your own issues and taking on someone else's it takes a certain amount of love, time, and patience. I expressed to him that when we started dating again everything he did for me, I never saw him being capable of. I was proud of him and happy I had someone like him on my side because he was very supportive especially when times were hard for me. How I felt like people tried to help in ways they could in the beginning, but didn't stick through the end, so honored his character wholeheartedly. Tristan and I was both trying to get accustomed to living with one another, it was something we both were being tolerate with, and we weren't hiding it. One even when Tristan came in he had been drinking a little bit more than I was comfortable with and we exchanged some unpleasant words. He made the statement in staggering words;" if I would have known that you had the level of issues you had I would have never dealt with you as far as getting you pregnant." When he said it he caught himself, but it was too late it was already said. "The fact that I laid down with him and he was living with his parents, wasn't working, driving, and didn't have any money" was on my mind to say as defense real snappy. I was judging him based on his resume, how he was to me in our past. "The fact that he was breaking down an oz of weed to help a friend sell," was all on my mind also, but I was not going to disrespect him like that because despite all that he was still there for me. I was glad to know that he thought the way he did and mad that I kind of knew that to some extent. He apologize right after he made his comment, letting me know," regardless of what I going to be with you, even though you have your situation I have mine too, and before everything happened you was with me in regard and was supportive." I listened to what he had to say, took the good words over the bad, and let it go. It was still in the back of my mind, but every couple has words with one another, it's the actions that count. Tristan's actions were way different than what he said to me that night. I always been a person that believed two people can never fail and should never fail. I knew I had to start getting more business connected with Tristan. He had goals that he wanted to accomplish and so did I. I started talking with him to see what type of plan he had so I could know where to start in assisting him with his endeavors. Tristan had a real estate debt that had to be paid and a business that needed to be established on paper. I was going to work my plan while doing everything I was capable of to help Tristan as well, with my experiences I knew if I applied them to him it would benefit us. I wanted him to be established as well as myself so no one was in anyone's shadow; I want a man that is a leader in his own rights. Us working together within the 45 days I was home Tristan's debit was one payment away from being paid, I made a settlement with Child Support for Mark, was signed up for the Fatherhood Program to help keep me out of jail, and Justin's attorney fees were half paid. Tristan's business documents were started, and we were starting to put money on the side to move in our own place. I was completely indebted to Tristan and his family for what they did for me and my children. I will not say Tristan' s mom was a peach pie, but I had so much respect for her character and what she did when everyone else turned away I will never say anything negative about her. She did what my mother could not and did not do, so the things she has done that rubbed me the wrong way I always turned the other cheek, just overlooking it. I looked at Tristan and I relationship as being undivided; I wanted to be his backbone. I once heard that a role that a woman has in her mate's life is to be a comforter, counselor, and companion. The woman is to be the reminder of foundation when he is going astray from his calling, having the ability to connect with him on any and every level mentality, emotionally and physically. I believe me concentrating on what I had to do to make me better understand what I was doing in this new relationship with so much baggage helped both of us. Tristan is an observant man, able to adapt to what's around him, and when I noticed that I operated in a healthy manner. I thought with a "rich mind" as some would say, not thinking or operating like anything was out of place in our lives. I moved and spoke like life was perfect as we knew it; it drew healthy events toward us I can say. I was thrown a baby shower by Tristan's mother, my mom and I invited people that we knew to come. I was surprised in the turnout and wondered why this support didn't come while I was going through one of the hardest times in my life. I thought about people only coming to see what jail had done to me or if I were destroyed in one way or another. I steered clear of the negative thoughts and just enjoyed what was going on in that moment, I'm glad I did because for a person that had only the basics on her baby registry (exactly 20 items). I was overwhelmed with many gifts; I had the nicest baby shower ever. I didn't have to purchase diapers until our baby was almost five months old. Everything from the highchair, car seat, two travel beds, stroller all the way to clothes, blankets, wash items, and even a bath robe. Tristan and I were in our place for about two weeks before the shower, and it was baby ready. Not even one week after the shower I was still collecting gifts pampers and such my water broke. I was admitted like 1:30-1:45p.m that afternoon, Malachi Charles did not arrive until 5 the evening of the next day 29 hours later. I chose the name Malachi because I was closing out the last chapter of my old life. Weighting in at five lbs three oz beautiful boy, his mom came in and was like he looks just like a little Tristan. I really didn't think too much about the comment. I had no doubt or thought about the baby not being Tristan's. I never thought if Tristan would have had a doubt, things did happen really fast for us. I think any man would have had some type of doubt, but I still take off my hat to the man for reacting opposite of his fears, how many of us say we do that? The day that I was being released from the hospital before we left we had to complete the birth certificate. Tristan went to turn everything in and came back with the DNA pamphlet asking me, "do our baby look like this one." I quickly replied, "no." I kind of thought he was implying something else, but I didn't fed anything into it. His mother was in state of shock at how much the baby looked like Tristan did as a baby that was all the DNA testing I needed. We worked together with getting the baby comfortable, Tristan was so much help, it was new for him and I could tell he had to get adjusted. It had been 12 years for me by then, I was completely starting over, but it's like driving a car you never forget. The mistakes I made as a young mother, I was going to correct them through this stage of being a seasoned mother that was the least I could do to show thanks to God. Tristan understood things I would explain about being a parent, we talked about when it came to his approach on things, and I saw a person that wanted more out of life. Tristan was going to be a great father. I had thought about things that I had experienced in my life and how things turned out. Maybe God didn't want me to get to a point without a partner, a person who was going to love me unconditional, give me love as closes to his as possible on this earth. We both had things to offer one another; I think I just had more of an open reputation of accomplishments than Tristan had. I introduced life skills that he didn't know, and he could give me a love I had never had. I perpetually thanked God for the occurrence he showed me earlier in my life and the instructions he wanted me to follow to change.

My semester ended in July and the school reimbursement I was expecting in August wasn't coming because my medical administrative assistant loan had gone into a negative status, so I had to pay six consecutive payments to qualify for more loan money to continue school with. I was thinking ok got to go back a little to go forward, and I then started calling back clients. One's that lived in that area, who had something going in their own lives that weren't going to be concerned too much about mine. I had child support, school payment to meet every month, and Tristan had overhead. The clients that I choose were the one's I started with that knew me from Raine's shop. I explained my absence in all honesty to all, but maybe three out of the 12. I picked 12 because that would let me make enough to meet my requirements every month. My clients were very excited to hear from back from me, the one's that knew the reason I was gone were very sorry something like that had happened to me. Some said if they would have known they would have come to see me or put money in the pot to help me out. I didn't bother calling anyone from the salon like Stephanie or the twins that I service regularly there, because I knew how they viewed me differently me, me being in jail I was not the kind of person they would associate themselves with. When Stephanie called the week of my baby shower to tell me Sage took the invitation home, forgetting to tell everyone about it until the last minute. Then Sage called me the night of the shower when I was unpacking everything to ask me, "what else do you need." Sage or the staff didn't send me even as much as a congratulations card. When I called Sage to let her know that I would not be returning, she was surprised and disappointed I could tell but was nice to use the address I gave her to mail my gift to mail my property that was there since I left. I sent her a thank you card attached with a kind letter and closed that chapter. I was disappointed that the mink strip was missing out of everything, but Stephanie was my first thought to have taken it, she helped pack things up I can image. Mackenzie was my second; both knew how to apply strip lashes. They probably assumed I would have forgotten I had them. I knew they were surprised I didn't come back, they never wanted me gone, but they were going to treat me another type of way, and I would rather start over than experience that on top of everything else that had gone on. Sage did not even trust me with a key before my incident to the salon when I was working there and everyone else working the same amount of hours had free will access. I can remember her suggesting I take my supplies with me one afternoon, because April or her would not be there to let me in to take care of my clients. I personally thought it was unfair to sometimes have to travel to client's home or have them meet me in neutral sites to service them when I was paying booth rent at a salon. It was very inconveniencing for me to spend gas for travel and sometimes buy supplies I may have needed, which I had at the salon to work with. On top of everything it looked unprofessional; no one else I the salon was treated like such, Mackenzie had a key once she first started, but that was probably because if anything happened Sage was sure her dad would cover the damages.

My clients started flowing as I planned and I was meeting monthly obligations. Tristan's birthday was coming up; I wanted it to be a special one, Tristan had been doing a great job holding everything down. He saw a bracelet he liked at the boutique across the hall from my mom's salon. The plaza had an side walk display one evening that we attended and I could meet a client from Sage's that helped me in the past get into the 100 Black Women Gala as a sponsor. She was very fond of me and Sage knew it. I was surprised to hear her say that night that Sage told her about my situation. I was thinking to myself "why would she tell her anything or even ask the lady for help?" Sage had once told me how she was broke, but had a lot of connections, and every time she came in she was trying to make some type of deal in order to pay for her services. I never mentioned that to her verbally, because I could tell she was there to see how I was looking, what my conversation was going to be like, maybe judging me because of where she knew I had been. I gave her a good report, so when she was to talk about me with them; I was looking good even after the storm and having the baby. I had enough to put Tristan's bracelet on lay away and get things started for his birthday. By the time his birthday came, I had the bracelet out, I got him a special cake, we had dinner, and he took pleasure in everything that I could do for him. We were growing to know each other, building a relationship; we never really had time to spend with each other before the Clayton County vacation. Life was moving along, but I always thought about the boys, it was mornings I would have to wake up early and just pray for them. Tristan would catch me in the living room crying sometimes from missing them. It was approaching a year's time since I had seen either Micah or Mark. I was communicating with Micah through Facebook and that shortly ended once the word got back to the co-parents. I heard that it was explained to him that I was on heroine from his uncle; my sister Butterfly got the information from Micah. I thought it would be best for me to keep my distant until the Child Support issue was clear; my presence just caused him stress at time with his parents. The jail situation really shook me up mentally, but I never expressed it to anyone. I gave my fears and concerns to God, trusting that he would fix the situation, if I stayed focus on him. Then I always thought of faith without works being dead, my mind was always all over the place about calling the house and even asking to speak to my children, I didn't want any more drama for any of us. Micah knew about me having another child from a Facebook message I once sent, he always been a really good big brother, but I wondered if he would accept his new brother. I only knew he was happy for me, he had heard some of the things said about me in the past. One about me not being able to have any more children, me knowing him he was probably thinking it was something else they lied on his mom about. Micah's thoughts of his co-parents were they were haters toward me, Micah and I relationship was open and sincere, we both never understood the drama, it was unnecessary.

Thanksgiving had come both Tristan's and I family shared the day together, I thought about Micah and Mark, prayed for them, and turned it over to God knowing that it was in the best hands ever. Four days after Thanksgiving me and Tristan was home watching television when Tristan phone ranged that was by me, he was in the living room on the Internet, so he didn't bother to answer. It rung again, so I picked it up, I gave him the phone, it was the concierge downstairs. Tristan let me know they said my mom was coming up, I was throwed off because she was popping up that was weird, I hadn't talked to her all that day. I started getting worried that maybe the Sheriff's had come, doing the eviction that day, she wasn't prepared, and didn't have a place to stay. Since I had been home from jail this was her second eviction notice on the same apartment. Her boyfriend left her with the entire responsibility; I could help her with a hundred dollars last time, but not this time. I had to let her deal with it completely, because she never paid me back like she said. It was always on my mind about her living arrangements, no one wants their mom 50+ moving every time they turn around, and by that age you want them more stable. I was thinking that's what had occurred with her with the call she was on her way up; I put Malachi in his crib and started calling her from my phone. No answer. I went to meet her in the hall, so when she got off the elevator whatever she was going through could hit me before my household. Well, when the elevator doors opened she got off with three police officers. She looked at me and said they need you to come with them, Child Support, I was stunned! When I walked back in the apartment with entourage Tristan was looking just as dumb founded as I was. My mom had a nervousness about her that was written all in her face and in her body language; she knew I was calling her shady. The officers were nice enough to allow me to prep the baby for Tristan and change my clothes. When I got in the room to change Tristan said,

"Why would she bring them here?" I comprehended where he was coming from, but couldn't entertain it like I wanted to; things were moving too fast and changing drastically right before my eyes. I kissed both my men and walked out. I just pondered over the fact that it's a 45 minute drive from my mom's place to mine, how did she feel riding over? I was confused because I was paying what I could every month and reporting to the program I was under to Child Support. I told the officer that it was a big misunderstanding, but they had one job once that order is made. The Judge signed a warrant for my arrest for missing a court appearance; I had no clue that the court appearance was still to proceed. My Fatherhood agent assured me that I was in the clear; she spoke with the judge in the private case, notifying them I was in this program, and paid the settlement amount at the office. I had money order receipts and my letter stating that I was exempt from incarceration. When I got in the officer's car I broke down crying, because I was mad, hurt, and confused. Fulton County Jail here I come, I had so many thoughts going in my mind, different emotions, but worry was not one of them. I was confident in my actions that I had been doing the right things by child support; it just had to be clarified with the judge. During process at the jail the clerk told me I could purge out for $7920 I heard her, but didn't. I didn't respond because I had documents from Fatherhood that the judge needed to see, I was not going to let hearing that large amount put fear or doubt in me. I was taking to IN200 in room 205 when I walked in; the room had all these scriptures from books and quotes about God all over the wall that the lady that was in there had done, I was so happy. The lady opened up to me about her personal problems, why she was there, and what she was facing as her consequences very quickly, all I could say was here I go, AGAIN. Not complaining, but fleshly wanting to deal with what I had going on first, I wasn't in there 24 hours yet. It took two days before Tristan got some time on the phone; once I could speak with him we got things started on what was going on. I vented to Tristan how I couldn't believe my mom brought the police to our place. The only other time I had heard or known that to happen was in the movie "Blow" with Johnny Depp, and he sold drugs. If the police were looking for me, let them know, I don't live with you, let them search your place to see, and leave. Call me and let me know I need to handle that was an option I would have expected her to do. Her riding in the car with the police was the kicker, she smoked weed more than a chimney and everyone she deal with personally was in the dope game, would she do that to them? I remembered her and I talking when I came home from Clayton County, Mason sent court papers to her address that she signed for. Mason skip traced her address thinking that's where I may have moved to. If he would have sent them to the last address he knew of, I would have got the documents like I got everything else that was forwarded. I tried to forgive her for being so distant the last time I was in this position, I expressed to Tristan I was tired of her ways, and her health was my only concern from this point on. I expressed to him how I loved her and would always respect her, but her character toward me at times I didn't comprehend or value. It was times she would speak about things I use to do and things I use to say, reminding me of the old me. I would correct or ignore her just wanting to move on in conversation and not disrespect her in any way, constantly forgiving her because it would hurt my feelings. I never reminded her of who she once was nor did I treat her in that manner. I was not perfect, by no means but I was a walking example of a better person than what I started off as and was proud of it. Tristan told me how hard it was to drive her home without saying anything disrespectful or out of line. I let him know he did the right thing, we were in a position regardless of what and was going to need everyone to help, and it was not the time for division, me leaving was enough. My mom had a couple of clients that worked at the jail I was in; she sent a message to one of them to bring me a document to fill out to give Power of Attorney over to Tristan so he could speak on my behalf to my agent at Fatherhood. I asked God not to take my new life away; I asked him what he wanted from me. I heard a voice say, "attention." It was a calling he put on me that I wasn't walking into with full potential. I was a light in a dark place that people needed. I worked on becoming that light once I came out of prayer; I turned on the switch. On the morning my bunkmate was facing court on charges that could send her back to prison; I woke up with her before she left to pray for and with her. The lady became very fond of my presence saying to me one day, "you are a comforter."

Now, the story on my case was, when I was in Clayton County I had a court appearance in Fulton County for the Child Custody Change and Child Support Arrears with Mason that was continued from our last court hearing. Apparently, if I were in jail, it was the responsibility of Clayton County to take me to the court appearance in Fulton, but they didn't. The judge dismissed the Child Custody case and the Child Support arrears were awarded. The papers served to me from Child Support Office in Clayton County that I responded to and settled out of court were something outside of the private action. Even after receiving the lump sum from the settlement, Mason reinforced what he was rewarded from the private action and had those papers served to my moms address thinking that was where I was living. They were to send the documents to the correct address, never did, and that's when the warrant was issued. Now the entire time I was following what my agreement was with the Child Support Office. My level of tolerance with Mason was extremely low, if anything bring me to court for not seeing my son that was court ordered just like child support. That would not have happened because having me out the picture was what he wanted, an example of that is. One of Mark's 7th grade teachers was a client of my mom and had been for many years. She knew the history and how much drama Mason once was. She informed Mark when school first started that she knew his mom and granny very well, being staggered that he was in her class. When she and I spoke she agreed to be my source to see Mark without the mess, so we waited a couple of weeks. Mark got impatient wanting to see me, told his dad that his teacher knew me. Mason went to the school and requested Mark be removed from her class, declaring we were going through custody battle. Mason's request was not granted, he had no legal documents stating that I could not see or come around our son. My information was not added to Mark's school information that was known from the previous school year. Me coming to see the teacher was how I was going to see Mark, I just backed off. I had someone that I knew personally to watch Mark to some extent, I was gratified toward God for keeping him in my circle somehow.

When they called for bible study, I woke up and was ready to go, the teacher covered the book of Genesis. How Abram had to trust the words of God when he instructed him to leave out of the country, leaving all his love ones, into the land that he had prepared for him. I was getting back into what I was not doing, not fulfilling my promise, getting more involved in church, and I took what I was going through as a reminder. Following what I accepted was going to get me where I needed to be. God had my children waiting for me down the road, even with me being out of their presence they knew my love for them. I had a chance to communicate with Micah on Facebook before school started and he wrote, "I know my mom love me." The things I was learning in online school and the training I would practice on others was what my kids were going to need when they came back around. Once my debit was paid and a good lawyer was in motion, I was requesting them back for more time. Tristan mentioned one evening on the phone how he really wanted me to get the boys, the drama is hurting them most of all, and we both agreed it was not cool. Sitting in Fulton Co. gave me more drive, I didn't understand why my family was the way they were toward me as far as support, and I knew I could do nothing to change them personally all I could do was continue to change who I was. Was I that bad as a person in the past for them not to want to support me? I stayed in Fulton County another week before getting transferred to Union City Jail, Fulton County was becoming over crowded, and they randomly selected 20 women to go to the other jail. Everyone who had experienced it before spoke about better food and housing. It was nothing like Fulton County; it would be more like a rooming house, but a jail setting. The food, and the privileges would be better, something you could relate to a little. When we got to the other jail, they assigned us to our room; I was in the room with seven other women. It was eight to a room, all the women were either studs, bi-sexual or curious. The comments started instantly, along with the invitations to shower together. I turned down comments that came my way, explained to them what they do is just that, I have or do not plan on being involved. I waited until the next morning to take a shower when no one was in there, I had a young lady come in there just to look and see what I was so shy about. When I came back into the room, the look on my face and way I responded to her was a clear gesture that I was not happy about what she did. The things that happened at night was wild, the sexual games they played were nothing you would feel comfortable sleeping through. I laid there like I was sleep, but I was awake the entire time listening and scared they would have wanted to try me in my sleep. I did not want to be in a situation where I was taking; I had that experience before and was not looking for another. I was in that room for about three days before I could move to another room. When I moved in the other room, it was a relief. The women in there were different; the room was not as crowded, five of us with three empty beds. I was glad to be in a better environment while I was there, I talked to the girls in the room in there for all violent crimes, one in particular I remembered hearing her story on the news. They could not take the fact that I was in there for Child Support; they thought it was the silliest thing ever with no court date scheduled. Tristan and I stayed focused on what we needed to do; ignoring what my mom had done, as we were still healing from the hurt. Tristan really had hard feelings toward her, I couldn't blame him, but I was in no position to deal with it like I needed to, I would have to deal with it when I was released, and settled in. I got back into my routine of reading and studying the word, I got a book or two from one of the other inmates to read in between my reading. Two I really liked, inspirational novels by James P. Gills, if you have never read Unseen Essential or Tender Journey, you must! Early in the morning while everyone was still asleep before breakfast, I would put in 30 minutes of exercising, and take a shower. Ladies in the pod respected my good habits under the circumstances, they stayed clear of bringing the drama in my direction and I appreciated that. I stayed in the room 75% of the time, I watched movies from time to time just to clear my mind, and wrote the rest of the time. I had decided to use the time to write in the book you are reading; I had some pages on the computer at home that I started when I was released from Clayton County. I would send everything to Tristan in the mail for him to put up for me; he was being such a good sport. I just knew he would have my bags packed, tired of supporting me through jail, but nothing in his demeanor changed about the way he felt about me. He just wanted the problem solved and people to start being more adult about life's affairs. We talked every other day, my thoughts about having another son without his mother was a waking nightmare. Malachi was completely incident coming into this world having to suffer for my past decisions, 10 days off breastfeeding before the police came, and picked me up. It had been a month before I could see Malachi at the new facility; when I did I just sat there and cried. Tristan told me how much of a big boy he was for his sister and brother in law who kept him while he worked. I was blessed to be connected to a person whom family loved them, not to say they didn't have anything negative to say, but their actions spoke louder than any word they uttered out of their mouth. Tristan spoke positive words while we waited through the beginning of the year, after the holiday, to contact the judge to see if I were on the court calendar. We were dealing with a lawyer I spoke with after I was released from Clayton County; I never retained him because at the time he was too expensive. The attorney did not have any news about the court appearance or a reasonable solution. We were thinking if we got the court appearance and explain to the judge that I was in a program under the Child Support program, what my status in the program was, and I was following the guidelines. This was our discussion to the attorney when I first got to Fulton County; I had all my documentation from the program. Tristan even got the evidence that I was in guidelines with the program, and child support couldn't step in and speak on my behalf, because it was a private action against me from the co-parents. The scenario was the same as Clayton County, just not as lengthy. It was my second year spending Christmas, New Year's and my birthday incarcerated. Tristan and Malachi was my birthday gift to say the most, I didn't even have that the previous year. The Monday after my birthday, we were tired of getting the run around from the first attorney, who was giving us bad suggestions, Tristan contacted another attorney, and I was on the schedule the same week. When I would pray that week, Psalms 63 was in my every moment of thought. I knew after this court appearance, my next time in a courtroom it would be for a custody change for Mark Byrd. I thought about it long and hard Micah would be 18 within a year's time, it would be no need to fight after he is at a point of making his own decision. I trust in God that he will choose to come back around basing his decision on our personal history. The morning I had court they called me after everyone else had gone to court. I was thinking maybe they didn't have me in the system, because of the short notice of the court date. I couldn't call Tristan and let him know what was going on because the phones were not turned on yet. I went into the room and prayed my fear and anxiety away. I had a letter that would help in my case from the Southern Human Rights Center explaining how they pulled my case investigating the regulations and policies the state of Georgia was not abiding with concerning indigent parents. The letter explained that in the State of Georgia by law I could not be incarcerated more than 60 days. A 60 day time frame would prove that the NCP does not have any assets and is incapable of paying the amount required to be released from incarceration. The information took me back to the incident in Clayton County, I honestly think Clayton County could have been aware of the law and that was why I was in there under two cases. It was a way to cover there tracks, when one of those cases was dismissed I was incarcerated less than 60 days. Then again I could be wrong, I am really not sure why I was held so long in Clayton, it was over, I was now dealing with Fulton, but I still thought about it. Fulton was not going to be like Clayton and that was one thing I was glad for. One of my bunkmates asked me, "are you ok," my response was, "God got me, if it is in his plans for me today I will be in court, and closer to home." No sooner than the words came out of my mouth, I tried to get myself comfortable in my bunk; they called my name and told me to get ready for court. The young lady jumped up the same time as I, and we met up for a hug, it was God's will. My heart was beating a thousand miles an hour; I knew it was the beginning of an unforeseen day with nothing, but good hope. Everyone else had already gone to sleep; I woke them up to say good bye, because I knew I was going home that day without knowing. I would have rather looked like a fool like that incident in Clayton County returning than to give the devil my hope. The ride over from Union City to Fulton County, I felt like it was VIP treatment. I was in a patrol car instead of a paddy wagon and the time of me having to wait to go to the court appearance was cut in half. When I arrived at Fulton I was in the holding cell for maybe an hour before the officers came to get me and to take me up stairs. When I got to the cell upstairs, outside the courtroom, my attorney came in to speak with me. I quickly gave him the letter, having all my documents with me from my room in Union City knowing I was not returning. He read over what was sent to me from the Southern Human Rights Center, agreed to the information, knowing it was an open, and shut case for him. When the officer brought me in the courtroom, Tristan walked in shortly after, and we proceeded. My attorney began to state my information to the judge when then walks in Mason, his wife, and attorney. I knew things were going to be messy seeing them walk in the door, but I have to say I was more confident having an attorney present. This was the first time in the entire 3 years of on and off court appearance that I had representation thanks to God establishing Tristan and I relationship and Tristan caring enough for my wellbeing. The opening argument from Mason's attorney was I was a hair stylist that performed services for celebrity clients and I grossed about 50k a year. My attorney leaned over to me and asked if it were true, I quietly responded if I made 50k a year I would not be in this position. The attorney that represented me knew Mason's attorney from previous cases and had an admirable level of respect for the gentleman, so I could understand him if he believed what he heard. The thought of Psalms 63 stayed in the back of my mind, because I knew this was going to be a show. The attorney then carried on with the argument speaking about the incident in Clayton County, the case with Justin, how I stayed in jail until I paid what I owed, and I should do the same in this case. I was curious to know why he would discuss a case that he did not represent that was in another county, but that goes to show you who was behind those words. If I can say the least about my attorney, he did his job defending me, he bought to the judge's attention I was in the Fatherhood Program and was in good standing with child support. The judge knowing the case had been carrying on from the previous year question my attendance from the last court appearance. It was then explained I was incarcerated; now it is the job of the system to transfer the prisoner to the court appearance they may have in another county. The fact that I missed the last court appearance was not from my neglect as much as it was the systems. The judge then started inquiring about my work status, correct address, who I lived with, wanting all my current, and correct information stated. The argument from the other party then became that I was not paying anything monthly to child support and I was not in good standing. The judge then asked me directly, "can you prove you are in positive standing with Child support and the Fatherhood Program." I was then chastised from the Judge for having another child not fully being commented to the care of the other children. It was comments that I ignored, because I could understand a person having that thought about my character in the position that I was in. By no means was I going to allow anyone to dictate who they thought, I was or form their opinion about me unless they could show me they could walk on water. The comments were hurtful but was I suppose to justify my character, absolutely not, I wanted nothing more but to go back home to continue my journey of healing and change. The judge then stated I had to the end of the day to produce the document from the Child Support Office that I was in good standing with them. I promised her I would be able knowing confidently that Tristan was going to leave there, go get the document, and turn it in. Within the hour Tristan did just as, I thought, the officer who informed me on the way back to the holding cell, "the judge would be disappointed if you do not have that document" leaving the courtroom, could not wait to show me my release terms.

I was being released on a reduction purge amount of $300, I was to re-enroll back in the Fatherhood program, school, and continue looking for employment. At a later date speaking with one of the Child Support agents, she remembered the case, stating Mason and his wife came up there, shortly after Tristan that court day. She expressed how much of an harassment they were to her about proving I was not paying the support. I say they were trying to bully her to produce what they wanted, she made an interesting comment that she thought the wife was more involved than the father in the process, I laughed in embarrassment that my case would have that much of remembrance to her mind with all cases she had to deal with daily. She was very happy to meet me after the picture they painted of me that day; she could now see the scenario more clearly. I was released after my paperwork was processed with full faith that that part of my life was over. Both parents had satisfaction in accomplishing their goal in what they thought diminished my new character, by all means under estimating who I was in the eyes of the all mighty.

Conclusion

I believe that my way to start fighting back for my integrity was to publicly expose it in a book, telling the story in actions I saw through my eyes. In order to solve the problem, I personally had, bringing awareness to others in the same position male/female, and get the life that I was beginning to have at one point back again. Some would say I was weak or I let the enemy win by not coming around my children sooner. I would say I had to lean not into my own understanding, listen to the instructions of God, and do a little work behind the scenes. When I pray about my children I hear a voice tell me all the time, "I AM IN CONTROL." When I hear that I feel secure in moving forward in my endeavors, God knows the boys are and will always be in my heart and thoughts. Writing this is my way of expressing how much I was hurt and to display to my children while I was absent I still kept them in mind. I ignore the comments that I hear about the choices I have made because we all have made some bad choices. I can say I had the courage to expose my rights and wrongs with the tenacity to correct the wrongs in the right way with time, patience, and diligence. I can say I am a woman of progressive and persistent adjustment; my growth through this entire venture has helped me and will help others. Showing those who know me, they can continue to talk about me, but respect my alterations, noticing how I have not stayed the same. Once I was released from Fulton County Jail, I re-enrolled back in the Fatherhood Program; I recognized I was the only woman in the class. The agent I was assigned to was very attentive to making sure I was on the right track, after I explained I was recently incarcerated for the second time. The agent noticed I had been in the program before and I was returning to the program, my agent after conversing with me for over a month or so through e-mail asked me to express my thoughts from my perspective as a woman on child support. She indicated how the men in the program always had comments about the mothers, how they were, and what they were doing to make matters worse for them. She also asked me to come in one morning as a guess speaker and share what I encountered.

The email:

Our Fatherhood guess speaker Paris D. (Child Support Participant)

- My name is Paris D. and I am in the **Fatherhood Program** in Atlanta, Georgia. I was placed on child support in 2005 after deciding it was time for the fathers to provide the welfare for our children to freely find my place in life. The fact that I was a young mother of two one in which I had when I was in the ninth grade and the other I had, in the twelfth grade. I put my family first, not painting the perfect picture, I was never able to fully grasp on aspects of my completion in my comfort zone. Thinking it would be a good opportunity to allow my children the experience of being raised by the father, I ran into the resentment of the step mothers.
- I was very relieved to know that this program being called **Fatherhood** was available for **mothers** as well.
- It took me to experience incarceration on two different occasions to realize hurt people, hurt people. I sit back and look at the situation and see that I have a purpose in this program. I will not allow my life to be altered without a fight, fighting with the same weapon that was use to destroy me.
- When I first entered the program, I was embarrassed, to even have this attachment, a program designed for men not commented

to their full responsibility. I as a woman have endured what men have been enduring for many years, and suffered the same consequences as a man has. I have also learned very valuable information about the system and the operations that are run. I am starting over in my life personal and business determined to gain everything tenfold making changes in others lives on my way. I am part of a program that allows me to come and express my feelings without judgment and helps me put things back in perspective while they are releasing energy it's more than fair to release some back.

- A room filled with the people with the same and/or similar issues, it's therapeutic for everyone involved. On behalf of every woman on child support rather she deserves to be or not men are not alone or discriminated upon. We are in this struggle for correction together for the wellbeing of relationship with our children.
- Thank you Fatherhood Program, with the push of this organization I am surely on my way to the top non-stop . . .

It was pouring down raining that morning with Malachi, I came in spoke, and as I spoke I watched the expression on their face. The men were in shock; I sounded and had similar stories as them. In my closing I made a comment referring to them that now, they've heard it from the opposite and they now know they are not alone, WHAT ARE THEY GOING TO DO? The information from the email and my visit went through the programs staff; the agent was telling me how her supervisor had a copy in his office. I felt relieved I could express my feelings professionally without getting all choked up. I knew from that day in that office, my healing was almost done, it was a time I could not talk about it at all without bursting with tears. The speaking event with the program my mother never knew about it, she would probably just ask me if I stuttered during the speech, which I didn't surprisingly. I had not shared the day with anyone except Tristan, and that was the only one I was suppose to share the day with, he was my real supporter through it all. I have discovered out of life, it does not matter how you were raised or how bad you had it growing up. When you become responsible for yourself at a certain age it is completely your responsibility to teach yourself everything you always wanted to know. Become the individual you have always seen in your mind regardless of what anyone has ever told you. I am still currently on child support, as of this day, and have not seen my two oldest children. I am pregnant with my fourth boy; second from Tristan and working toward clearing the child support arrears completely. Micah will soon be 18 and I am in clear hopes he wants to come live with me or even come around, so I can re-establish myself in his life as his mother. I pray that my boys forgive me for the bad decisions that I have made with my last reading of Micah's Facebook page, he vented to me, how he was F****ing serious about me sending him messages, and how it had been two years since he had seen me. It hurt me to know his patience had gotten weary, but it is expected from a teenage child who is completely frustrated with the affiliation with his mother. I can image it is hard trying to have a relationship with both parents and one parents mistreats you for not falling suit in the way that they feel about the other co-parent. I feel like my son has to dislike me or be distant to keep contentment toward him in the home he lives in. I can only pray that the connection I have with my mother despite what I truly feel about the person she is; he can see it in his heart to have for me when he comes to the healing point of his life.

These are questions I often ask myself:

Do I worry about what my children think about me being absent so long, absolutely? I think about everything they have heard that they have no other option, but to believe because of my absence. Do I care about them being jealous of my new family and their other siblings, yes? Can I trust God to work with them in the convert and the direction they will need, yes? Will I be there as support in what they need when we unite, yes? Can I handle what they will say when they express their hurt, concerns and pain? I have no other option, if it's respectful. Will I listen and be patient through the process, yes? Can I deal with what my critics will have to say about me, yes?

I have been preparing for them for a while with the help of family criticism coming first. I look at what I saw from others I admired as a preview of the latter of my life, God was showing me what I will look like, act, and deserve for my dedication I had to him even with flaws. I pray for everyone that was involved in the cases because after everything we have been through and the level of expertise involved we have not yet to have a counseling section. I think about what could have happened in my career, if I had not went to jail, but I find joy in discovering my new career. I thought maybe it was not in God's plan for me to follow down the path of my family history, I could have been created for something more.

CPSIA information can be obtained at www.ICGtesting.com
Printed in the USA
LVOW091641180512

282342LV00005B/51/P